JUDGMENT DAY

The warrior couldn't help thinking that guilt was something a higher force had bestowed on men and women to stop them from being worse than animals. But that gift was sometimes rejected. When left untainted by human hands, Nature's assets were a beauty to behold. With the emergence of man, the natural balance was destroyed and an accounting procedure was introduced.

As an efficiency expert on the evil that man could inflict upon his fellow man, the Executioner ranked high when it came to evening up the score.

DON PENDLETON'S
THE EXECUTIONER®
FEATURING MACK BOLAN®

EVIL
KINGDOM

A GOLD EAGLE BOOK FROM
WORLDWIDE®

TORONTO • NEW YORK • LONDON • PARIS
AMSTERDAM • STOCKHOLM • HAMBURG
ATHENS • MILAN • TOKYO • SYDNEY

First edition June 1991

ISBN 0-373-61423-3

Special thanks and acknowledgment to
Mel Odom for his contribution to this work.

EVIL KINGDOM

The man who is tenacious of purpose in a rightful cause is not shaken from his firm resolve.

> —Horace
> 65-8 B.C.

A frontline warrior has to stand firm despite the odds. To give ground in *this* war is to take away the future of millions.

> —Mack Bolan

To the frontline warriors in the
everlasting war against drugs

PROLOGUE

Silvery moonlight streamed down over the long trail like skeletal fogs. The wind whispered through the trees, bearing an unaccustomed chill.

Chance Burdett felt his horse shift under him as he rested his hands on the pommel and leaned forward to relieve some of the ache in his lower back. The caravan stretched down the steep incline, weaving back and forth through the dense jungle like some kind of giant, segmented worm. Straining engines whined above the clopping of the mules, struggling to drag the loaded two-wheeled carts up the ridge.

The mules and their peasant drivers shone in stark relief in the headlights of the four jeeps. The cart drivers had their wives and children out in front with lanterns to mark the way. Sparks flared briefly in the darkness as the occasional iron-shod hoof scraped across a flat rock.

Burdett checked his watch and reached for his walkie-talkie. "Reynaldo."

The answer came back at once. *"Sí."*

"We're behind schedule here. It's almost five o'clock."

"I know, Señor Chance, but there's not much more these mules can take without lying down and dying. The drivers aren't doing much better."

Burdett grinned mirthlessly and hit the talk button again. "That sounds like an excuse, amigo, and you know how Costanza feels about excuses."

"*Sí.* I'll see what I can do to hurry them."

Burdett replaced the walkie-talkie and reached back for the CAR-15 booted in the customized rig under his right leg. He tipped his hat back with his free hand and scanned the surrounding terrain. The assault rifle rested butt first on his thigh, more a comfortable prosthesis than a piece of equipment.

He clucked lightly and the horse moved forward, finding sure footing back down the overgrown trail. He pulled up as the first mule cart came abreast of him. Easing his feet out of the stirrups until only the toes of his boots clung to the edge, he picked up the walkie-talkie.

The cart driver glanced at him briefly as he pulled his mule to a halt. Gray trail dust stained the old man's dark features. *"Señor?"*

"Go on," Burdett ordered.

"No, *señor.*" The old man took off his straw hat and held it against his chest. "This is a bad place." He pointed at the cart animal, whose long ears were twitching back and forth. "The mule, he knows these things. He can scent death for a long ways. This mule, he's a very smart mule."

The rest of the caravan ground to a halt behind the old man. His wife moved to his side, wrapped in her shawl and carrying the lantern. She spoke to the old man in Spanish.

The cool wind brushed against Burdett's neck again, racing down his spine.

"Señor Chance?" Reynaldo's voice was quietly curious.

Burdett raised the walkie-talkie to his lips. "Got a problem. Haul your ass up here and get ready to back my play." He glanced farther down the slope as the lead jeep peeled out of the formation and swept through the rough terrain beside the trail. Reynaldo drew his gunner's attention to the .50-caliber machine gun mounted at the rear of the vehicle.

The cart drivers and lantern-carriers watched the jeep swing into line in front of the lead mule.

Burdett lowered the CAR-15 until it pointed at the driver's midsection. "Go on, old man."

The man waved his hands, still holding the long reins working the mule. "But, *señor,* that way holds death. The mule, I'm telling you, he knows. There are ghosts, bad spirits."

Baring his teeth in an impersonal shark's smile, Burdett said, "Old man, if you don't get that mule moving, I'm going to shoot him. Then you'll have to pull that cart yourself, or I'm going to shoot your old lady. I was hired to get a job done tonight, and you can goddamn well believe I intend to see it done. Tonight." He pointed the assault rifle's muzzle at the mule's head.

The old woman wailed at her husband, pleading with him to do as he was told before he got them all killed. She cursed the mule with a colorful command of the language that impressed Burdett. The old man put his hat back on and clucked to the animal.

"Reynaldo."

"*Sí,* Señor Chance."

"You got point for the moment."

"*Sí.*"

"Do all these people believe in fucking ghosts?"

The jeep rode unevenly as it continued slowly up the incline. The thick barrel of the .50-caliber machine gun jumped to a separate rhythm as the gunner tried to keep it steady.

"You must remember, Señor Chance, that these people believe in many things. They're peasants, not educated men such as you and myself. They believe in the things their fathers told them, in the things the Catholic church tells them. Maybe, if you think back, you will remember ghosts of your own."

"It's not ghosts I'm worried about, amigo. It's those people who've been hammering away at Costanza's little jungle empire. The reason we're packing all this cocaine on this little cross-country trip to La Guajira is because somebody blew up Costanza's private airstrip yesterday and tore up the Trans-Global Security training facilities before that."

"*Sí,* but they did a much better job on the airstrip."

Burdett controlled his anger, realizing the growing fear inside him only pushed at the restraints he held in place.

"You think these people would know of Señor Costanza's decision to send us this way to La Guajira?" Reynaldo asked.

"I don't think I want to rule out that possibility," Burdett said dryly. "And I wouldn't put it past the boss to stake us out like a Judas goat." He heard the old man's words in his mind: ghosts, bad spirits. He'd thought the North Vietnamese snipers were ghosts, too, that first year, before he learned to move like them. The horse's ears twitched nervously. Animals knew things, sensed things before most people could. "Take your people forward, Reynaldo, and check things out. Maintain constant radio contact."

The man waved from the passenger side of the jeep, then the vehicle spurted forward, gray clouds of dust trailing behind.

Burdett raised the bandanna hanging around his neck and snugged it over his nose, narrowing his eyes as the cloud of dust enveloped him. He waved the assault rifle toward the old man. "*Vámonos, amigo.* We're burning daylight."

The jeep jumped erratically as it continued its climb.

Trying to shake the chill that clung to him, Burdett lifted the walkie-talkie and said, "You know, amigo, if it hadn't been for this emergency run, you and I would be terrorizing the women of Medellín tonight."

Reynaldo chuckled. "True. Let's hope they're all showing some common sense and decency and have decided to rest up at home until our return."

Burdett laughed, realizing it was what he needed to do. The business with the airstrip and the other unexplained goings-on involving the cartel members was bullshit he didn't need on his mind. He took a deep breath and looked up at the Colombian night filled with stars. He saw the man resting in the fork of the tree at the crest of the ridge by accident and reached for the walkie-talkie. Then something slammed into his chest and tore him from the saddle.

He died before the sound of the shot reached him.

CHAPTER ONE

Mack Bolan rode out the Galil's recoil as the riderless horse galloped out of his field of vision. Shifting slightly in the tree, he kept the folding buttstock of his weapon to his cheek as he sighted in on a lantern hanging from a bar over one of the mule-driven carts loaded with Costanza's latest shipment. He let out half a breath, used Kentucky windage on the open sights and squeezed the trigger.

The kerosene lantern exploded into dozens of flaming shards that rained down over the bales of hay covering *la merca*—the merchandise. The fire spread rapidly. The peasants Burdett and his men had shanghaied into handling the transportation back in Medellín freed their animals and fled into the jungle.

The Executioner touched the transmit button on the throat/ear headset he wore. "Jack?"

"Yo."

"The mines."

"You got it."

An eruption of flames and dirt fanned to life behind the three jeeps at the rear of the caravan. Trees fell across the trail, severely limiting movement.

"Now," Bolan said, gripping the handle of the machete sheathed in the soft bark of the tree to his left, "let's go for the heavy artillery. On three." He counted down, then swung the big blade into the coil of vine hugging the trunk to his right.

The gunner in the jeep below had found Bolan's position now. Fifty-caliber slugs ripped through the foliage as the driver manhandled his vehicle toward the tree.

The vine parted easily, pulling away with the immense weight it supported. Bolan watched the bole of the tree appear seemingly from nowhere, glaring white where branches had been stripped away, arcing from the other vines tied to either end. His and Grimaldi's timing hadn't been exact, but it had been close enough.

Nearly two tons of tree smashed into the jeep, caving in the front end and imploding the windshield. The vehicle vanished into the darkness, flipping end over end, the tortured sound of wrenched metal ripping through the night.

Leaning back to the gunsight, Bolan targeted the glowing lanterns. He squeezed off rounds in rapid single-shot, and pools of fire dropped to the rocky ground.

"And to think," Grimaldi drawled through the headset, "I thought we weren't going to find a use for that chain saw." The pilot sprayed the jeeps with discretionary bursts. Although the peasants involved weren't totally innocent, they hadn't been packing weapons, either. The Stony Man warriors were drawing a hard line in their covert war on the Colombian cartels, but they weren't about to step over it at the expense of innocents.

Dropping the empty clip, Bolan shoved another into place, then stood and slung the weapon over his shoulder. Clad in a blacksuit and Kevlar body armor, his face tiger-striped with camouflage cosmetics, he was a long, lean shadow in the tree branches. He kicked loose the rope beside him and grabbed it in gloved hands, following it down to the ground. Then he tapped the transmit button. "I'm down."

"Me, too," Grimaldi replied. "Don't count on my being there soon, Sarge. I'm going to be busy ducking civilians for a few minutes. They must have picked my side to run to."

"Stay in touch," Bolan said. He let the shadows take him, his movements in the jungle as sure as any animal's, trained by surviving in a war zone. The Beretta 93-R rode in a shoulder rig while the big Desert Eagle .44 filled a military-style holster on his right hip. Other ordnance was concealed and carried in pockets of the blacksuit and canvas pouches attached to a military belt. Perspiration streaked his face. Burdett and his crew of killers had been behind schedule, and sitting in the tree waiting in the muggy heat hadn't been pleasant.

The flames leeching life from the hay bales had climbed to an impressive height, lighting up the jungle, yet deepening the protection of the shadows.

Bolan slid the Galil forward and switched it to 3-round burst and listened as one of the whining jeep engines closed in on him. Voices screaming in Spanish rose above the noise.

A cracking branch alerted Bolan to the presence of someone behind him. The warrior whirled to confront his attacker, who held a knife in his fist. Without hesitation the man lunged at Bolan. He blocked with the

Galil, following through with a butt swipe with the assault rifle that stretched the unconscious man on the ground.

A row of .50-caliber rounds punched through the underbrush as the lights of a jeep swung toward him. The Executioner went to ground as the bullets passed overhead, shredding branches into confetti that rained gently onto the ground. He pushed himself to his feet and charged after the passing jeep. The rear gunner spotted him and tried to swing around the big machine gun. The warrior tugged a fragmentation grenade from his harness and lobbed it overhand into the rear of the vehicle as the gunner tried to yell a warning and fire accurately at the same time.

The grenade detonated seconds later and threw all three bodies from the vehicle. The flaming wreckage became airborne when it hit a boulder too large to straddle. It rolled down the hill until it was stopped by a row of trees.

"Sarge." Grimaldi sounded tense.

"Yeah."

Relief evident in his voice, the Stony Man pilot said, "Never mind. I was thinking something foolish."

Bolan felt the beginnings of a grin despite the seriousness of the situation. They'd been together on the Colombian strike for three days. The action tonight was starting to look like a cakewalk when compared to some of the things they'd faced. He ducked his head long enough to wipe the perspiration from his eyes as he tracked the two remaining jeeps.

He responded to movement to his left, merging with the underbrush. Slinging the Galil, he gripped the haft of his Cold Steel Tanto, slid it from its boot sheath and waited as the person stepped into his reach. He curled an arm around the skulker and felt the soft curves that told him his prisoner was a woman. Clapping a hand over her mouth, Bolan stopped the knife's descent and concentrated on keeping her from screaming. In the moonlight he saw she was all of fourteen or fifteen, and frightened for her life.

"Quiet," Bolan whispered. "I'm not going to hurt you." He tried it in Spanish. She didn't relax, but the struggling stopped. He released her slowly, holding a finger to his lips. Her eyes were jet-black, and she shivered at his touch. He sat her in the underbrush and said, "Stay here and you'll be safe."

She nodded uncertainly as she chewed her lower lip and darted quick glances down the incline. Bolan sheathed his knife and swung up the Galil as he moved away.

The girl bolted as soon as the warrior was out of sight. Her screams were shrill and didn't go unnoticed. One of the jeeps roared in her direction, skidding around on the loose rocky soil until the headlights caught her in full flight. The Executioner shouldered his weapon as the rear gunner and the guy riding shotgun made their moves. He flicked the Galil on full-auto and raked a clip of 7.62 mm rounds across the front of the jeep.

The driver pulled his vehicle hard left in an attempt to dodge out of the line of fire. Crumpling in slow motion, the shotgun rider pitched out of his seat and disappeared into the vegetation.

Bolan reloaded on the run, moving toward his target. He hadn't been able to see if the girl had gone down. Flicking the assault rifle back on tri-burst, he stitched the right front tire of the vehicle.

The jeep jerked out of control and smashed into a tree. The surviving vehicle roared from a pool of darkness, its lights out. Ragged muzzle-flashes from the big .50-caliber machine gun mounted on the rear deck illuminated the dark faces of the jeep team.

Trying to whirl to confront the new attack, Bolan felt an anvil slam into his chest and knock him from his feet. The Galil spun from his hands as he dropped to the ground, his lungs fighting to draw another breath. The Kevlar armor had done its part to keep the bullet from piercing the flesh beneath, but the warrior would be badly bruised for some time to come.

Unable to find the assault rifle, the Executioner drew the 93-R and stayed under the line of brush. He listened to the steady roar of the jeep's engine as the driver pushed through the undergrowth to the spot where he'd gone down.

The machine gunner was a crouching shadow while the shotgun rider flanked the vehicle to the left. The driver of the other jeep hung upside down from the burning carriage. Staggering through the underbrush, the surviving member of the team leaned down, then came up with an M-16.

Closing in as quickly and quietly as he could, Bolan raised the Beretta into target acquisition on the second jeep's flanker ten yards away. Ignoring the sharp pain in his chest that was only now starting to fade, he squeezed the trigger and watched the man collapse to the ground.

The machine gunner responded immediately, raking a vicious arc of fire that shook and shattered trees and bushes. Nocturnal noises faded as the .50-caliber drumbeat reverberated through the jungle.

Bolan took cover behind a tree as the jeep cut back in his direction. The 93-R was equipped with a flash-hider so the team had to be guessing, but the jeep's driver homed in on his position.

"Sarge."

Hitting the transmit button, Bolan said, "Yeah."

"We got company."

Bolan stripped away the ear/throat assembly as he listened to the sound of rotors filling the night. Searchlights kicked to life as a pair of helicopters swung into view, illuminating warped ovals of jungle. He dodged as one of the searchlights swept across his position, a hail of bullets hot on its heels.

HAL BROGNOLA AWAKENED slowly with a feeling of disorientation he hadn't experienced in years. He blinked at the darkness and tried to remember where he was. Realizing he was on a couch narrowed the possibilities to three instantly—he was either at home in the den waiting for a call and not wanting to wake his wife, he was in his office, or he was at Stony Man Farm.

His memory cleared at once as he levered his feet to the floor and sat up with a groan that came from the heart. He closed his eyes as the headache ripped through his temples again. Massaging his forehead with a knuckled fist, he took two antacid tablets from his jacket pocket and popped them into his mouth.

He pressed the intercom button on the wall and said, "Aaron?" During the few seconds it took to get the answer, his mind summoned up images that only served to increase the pressure in his head.

"Yeah, Hal?" Kurtzman's voice was deep and scratchy.

Brognola felt guilty for taking the nap. He wasn't the only one at the Farm who was logging long hours. "Anything happen?"

"You'd have been the second person I called if it had."

"The second?"

"Barb's coordinating the action. You put her there. It's time you get used to the idea."

"She there?"

"Yeah. Want to talk to her?"

"No. I'll be right in."

Barbara Price cut in immediately. "Why don't you take some more down time? We've got everything under control here."

"Yeah, yeah, I know, but I'm okay. I've had all the sleep I need."

"You've been in there twenty minutes," Price chided. "I'd hardly call that all the sleep you need. You've—"

Brognola cut her off. "I'll be right there." He switched off the intercom and stood. He was wobbly at first, punchy under the weight of too many hours and too many worries, then the motion warmed him and he let the reflexes take over.

He paused in the kitchen long enough to get a quart of orange juice from the refrigerator and a glass, then walked to Kurtzman's office—"world" was the term that would have suited the room better. Banks of computer equipment filled every available space. Even the air seemed to hum. Brognola couldn't have begun to name or figure out the function of most of the components of Kurtzman's environment, but knew Stony Man couldn't have had a more learned man at the helm.

Kurtzman was on a raised dais near the center of the room, almost encircled by a horseshoe-shape table filled with keyboards, phones and other electronic setups. He was a big man even in his wheelchair, fleshing out his nickname of Bear.

If Kurtzman had been cast as the Beast, however, Barbara Price would have been chosen as the Beauty. Honey-blond hair fell to her shoulders, framing a face that would have graced magazine covers if she'd chosen another line of work. She was dressed in navy blue and white sweats and looked ready for a day at the gym rather than ramrodding a sensitive operation in South America that could have worldwide repercussions.

Brognola checked his thoughts. Hell, they were hoping for repercussions that would be felt around the world. They just didn't expect the cost to be so dear and strike so close to home so soon.

"Coffee?" Price asked.

Brognola held up the orange juice. "No thanks. Juice?"

"Yes." Price emptied her cup in the sink beside the coffee maker and approached him.

He poured. Close up he could see the dark purple smudges under her eyes. "Any word on Lyons?"

"No." She sipped the orange juice. "Leo's made it to Miami, but he hasn't hooked up with Politician or Gadgets."

"Have they checked back in?"

"Not since they broke into Maria Teresina's house and found the body."

Brognola directed his attention to Kurtzman. "Aaron, don't we have some people in Dade County who owe Justice some favors? Get hold of them and have them put their ears to the ground."

"The lady's already got me working it," Kurtzman said, fingers still dancing over the keyboard.

Nodding, Brognola looked at Price and said, "Sorry. Old habits are hard to break."

"Just means you care," she said. "Nothing wrong with that."

His voice was rough when he replied. "Yeah, there is. If I step in at the wrong time, I could confuse the issue and get somebody killed. I sidelined myself from this so that I could deal with the Washington end of things in case the operation gets compromised before we're able to pull out."

She smiled at him. "Not to worry, Hal. I might act soft and demure most of the time, but I've got a mean side to me, too. Otherwise you'd have never chosen me to head up this operation. Rest assured that if you get underfoot, I'll let you know so fast it'll make your head swim."

Despite the tension and all the unanswered questions, Brognola couldn't help but smile back at her.

"We still don't know if the body was Teresina's," Price remarked.

"Gadgets said there wasn't enough of it to make an ID." Brognola's mind filled with images of what might have happened to Carl Lyons. Memories started filtering in then of the times when he was younger and considered the ex-LAPD cop a kid. He shut them off before the acid could start bubbling in his stomach again. "If they killed Lyons, why didn't they leave him behind?"

"Whoever did this might have been looking for information," Price said in a neutral voice.

Data continued to scroll across the half-dozen screens Kurtzman monitored. They changed at his command, zeroing in at times, shifting perspective completely at others.

"If they were, Lyons could have wandered in as an unexpected bonus," Price went on. "Mack's got Costanza fighting with Mercado and Rodriguez. We know from Gadgets that Teresina was suspected of being La Araña, Costanza's representative in south Florida, fingered by Ernesto Ramos—"

"Who was Mercado's man," Brognola finished. "I know. It makes sense that Mercado would want to put La Araña out of business here if he thought he was going to be whacked by Costanza. I just don't like the idea of our guys getting caught up in a cross fire we devised."

"We knew it was a possibility when we set up the parameters on this mission," Price said softly.

Brognola shook his head. "Ten days. We scattered them from Panama to Colombia to Florida and expected them to pull off the impossible. Only three days into it and we might have already lost Lyons.''

Price waited a beat, then said, ''They're good men, and they knew the risks when they agreed to this.''

Brognola nodded. ''I know, and we might have signed the death warrants on all of them.''

CHAPTER TWO

Using the fork of the tree he'd taken cover behind as a brace, Bolan steadied the flare gun and aimed at the closer helicopter. He fitted the communication apparatus back into place and pressed the transmit button. "Jack."

"Yeah?"

"Take deep cover because we're about to lose the darkness for a few minutes."

"Give me ten seconds."

Bolan started counting down the numbers as he kept the flare gun centered on his chosen target.

The second helicopter had dropped to within fifteen feet of ground zero and uncoiled a rope ladder from its belly. Men began to climb down, carrying automatic weapons and fire extinguishers, letting the Executioner know that even if the caravan had been a trap manufactured by Costanza, the bait aboard wasn't expendable.

With ten seconds gone Bolan squeezed the trigger of the flare gun and hoped the stubby barrel would give him the accuracy he needed. He fell back as soon as the round ignited. Autofire lashed the tree he'd taken refuge behind as the gunners tracked his position from the streaming tail of the flare. The door gunner leaning out of the target helicopter stopped firing almost immediately.

A lambent emerald green washed over the area and chased away the shadows. The Executioner dived behind a fallen tree big enough to hide and protect him, his right hand drawing the Beretta as he glanced toward the helicopter.

The door gunner clung to the frame of the aircraft as green flames from the flare chewed voraciously at his clothing. He flailed at them with his free hand, legs dangling over open space. The pilot lifted up on the stick and dragged the gunner through the airstream. Emerald comets flew from the man's clothing, and seconds later he fell, screaming terror until he hit the earth.

In the vacuum left by the sudden silence Bolan moved quietly through the brush. He leathered the Beretta and drew the Tanto as he closed in on the nearest man. The guy peered at the darkness without seeing death reach for him with gloved hands and mat-black combat steel. The Executioner wrapped his free arm around the man's throat, shutting off a scream, and slipped the blade between the third and fourth ribs. The man shuddered and died.

Claiming the dead man's M-16, Bolan cleaned the knife on the guy's clothing and sheathed it. He stripped the extra magazines from the body and dropped them into a canvas pouch tied to his belt.

The soldiers with the fire extinguishers dashed frantically up and down the line of carts, desperately trying to put out the dancing flames. The Executioner circled around to the unmoving jeep. The .50-caliber machine gun mounted on the rear deck seemed to have survived the crash. If it had, the Executioner had a use for it.

Five men had crawled from the belly of the second helicopter, and their attention was still focused on the cocaine caravan. Their voices were shrill and harsh as they spoke and ran between the carts. Light from the helicopter hovering above them kept them visible.

Craning his head to the right, Bolan picked up the other two ground players. They remained with the jeep, circling the area where Bolan had last been.

The Executioner shouldered the M-16, drew the Beretta again and made his way to the overturned jeep unobserved. He checked the feed and function of the big machine gun with a practiced touch and, satisfied that everything was in place, he tested the balance of the wreckage. It felt solid, jammed tight against the bulwark of trees. Moving to the rear of the vehicle, he uncapped the two jerricans of gasoline from the rack and gently eased them away from his position. The liquid spilled quietly from the metal containers, and the cloying smell overpowered everything the jungle foliage had to offer. He found the folding shovel in the kit just as the remaining jeep swung back toward him. The helicopter followed, trolling the treetops like a Macy's parade balloon.

Connecting the two halves of the shovel, he slid it under the side of the jeep and placed his shoulder against the seat. He shoved, feeling his feet sink through the mulch and rocky soil, for a moment doubting he'd find solid purchase. He refused to give in. Forcing the tiredness and pain away, he renewed his efforts. The metal frame of the seat bit into his flesh.

The balance of the vehicle gave way with a metallic creak as the crew of the jeep spotted him. Bolan vaulted onto the rear deck of the wreck, drew the flare gun and fired into the pool of gasoline that had raced down the slope into the path of the approaching jeep.

The flare hit the volatile liquid, igniting it with a gentle whoosh that created instant havoc. Flames leaped from the underbrush and curled around the jeep, cresting the top of the vehicle in a solid wave. The driver veered away.

Bolan drew back the bolt as he thumbed the .50-caliber's trigger. He felt the big machine gun wobble in his hands, evidently torn loose from its moorings on the rear deck. Orange tracers tracked through the night sky toward the helicopter directly above the hell zone. Fifty-caliber rounds chopped holes in the Plexiglas bubble and drilled through the pilot.

The helicopter fell away from its flight pattern and crashed into the treetops. It ruptured into a huge orange-and-black ball of fire that kicked metal fragments in every direction. The explosion was deafening.

The jeep circled the flames racing toward it. On the rear deck the gunner tracked the machine gun across the body of Bolan's vehicle. More gunfire came from the direction of the men flanking the stalled caravan as they dropped their fire extinguishers and reached for their weapons. Bolan threw himself from the jeep as a lethal mixture of .50-caliber rounds and 5.56 mm tumblers pummeled the bodywork of the vehicle.

"Hey, Sarge," Grimaldi's voice whispered in his ear, "you planning on running this mission solo or can anyone join?"

"Be my guest. At the moment I'm willing to listen to a really good idea."

"How would you like to own a jeep that works?"

Bolan paused, watching the circling vehicle plow through the underbrush. "I'd like that just fine."

"Figured you might after seeing how much mileage you could get out of the nonmobile kind. I'm on the driver now, so if you can take care of the gunner, I think that can be arranged."

Bolan assumed a seated position against the bole of a tree. So far no one had spotted him since his departure from the jeep. He tried to find Grimaldi in the darkness and couldn't. The night was both friend and foe when a soldier went on a mission that wasn't solo. He raised the M-16 and flicked the fire selector to single-shot. The machine gunner wasn't making much of a target, and the muzzle-flashes threw off target acquisition even more. He let out his breath slowly, relying on the years of combat missions to guide him, realizing Grimaldi would be doing the same. "Say when."

"When," Grimaldi said in a voice that wasn't as light and airy as before.

Bolan saw the pilot break cover. Grimaldi was a dark shadow twisted and colored by the leaping flames in front of the jeep, arms pumping at his sides. The Executioner waited until the machine gunner on the rear deck turned to bring the Stony Man pilot into his arc of fire. The Executioner let out half a breath and started squeezing off shots a half second apart.

The .50-caliber machine gun flared briefly, tearing clumps of grass and bark from the jungle floor in Grimaldi's path. Twelve shots into the M-16's clip, the machine gunner crumpled and peeled away from his weapon, falling out of the vehicle. Bolan picked himself up and ran, switching the M-16 to tri-burst.

Grimaldi flung himself bodily onto the driver, a knife flashing in his hand. There was a brief struggle as the jeep veered out of control. Even as Bolan caught up and grabbed hold of the rear of the jeep, Grimaldi's knife flashed once more, burying to the hilt in the driver's throat. The pilot grabbed the dead man's uniform shirt and pulled the body from the seat, gaining control of the vehicle in time to keep them from smashing into a boulder.

Autofire licked through the brush at them, tearing through the window. Grimaldi kicked the windshield down. Bolan stripped off the ear/throat walkie-talkie and slipped it into a slit pocket of the blacksuit, then knelt to inspect the box feed on the machine gun. Everything seemed in order.

"Are we operational back there?" Grimaldi yelled above the sudden increase in autofire.

"As good as it gets," Bolan replied as he loosed a withering blast that drove some of the caravan rescuers to cover.

"Then hang on," Grimaldi said, "because this is where it starts to get really hairy."

The remaining helicopter veered away, heeling in midair as it spun around and began a sideways drift back toward the jeep. Tracers bit into the earth in front of the ground unit as the door gunner measured the distance.

Grimaldi cut the jeep instantly, ducking back through the crackling flames of the gasoline fire Bolan had started. There was a wave of heat, a sensation of no air to breathe, then they were through, fire clinging to the tires.

Bolan worked the machine gun as Grimaldi steered them through the trees and onto the trail the caravan had been following. The big weapon bucked in his hands as he directed a hail of fire that kicked life from two of the enemy soldiers and deposited them onto the ground in crumpled heaps.

Then the helicopter drifted in for another pass. Cursing, Grimaldi turned the jeep back down the trail, shifted gears and floored the accelerator. Bolan found himself hanging on to the machine gun more for support than for any offensive stance as the jeep bounced down the trail and struck the first cart. Fire, hay and football-shape packages of cocaine scattered at impact, drifting across the interior of the jeep.

Leaning with the machine gun, Bolan put down the remaining three men in twin bursts before they reached the safety of the jungle. The carts and their contents were reduced to rubble as the jeep continued to plow through them.

The helicopter swung about as Bolan gave it his full attention. His initial burst ripped the door gunner from his post, and he tracked the .50-caliber rounds toward the whirling blades as the pilot presented him the rear section.

An almost inaudible pop hissed from the helicopter's main rotor, then fire tried to climb up the bent and broken blades. Unable to go up, the flames turned and scaled back down the helicopter, resembling a huge orange-and-yellow hand as fiery fingers reached inside the Plexiglas bubble. The internal explosion ripped the chopper apart.

Bolan hopped out of the jeep as Grimaldi brought the vehicle to a halt against a tree. They looked back toward the caravan. The surviving carts had been rammed into the brush on either side of the trail. As he unhooked one of the jerricans from the jeep, the Executioner said, "If you ever decide to give up your wings, Jack, I see a great future ahead of you as a demolition derby driver."

The pilot flashed a thin grin. "What next?"

"Grab that other jerrican. We've still got a job to finish here." He poured a line of gasoline over the broken carts and the trail.

Grimaldi followed, pouring from the other side.

"Scorched earth," Bolan announced as they neared the top. "I want Costanza to know what he's in for."

"Really think you're going to make the guy have a change of heart?" Grimaldi asked. "Costanza's been in the cocaine business a long time, and he's not exactly a pauper because of it."

Bolan tossed the empty can to one side and removed a lighter from one of the pouches on his belt. "No, I can't make him change his mind, but I can scare the hell out of him. If he panics, he'll make mistakes. His mistakes are what it's going to take to keep Able, Phoenix, and you and me alive." He knelt and touched the flame to the gasoline. It caught at once, roaring furiously back down the trail. He watched the flames lick at the carts, hay and cocaine, knowing what the fire didn't destroy, exposure to the elements would. There was no satisfaction in him as he turned from the trail, only the knowledge that one more step had been taken in Stony Man's assault on the cartels. He didn't allow himself to wonder how many more steps were going to be taken before someone on the Stony Man team slipped and fell. And he couldn't complain about the heat. He was turning that up himself.

The first scream drew him into the brush for cover. He unlimbered the M-16 as Grimaldi faded into the night less than six feet away.

"FATHER, FORGIVE ME for I have sinned."

Sitting on the other side of the worn curtain of the confessional, Father Julio Lazaro touched the crucifix at his throat. Though they spoke in whispers, he knew her voice just as surely as he knew her face. Only here, on the other side of the curtain, he wasn't supposed to know her at all. "Daughter, tell me how you have sinned."

Her voice was tight with emotion. He knew she'd be crying, that tears would be running down her round, aged face to gather at her chin.

"I have picked the coca leaf again this week, Father."

He shuffled, fighting the pain in his stomach. It had grown since he'd first noticed it, getting to the point where it was sometimes hard to put out of his mind.

"Father?" The curtain rippled slightly.

"Yes, daughter, I have heard you. Why did you do this thing if you know it to be against God's will?"

She snuffled. He imagined her biting on her knuckles as she always did when she was troubled.

"To feed my family. Without the work I do toward the harvesting of the coca leaf, my children would go hungry."

He knew her words to be true. She had five children still at home, some of them very small. They sat in his church and listened to him deliver God's words.

"Still, this is not what God would have you do."

"Yes, I know this in my heart."

And she did. Father Lazaro had seen to the burial of her second oldest son, a victim of the cocaine addiction that had come with the cartel harvestings. He massaged his temple as another spasm racked his stomach. He curled an arm around himself in an effort to ward off another attack. "What would you have of me, daughter?"

"I need to be punished, Father. I know this. I have been a weak person." She sobbed quietly now.

Although he kept the tears from his eyes, his heart wept for her. He couldn't help but wonder what kind of place his country had turned into if women who did what they had to in order to survive had to feel as if they'd failed God and themselves. "You'll instruct your children along the proper path, daughter, and you'll say three prayers to the Virgin Mary, and you'll be forgiven."

"Yes, thank you, Father."

He waited until she'd gone, then stepped from the confessional. Fifty-seven years had left their mark on him. His hair was no longer the ebony of his youth. Instead it had grayed. Now, on most mornings when the pain was truly with him as it was today, he could see that his skin was losing its color, too, becoming as gray as his hair. He was thin to the point of emaciation, too thin, he thought at times, to contain the pain that filled him to overflowing. His priest's clothing hung about him like a tent. He'd have to see about having Sister Yanett take them up for him.

"Father?"

He turned to face Sister Gloria. For a moment he could see the smiling young girl she'd been so long ago, instead of the worn woman she'd become. He'd never felt physical attraction for her, but had always cherished her smile and her manners.

"You're well?"

He waved her concern away. "A minor discomfort, nothing more."

She studied him. "You never said what the doctors told you in Santa Rosa de Osos."

"No," he said without inflection.

She nodded quietly. "There are others here who would like you to hear their confessions."

"In time," he said, biting down on the pain rattling his insides. "First I want a drink from the well, and a few minutes to see to my own soul."

"Of course, Father. I'll tell them." She bowed slightly and walked away with a rustle of cloth.

Father Lazaro used the side entrance to the church, coming out on the north side. The church was made primarily of native stone and mortar, crafted of native artifice instead of the imported engineering the cartel members used for their mansions. Where the drug barons had landscaping and beautiful flowers, this house of God had only the jungle, and the moss and creepers scaling the stone walls.

He walked to the well in the twilight of dawn, the pain inside him coiling through his intestines like a thorned vine. Pausing at the well, he grasped the handle and breathed shallowly until most of the attack passed. Perspiration cooled his face as he twisted the handle and brought the bucket up. He used the ladle hung under the circular thatched roof to drink from after setting the bucket on the edge of the well.

He hung the ladle and stared at the thin reflection of himself in the undisturbed depths of the water in the bucket. Thoughts of his own impending mortality and the woman's confession wouldn't leave him.

"I'm but one priest, Father," he prayed out loud. "Perhaps less than that. I'm dying, and will be in my grave in another six months. At most a year. Am I to spend the last of my days listening to these people, our children—Yours and mine—live the life that has been theirs ever since the harvesting of the coca leaf began? How many mothers must I listen to who ask for forgiveness for merely ensuring their family has something on the table?"

He stopped as his belief trembled before his reflection. "This country is dying, Father, and dying because of a leaf You have placed here. I don't question Your judgment in this matter, but couldn't there have been something left to take care of the faithful? You know I don't ask this for myself. I ask it for the children. Your children if You would have them. I know so many things. I know so much of the traffickers' business from listening to my people confess. Yet what can I do to help them? Is there anything one dying, old priest may do to save his flock?''

A leaf hit the water in the bucket and made him blink.

Without thinking he reached in after it to take it out. Then he noticed the ever-widening ripples that finally touched the wooden sides of the bucket. "This is my answer, then?" Tears of joy filled his eyes as he realized even the weight of a falling leaf could be felt in many places. He closed his eyes and prayed, giving thanks, asking for the strength to make a difference.

When he opened his eyes, he saw the line of smoke coming from the east. He wondered what else the wind might blow in later besides leaves.

CHAPTER THREE

"Goddamn it, Mack, he's only a boy," Grimaldi cursed as he pushed his way through the brush toward the tree where the woman cradled the small form protectively.

Bolan followed, flanking the pilot and never forgetting they were in enemy territory. The sky was lightening, caught in the gray ambiguity between night and true dawn.

The woman spoke Spanish, tears tracking down her cheeks. "Stay away from us." The boy moaned again, shifting slightly in her lap and staining her white blouse crimson in a new place. She brandished a small knife as Grimaldi neared.

The pilot laid down his weapon and showed the woman his empty hands. He spoke in Spanish. "Please, lady, let me look at the boy. Maybe there's something I can do."

"If you come any closer, I'll kill you," the woman threatened.

Grimaldi hardened his voice but didn't move away. "Do you think you can take care of him?"

She didn't look away.

"Do you want him to die?" Grimaldi pressed. "Because if you just sit here with him, that's exactly what's going to happen."

Bolan watched. It was Grimaldi's play, and of the two of them, the pilot looked the less imposing.

"Can you help him?" the woman asked at last.

"I don't know," Grimaldi replied, "but I can try." He moved closer, touching the boy gently.

Bolan heard the footsteps close in on them and tightened his grip on his M-16.

"Caught one in the upper chest," Grimaldi said in English. "A ricochet from a 5.56 mm from the looks of it. In and out. Must not have been tumbling at all. Lucky kid."

"Not as lucky as he could have been," Bolan commented. The footsteps had paused, but were closing in again. He kept the barrel of the assault rifle motionless.

"Yeah," Grimaldi agreed as he took his shirt off and began tearing it into strips.

A middle-aged man stepped out of the brush, carrying a pistol. "You will stand away from the woman and boy, *señor*," the man said in broken English. He motioned with the pistol.

Bolan left the barrel of the M-16 pointed where it was. The number of footsteps told him there were still others in the brush. Even if he could fade into the jungle, Grimaldi was on his knees, unable to maneuver quickly. Movement on his part could signal the pilot's death.

"Drop the rifle," the man told Bolan.

"Your fight's not with us," the Executioner said.

"It didn't appear that way only minutes ago," the man replied tightly.

"Luis." The woman's voice was sharp and imperative.

"Consuela, stay out of this. This is men's business."

"Not when my son may be dying, Luis. They can help him. Let them."

Grimaldi said nothing, leaving his hands on his thighs.

Bolan said, "I heard you coming, amigo. If we'd wished to harm you, we wouldn't have stayed here in the open to wait for you."

"You lie."

"No." Bolan moved his hand slowly. "There are four of you. The other three are there, there and there."

The three chagrined men stepped into the clearing, still holding their weapons on Bolan and Grimaldi.

"Our fight wasn't with you," the Executioner went on. "We knew Costanza's men forced you to work the caravan tonight. We wished no harm to any of you."

"Yet young Tito lies there, perhaps dying." Luis's stare was hard and unforgiving.

Bolan stared back at the man. Never had his personal war been waged on innocents, and he wasn't about to begin now. He held on to the M-16.

"We can save him," Grimaldi said, "if you let us."

"Luis." The woman's tone was pleading. "He is my only son. For the love of God."

A nerve quivered high on the man's cheek. "May God damn your soul if I'm wrong." He lowered his weapon.

Bolan shouldered the assault rifle and crossed the distance to Grimaldi's side. The wound still seeped blood. He could tell from the pulse in the boy's neck that his blood pressure was dangerously low. He'd seen more than his share of death and near death, from Vietnam to whatever lands his private war had taken him, and knew if they expected the boy to live, he'd have to receive medical aid soon. He took his map case from a thigh pocket of the blacksuit and flipped it open. The four men from the brush crowded in around him as he spread out a map of the area. A penciled X marked their present location.

"You are DEA?" Luis asked.

"No," Bolan said as he traced the Río Nechi with a forefinger. He blinked, trying to clear the fatigue blur from his eyes.

"Yet you attack Señor Costanza's load of cocaine and burn it into the ground."

"Yes."

"Luis," one of the other men cautioned, "it's none of your business."

Bolan pointed at the map so that they could see. "According to this, Santa Rosa de Osos is the closest town with medical facilities."

"Yes," Luis said, "but there's another place." He touched the map. "Here. Father Lazaro lives here in the house of God. He knows much of medicine."

"Sí," another man said. "He treated my boy Juan for a gunshot wound. This priest, he has healing hands."

Bolan marked the spot indicated and put the map away. If the men were right, it would save miles off his trip. And hopefully save the boy's life. He put the grim thoughts away, telling himself not to count the journey over until he'd made the last few steps. "I'll be back in a minute, Jack."

Bolan melted into the jungle. The four men hadn't been the only thing he'd heard. Five minutes later he found Burdett's horse eating leaves from a tree. He kept his voice soothing until he had the animal's reins in his hand, then led it back to the clearing.

"I've done the best I can," Grimaldi said as he stood.

Bolan nodded. "I'm going on with the boy alone," he said as he checked the gear on the horse. The canteen was almost full. He tossed the bedroll into the brush, followed by bags of ammo magazines. If he came up on someone else, a running firefight was the last of his options. "I'll wait for you at the church. You're going to have a tougher time getting there with the jeep than I will going cross-country."

"I don't like the idea of splitting up."

"Neither do I, but that isn't one of the options. This boy needs medical aid as soon as we can get it to him, and we need that jeep." He tightened the saddle girth.

"Why don't you bring the jeep?"

"Because I'm better in the brush than you are," Bolan replied. He put a foot in the stirrup and pulled himself into the saddle. The horse snorted and shifted under the weight.

"You know," Grimaldi said, "if it wasn't true, I might take offense at that."

Bolan grinned. He took up the reins and looked at the woman. *"¿Señora?"*

She came forward, holding the boy's body close to her chest. "Please be careful with him. He's such a small boy. My baby." Tears ran down her face.

Leaning forward, Bolan took the boy's slight weight into his arms. The Executioner hadn't been the only name Mack Bolan had been given in Vietnam. There were a great many who had known him as Sergeant Mercy. Flip sides of the same soul, and the man had earned them both.

Grimaldi pulled the mother away gently. "Good luck, Sarge."

"I'll see both of you there," Bolan said as he urged the horse into a walk.

"¡Vaya con Dios!" the woman called out, and the men echoed her.

Sergeant Mercy settled into the rhythm of the horse's stride, monitoring the boy's breath blowing gently against the inside of his arm.

"FATHER, FATHER!"

Father Lazaro looked down the dirt road toward the direction of the boy's voice. The midmorning sun burned down on his face when he looked up from the vegetable garden behind the church. The last of the bad pains had passed hours ago, leaving him free to work as he pleased.

"The river," the barefoot boy said excitedly, "she has been very generous this morning." He held up a stringer of fish proudly. The cane pole and red-and-white bob jerked animatedly over his shoulder.

Lazaro brushed the dirt from his palms as he stood to admire the boy's catch. "Yes, Pepe, the river has been very kind to you this morning. You should remember to give thanks."

"I will, Father."

"But," Lazaro went on, "your mother has been looking for you most of the morning. She expected you to do your chores, not run to the river as you have been doing."

"I know, Father, but I've been learning the river, the fish. I think she'll be proud of me for catching dinner instead of washing clothes."

Lazaro smiled in spite of himself. "I think so, too." He tousled the boy's hair and tried to remember when his own life had seemed so simple and unencumbered.

"Of course," the boy went on to say, "I want you to have the biggest fish for your own table."

Dust blew across the dirt road, sweeping against Lazaro's garments. Figures rippled in the haze. He replied without looking at the boy, not letting the chill that touched him reach his voice. "No, Pepe, the biggest must go to your own table. Leave one of the smaller fishes with Sister Gloria, and I will have it today."

"If you insist, Father."

"I do. Now get along. Your mother is still looking for you."

The boy fled, yelling his excitement to others his own age in the small gathering of handmade houses around the church.

Father Lazaro tucked his hands inside the sleeves of his robe and went to meet the wavering figures.

A big man, dressed in black and carrying weapons, held a small child in his arms. He led a white-lathered horse. The man's steps were heavy, as if it took concentration to make the next one.

The man was covered in death. The priest could sense that now that they were closer and his vision was more sure. The man's eyes held graveyards behind them, with tombstones that were weights tied to his soul.

"Are you Father Lazaro?" the big man asked.

"Yes."

"I need help for the boy," the man said. "I was told you knew about gunshot wounds and had medical equipment."

"Yes." Lazaro caught the attention of a teenage girl. "Maria, run and fetch Sister Yanett."

"Yes, Father."

"Quickly, please."

The girl ran.

"This way," Lazaro said, taking the man by the elbow and wondering why one tied so closely to death would try so hard to preserve life.

CHAPTER FOUR

Gary Manning sat in the Volkswagen van with Yakov Katzenelenbogen and wished the hell the older man would stop smoking. Yellow curls of smoke from the unfiltered Camel hit the bug-smeared windshield of the vehicle with astonishing regularity.

Katz was quiet. But then the Israeli ex-Mossad agent usually was unless he had something useful to say.

Shaking his head, Manning poured himself another cup of coffee from the red thermos between their seats. He blew on it, then sipped it, anyway. He refused to curse when it burned his lips.

"Stop fidgeting," Katz said.

Manning glanced irritably at the leader of Phoenix Force. They spoke French because it was a common language between them that passersby probably wouldn't understand. "I'm not fidgeting."

Katz didn't say anything.

Catching himself just as his foot started to tap the floorboard again, Manning glanced at the Israeli with renewed hostility. He hated being left out of the action, especially since McCarter was inside the condominium across the street, wandering around at something less than one hundred percent. But his lack of Spanish had designated him as a baby-sitter on the operation. It had also put him behind the wheel.

Manning knew that he and Katz didn't look the types to be hanging around a dirty microbus during a sweltering day. He figured if one of Hector Mendoza Caseros's stormtroopers took one look at them dawdling in front of the prestigious condo club, they'd be history. "I'm not fidgeting," he repeated. He focused on the rolling blue of the sea on the other side of the buildings, staring wistfully at the multicolored sails ballooning in the wind.

"I heard you the first time," Katz said, not moving.

"Then why didn't you say something?"

"It would have only started this argument."

"What argument?" Manning gave the man a look of disbelief.

"The one you're still attempting to initiate because you're bored." Katz crushed out his cigarette and lit another.

Manning waved away the sudden cloud of smoke. "My God, are you trying to choke me? What is this?"

Katz gave him a thin grin. "A proposal for disarmament. You shut up and I'll pause between cigarettes."

"I mean, come on now. It was me who turned up Armand Kingston. If it hadn't been my connection to the security section of the import-export business where I used to work, we wouldn't have found this guy at all."

"True," Katz agreed.

"It's not fair that I have to sit out here and wonder what the hell's going on in there."

"If this Armand Kingston does have ties to the Santeria religion that entices Caseros so much," Katz said, "perhaps David and Rafael are being properly entertained at this very moment."

"Terrific," Manning grumbled, turning back to watch the condo unit. "Now I have to worry not only about what they're doing, but whether they're even still alive to do it."

"They serve who also stand and wait, Gary," the Israeli reminded him.

"Yeah, but they who serve while standing and waiting rarely get to make the rest of the party. Ask any bartender. Me, I'd rather be a cocktail waitress."

"You haven't got the build for those short dresses."

Without giving any indication that something was wrong, Katz reached under his jacket, pulling his H&K 9 mm squeeze-cocker into his lap and stubbed out his cigarette in the overflowing ashtray.

Feeling a sudden gust of cool air curl around his nape, Manning glanced at the side mirror as two black limousines cruised to a halt on either side of the street. There was a moment of conversation between the drivers of the vehicles, then one of them continued on inside the condominium area proper. The other disgorged six men dressed in the uniforms of the Panamanian infantry. Most of them were armed with Uzis, though two carried CAR-15 assault rifles, letting Manning know the group intended some serious action.

"It would appear," Katz observed, "that Caseros has made our man from the photos Pablo Arevalo showed David."

"Yeah, well, our favorite Panamanian president did have a starring role with a cast worth billions and billions." Manning reached under his jacket for the Beretta 92-F but left it in the breakout leather.

Citizens scurried out of the way with practiced movements. One woman flattened herself and her three small children against a bullet-scarred wall as a trio of national army men double-timed it down the sidewalk. Once they were past, she hurried her charges on without looking back.

"I can't raise David or Rafael," Katz said. "Calvin has already spotted them. The people we've seen aren't alone."

"That means David and Rafael walked into a trap, and we let them. Damn it."

Katz nodded. "Still, Caseros's people have to spring it closed, and that won't be easy."

"No, because we won't let it be." As he watched, the three remaining men of the ground team headed in the direction of the microbus. "Ideas?"

"Start the engine," Katz instructed. "If we can pull away from here, buy us some maneuvering room, so much the better. At least we'll be mobile."

Manning switched on the key and listened to the engine rumble to life. Encizo had done some work on the microbus after they'd purchased it, making sure it was considerably more roadworthy than it appeared.

One of the uniformed men stepped in front of the vehicle and pointed his CAR-15 at the windshield. Another man brandished a pistol at Manning from the sidewalk. "Your papers," the team leader said in English. "Let me see them."

Manning raised an eyebrow and spoke in French. "Sorry, but I don't speak the language."

Puzzled by the language so similar to his native tongue, the leader stepped forward and said, "Passports," in a clear voice. He repeated himself in Spanish.

"I think we just landed in deep shit," Manning observed quietly.

Katz agreed.

Smiling, Manning put on his best Clint Eastwood voice because McCarter wasn't around to rag him about it later, and pulled the Beretta free, saying in English, "Feel lucky, punk?"

"WE'RE NOT TERRIBLY well equipped," Father Lazaro said as he finished dressing the boy's wounds, "but we've been well trained through necessity."

Bolan watched the procedure, noting that the boy's breathing had eased. He felt tired from the previous night's activities and the long trek through the jungle alternately riding and leading the horse as he carried the wounded boy.

They were in the priest's small office in the back of the church. The boy had been made comfortable on cushions piled atop the scarred desk. Books in Spanish, English and Latin lined handmade shelves along one wall, their bindings wrinkled with age, but still holding the yellowed pages. Most were on theology, but many were by Ernest Hemingway.

The priest washed his hands in a ceramic bowl that one of the two nuns assisting him held out. He smiled as he looked at the younger of the sisters. "Did you

notice the fine stitches Sister Yanett gave the boy?''
Father Lazaro asked.

Bolan nodded.

"She's the finest seamstress in the whole village,"
the priest went on. "When the wound heals, the scar
will appear much smaller because of her skills with the
needle.''

The nun blushed and took the washbasin away.

"Come," the priest said, "we'll let young Tito sleep
now." He mopped his neck with a gray handkerchief,
then put it in his pocket. "Sister, if you'll watch him.''

"Yes, Father.'' The older woman curtsied and
bowed her head. "And I'll pray for his recovery, as
well.''

The priest stopped at the bookshelves, turned aside
a copy of *The Old Man and the Sea* and took out a
bottle of whiskey. "You look like a man who could use
a stiff drink," he said to Bolan, handing him a glass.

Bolan followed the older man through the back door
and into the heat of the noonday sun. Scrawny dogs
and chickens lounged in the shade offered by trees
along the edge of the encroaching jungle. The scant
breeze was laden with too-sweet scents, advertising de-
cay.

"Here," Father Lazaro said, waving to a pair of
handcrafted chairs behind the church.

Bolan sat, the chair groaning slightly under his unaccustomed weight. The breeze felt better here, more
soothing.

The priest poured a healthy shot of whiskey in each
glass, then seated himself, putting the bottle between

them on the ground. He sipped, made a face and looked out over the church grounds.

The whiskey hit the bottom of Bolan's empty stomach with the intensity of napalm, and he coughed.

"Sorry," the priest apologized with a slight smile. "I should have warned you. This is native brew, not necessarily for the untrained palate."

"Unexpected," Bolan said, "but good." He stretched his legs before him, letting the whiskey do its job of relaxing the inner man. He checked his watch again. Grimaldi should be arriving soon. He didn't allow himself to think that the pilot might have encountered trouble. Still, Costanza wouldn't dismiss the caravan disaster without an investigation of some sort. Doubtless there was already an army en route if not actually on the site by now.

"You aren't of this country," the priest said, holding his glass before him in both hands. His eyes met the warrior's full measure.

"No."

"Yet you are here now."

"Yes."

"Why?"

Bolan shifted in the seat. "I don't want to be rude, Father, but that's business of my own."

"And the child you carried in here today? Was that business of yours?"

"Of a kind."

Father Lazaro nodded and leaned back in his chair. "I've seen many Americans through this part of Colombia in recent years. Most of them seem to be seeking their fortunes by working the coca leaf."

"But not all of them."

"No, not all of them." The priest hesitated. "I don't think you're one of these men, yet I see death all over you. You wear death in your eyes, in the way you carry your body, in the way you hold your head when you listen for noises." He reached forward, encircling the warrior's wrist with thin fingers and turning his hand palm up. "You hold death in your hands. You're scarred, on the outside as well as the inside."

"Yes." Bolan knew it was true. He'd learned to avoid seeing it in himself when he was shaving, but his missions weren't without personal cost.

"Even with this death that seems linked to you," the priest went on, "I don't think you pursue riches through the white powder, the cocaine."

"I don't." Bolan sipped the whiskey again, easing it down slower this time.

"You have the mannerisms of a soldier."

"I was. Once."

"And now?"

Bolan grinned. "Perhaps I still am."

The priest's eyes were intensely black. "And what war do you work your skills in?"

"My own."

"You must have much confidence if you can declare a war to be your own."

Bolan didn't say anything. He wondered what the priest was leading up to. A group of children carrying wet laundry from the direction of the small river crossed in front of them. Dust clung to their damp legs. Their voices were animated, filled with giggles.

"I care about these people," Father Lazaro said. "I have been priest to their families for generations. I took my vows at an early age after La Violencia swept through my country. I had hoped to help promote an era of healing with my voice and my hands. Instead, after political power, my countrymen learned of the power contained in the coca leaf."

Bolan finished his drink and was poured another without asking.

"I have listened to a good many confessions over the years. I have heard of heartbreak, of sorrows, of fears, of guilts that might break the spirit of lesser men." Father Lazaro looked down the twisting dirt road leading from the church. "I can truthfully tell you that none have challenged my heart as much as the confession I heard this morning."

Bolan waited, sensing the emotion in the older man's words and being moved by it.

"The woman came to me and told me she had sinned by picking the coca leaf that causes so many deaths. I know her. The only reason she works in the fields is to feed her family. Her husband is a good man, a hard-working man, but they have many children. It takes both of them, and the older children at times, to see to their needs. This woman is carrying a double burden of guilt. She must care for her family, and she must care for her soul. Which must she place first? Do you understand?"

Bolan nodded. "I understand."

"So I talk to her in the confessional, then we leave, each with our own thoughts. Still, even though I know who she is, I must not admit this when we meet face-to-face. I can't console her as a friend would. The curtain between the booths still exists for us." Father Lazaro sighed and drained his glass. "The boy in there, he isn't the first I've treated who has been a victim of the cocaine trade. Many have died in that room, and we have buried them behind the church. Some of them have no names because we never knew them. Even here, tucked away in the jungle as we are, death touches all around us."

"Death is a natural part of life, Father," Bolan said in a gentle voice.

"Yes, I know this, and I accept it. But today I prayed for knowledge of what to do about the things I have seen." The priest looked at Bolan. "Do you pray?"

The Executioner nodded. "When I feel I'm not being hypocritical."

"A man of war always knows of God, as well."

Bolan smiled slightly. "Just as a man of God knows of war and fear."

"Yes." Father Lazaro raised his glass. "Your health, my friend."

"And yours."

They drank.

"This morning I received an answer to my prayers," the priest said, studying Bolan silently. "And I don't think your arrival here was purely chance, either."

Bolan said nothing.

"The privilege of confession is a sacred thing," the priest said, "and I don't want to break it. Still, there are a great many things I have learned that I feel must be passed on to the right ears, things that will help someone who is attacking Luis Costanza and others of the cartel." He paused. "There were others who arrived here before you. They told me of the attack on the caravan by the men dressed in black, and I have heard on the radio and seen on television shows how other attacks have been made on Costanza's, Mercado's and Rodriguez's holdings in Medellín and Bogotá. I think I'm looking at one of the men responsible. If you're interested, I have much to tell you of the operations those men are conducting in the jungle. I can tell you the location of labs where they prepare the cocaine, of managerial people involved, of travel routes, and many other things."

Bolan set his glass down. "I'm listening."

"THIS IS ALL too bloody easy," David McCarter said as they stepped off the elevator on the eighth floor of the condominium. He touched the familiar lines of his Browning Hi-Power, tucked into the waistband of his pants. The windbreaker he wore concealed the weapon from view. McCarter had a narrow face with high cheekbones. The yellow-lensed aviator sunglasses he wore helped soften the bleak hardness of his features and, combined with the longish light brown hair trickling over the tops of his ears, served to take almost ten years off his age.

"Grouchy this morning, aren't we?" Rafael Encizo asked. The Cuban-born member of Phoenix Force was a compact study of control. His hair was black and curly, framing a face that could easily pass for Indian. The first signs of hardness were the flat brown eyes and the white scar beneath his mouth.

"No," McCarter said gruffly, "just bloody cautious after what happened yesterday." The nightmares that had visited him before dawn were still sharply etched in his memory. He was no stranger to torture, but he knew it would take time to scar over the experience. Pain in his rib cage still surged throughout his body whenever he moved. The cigarette burns across his chest had turned an ugly gray-yellow by this morning and looked as if they might become infected. He had noticed Katz watching him as they prepared for the raid on Armand Kingston, and had known if he'd shown any evidence of weakness, Phoenix's team leader wouldn't have let him work the inside part of the job. And there was simply no way in hell he was going to sit in the microbus with Gary Manning.

"What are you smiling about?" Encizo asked as they rounded a corner.

"I was just thinking about Katz trapped out there in that VW with Manning." McCarter snorted derisively. "Hell, mate, if Caseros's men had wanted to really threaten me with a fate worse than death, all they'd have had to do was capture Manning when they got me and throw us in a closet together. I'd have told them anything they wanted to hear inside of ten minutes."

"Manning probably wouldn't have lasted that long."

McCarter looked up sharply. Encizo was so bloody quiet that a man didn't often realize he was setting himself up.

"Here," the Cuban said.

McCarter looked at the door and saw the gilt numbers 804. He checked the hallway with his peripheral vision, having to move his head somewhat because the swelling of the cut under one eye hadn't completely gone down. Seeing no one there, he reached under the windbreaker and drew the Hi-Power, flicking the safety off immediately.

Encizo produced his Beretta 92-F and reached for the door, jiggling the knob gently. Nothing happened. "Locked," he grunted, reaching into a pocket.

Still in a nasty mood, McCarter said, "Why don't you just ring the doorbell and tell him your story about being an insurance investigator looking into the matter of the fire on his boat?"

Inserting a lockpick into the door, Encizo said, "Because Kingston isn't like the office personnel in the condominium. He knows he doesn't own a boat." The lock gave a satisfying snick.

"He might," McCarter insisted. "We don't know that he doesn't."

Encizo ignored him. "I got the left and high."

"I got the rest of it, mate." All playfulness was gone from McCarter's voice now. "Hit it."

The Cuban swung the door open, extending his arm inside with the Beretta. Dropping to one knee with a grunt of pain, McCarter covered the room, holding the Browning in a modified Weaver grip. Nothing moved inside the room. The living room was large and spacious, befitting a member of Caseros's personal guard, and windows let in a lot of morning sunlight. The stereo played softly, some kind of blues piece.

"I got your back," McCarter said as Encizo moved into the apartment. The Briton closed the door behind them and threw the dead bolt. A familiar smell tickled his nostrils, but he couldn't place it. "Looks like no-body's home."

Encizo kept his 9 mm pistol pointed straight ahead, up and ready. "The man was here when Manning placed the call twenty minutes ago."

"Maybe Manning called the wrong number. Didn't ask who he was talking to, just hung up when a man answered. Be about up to bleedin' speed for this operation. Manning calls the wrong number, so we waste our time hitting this place while across town some guy's giving his wife hell over some boyfriend that doesn't even exist."

"The man likes his music," Encizo said, gazing at the well-stocked shelves by the stereo in true admiration.

"Yeah, well, we aren't here to see what the man thinks of the American Top 40." McCarter's surliness had returned full force, and he didn't try to hide it. "I got the rear rooms. Try to keep your mitts off his Elvis collection."

When he found the body in the bedroom, McCarter placed the unidentified smell. Armand Kingston had been a male black in his middle forties, blocky and big, with an American football history in his past. Someone had reduced Armand Kingston to a lump of disfigured meat in the center of a bloodstained bed.

The Briton walked to the bed, holding a handkerchief over his nose and mouth. Someone enthusiastic had taken his time with his knife. He knew there was no way in hell Kingston had been able to take Manning's call. McCarter retreated, pausing in the hallway as Encizo looked up at him. "We're made."

"Kingston?"

"In here. Looks like something out of a Clive Barker novel."

Encizo held up an old Buddy Holly album.

"Go ahead," McCarter said sarcastically. "Kingston bloody well won't mind."

Shaking his head, Encizo began, "That's not what this is about—"

The rest of his words were lost as a shotgun blast blew a hole through the door.

LYING ON THE ROOF of the building across the street from the condo, Calvin James used binoculars to keep watch over the window they'd decided belonged to Armand Kingston. He stayed under cover of a maintenance tarp he'd carried with him to check, supposedly, the building's HVAC units. He wore an orange coverall, which he'd swiped from the actual company that performed maintenance on the condo buildings earlier that morning.

His walkie-talkie crackled with static, but so far there had been no other communications from Katz or Manning. McCarter and Encizo were buried too deep inside the building to attempt outside contact.

The sounds of shots being fired out on the street drove him under the tarp. Katz and Manning were out of his field of view, but if they were in trouble, it stood to reason that McCarter and Encizo could be, as well. He came out with the Beretta M-21 semiauto sniper rifle he'd carried up in his toolbox. He'd opted for the M-21 because the distance between the buildings wasn't so great, and because the weapon sported a 20-round box of .308 Winchester bullets. He focused on Kingston's window. Nothing moved.

The sound of the shot arrived after the bullet that dug out a fist-size chunk of tar and pebbles near James's left elbow. Shifting the M-21 on its bipod, he searched for the sniper as the crack of the weapon echoed through the still, hot air. A glint of light drew his attention to the top of the ten-story building McCarter and Encizo were in.

The sound of helicopter rotors nearly deafened James as he trained the scope on the area where the brief spark of light had been. The backwash from the rotors beat at his clothing, stirring up dust and loose pebbles that stung his face. He ignored the helicopter for the moment because *it* wasn't shooting at him. The image blurred as he adjusted the scope's magnification, then it cleared on the bright flash of the enemy's scope.

Unable to see the man's face, James aimed for the bright blur, knowing death for one of them could only be a heartbeat away.

CHAPTER FIVE

Reports from Manning's Beretta were earsplitting inside the confines of the microbus. The 9 mm parabellums cored through the soft metal of the door and into the officer standing on the other side. The man dropped immediately, clutching helplessly at the gaping wounds blasted into his stomach, then died.

"Get down!" the Canadian roared as he let off the clutch and steered for the soldier carrying the CAR-15.

Katz twisted in the seat, leaned out the window and fired with his arm braced across his metal prosthesis. Autofire raked the front of the Volkswagen. One of the rounds punctured the bodywork and clipped Manning's boot heel, knocking his foot from the accelerator. Then the front tires crunched over the soldier's body and the gunfire stopped.

Pulling the steering wheel savagely, Manning directed the microbus into the flow of oncoming traffic. Horns blared as drivers locked their brakes and fishtailed through all four lanes of traffic. The sound of collisions trailed in their wake, punctuated by sporadic bursts of gunfire.

"Suggestions?" Manning asked, darting a look over his shoulder. The black limousine, scarred from the bullets Katz had pumped into it, moved sluggishly from the curb and took up pursuit.

"Keep your eyes on the road ahead of you," the Israeli replied as he braced himself.

Manning glanced quickly ahead as a large flatbed truck loaded with crates of fruit slewed into their path. Unable to totally avoid the vehicle, he floored the accelerator and shifted into second, knowing momentum might mean the difference between getting through or getting stuck.

The microbus caught the rear outside corner of the flatbed and shivered as the metal screamed through the row of windows and sheet metal on the driver's side. The dual wheels of the truck's rear axle slipped across the pavement, and fruit spilled from the crates in a colorful rainbow.

Manning downshifted, double-clutching for power, then released the clutch and felt the entire driveline jerk as the microbus ripped free of the truck with a metallic screech. He glanced back at the damage as he swerved around a stalled late-model Chevrolet. A long tear ran down the side of the VW.

"Shit," he said with real feeling. Manning glanced back at the road and cut off two advancing cars as he made a left at the intersection. "There goes any chance we had of getting away unnoticed in this thing."

"At least you're remaining optimistic," Katz replied.

The Canadian looked at him expectantly.

The leader of Phoenix Force was busy opening the catches on one of their equipment cases. "You still believe we're going to get away." Katz gave him a cold smile.

Seeing the traffic blocking the next light, Manning laid on the horn and pulled over onto the sidewalk. People scattered from his path. "Yeah, we're going to get away. The only thing that worries me is what McCarter's going to say when he sees this goddamn van. I'll have to listen to him ride me for weeks."

"It could be worse," Katz said as he slipped between the seats and quickly assembled the M-249 SAW. "We could all be captured and thrown into prison together. Perhaps you and McCarter could end up manacled together for years."

The microbus jumped as it hit the end of the sidewalk and collided with the street again. The fact that Manning hit no one when he swerved again, this time to the right, was partly skill and partly luck.

He glanced toward the driver's outside mirror and felt foolish when he realized it had been ripped off by the flatbed. The rearview mirror revealed Katz falling into position across the rear seat as the first limousine charged into view. It was black and polished chrome, flying tiny red, white and blue flags of Panama from the front fenders. A second limo followed a heartbeat later, powering through the stalled traffic like a large black shark.

"Keep us steady," Katz ordered as he lined up the squad automatic weapon.

Manning concentrated on his driving, suddenly aware that the blue of the ocean was to his left, covered with white triangular sails sporting colorful stripes and schemes.

The SAW cut loose with a full-throated roar that scattered brass all over the microbus's interior. Man-

ning bit back a curse as he yanked one of the hot cas-
ings from the back of his shirt and hurled it to the
floor. The M-855 hardball fired by the Belgian Fab-
rique Nationale light machine gun was capable of pen-
etrating a steel helmet at over fourteen hundred yards.
With the 200-round magazine clipped in place, the
weapon was nothing short of devastating. The 5.56 mm
rounds crunched through the front end of the lead
limousine. Both tires blew at roughly the same time,
dropping the carriage inches and throwing the vehicle
out of control. It spun helplessly for a moment, then
smashed into a lamppost, which crashed on top of it
moments later.

The second limousine, already bearing scars from
the previous engagement, pulled around the other in a
sudden burst of acceleration. Bullets from the SAW
chewed into the side of the limo and spit safety glass
over the occupants.

Abruptly there was nowhere else for Manning to go.
A phalanx of military jeeps swarmed across the street
in front of him as guardsmen knelt behind the protection the vehicles provided. It looked as if they were
rushing headlong into a firing squad.

"Katz!"

The SAW ceased firing. "The docks. It's our only
chance."

Manning cut the wheel hard left, downshifting into
first and grinding the gears as he let the transmission
help slow their acceleration. There was a moment of
indecision, as if the microbus might flip over on its
side, then the wheels along the left side banged back

down. The wooden dock was rickety and rough, and Manning saw that it ended too damn soon to stop.

"Katz, we don't have—"

The Israeli scrambled back between the seats, abandoning the SAW. "Don't stop. We'll take our chances with the water."

The big Canadian nodded tightly, shifting into second as the microbus slammed through the chain-link gates designed to keep tourists out. Chains fractured, links popping against the Volkswagen's body like hailstones.

The microbus hit the end of the dock and sailed into the air, describing a short parabola that filled the windshield with nothing but ocean just before impact. Katz opened his door and threw himself out before they hit the water. Something hit the back of the van with a liquid thump, and heat flooded the interior, followed instantly by flames.

Releasing the useless wheel, Manning reached for his door and jerked the handle, only to find that the impact that had ripped the side open had also sprung the latch. Trapped, he went down with the microbus. Water slammed into the windshield and tore it loose, ramming it back toward the Canadian. Manning had one lucid moment before blackness swallowed him, then he was lost in the undertow, dragged deeper and deeper.

JACK GRIMALDI STUMBLED out of the jungle with Tito's mother in tow, the pilot looking somewhat rough and worse for the wear. His jaw was darkened by dirt and a five o'clock shadow, and dust covered the lenses of his aviator sunglasses. His Galil was in hand.

"My son!" the young mother cried in Spanish when she saw Father Lazaro, who went to comfort her.

Bolan closed his current war journal after glancing at the neatly written and copious notes Father Lazaro had given him. Combined with the intel he'd gotten from Stony Man and Kurtzman's electronic marvels, he figured he was in possession of invaluable information. The problem he faced now lay in being able to utilize it to its fullest advantage. He stood and shoved the slim volume into a thigh pocket of the blacksuit.

"The boy?" Grimaldi asked when they met in the center of the dirt road.

"He's hanging in there."

"Glad to hear that." The pilot jerked a thumb toward the jungle. "They got a goddamn army out there searching for us."

"Costanza's men?"

"Yeah, and with Ortega leading the operation, you can sure as hell bet they're leaving no stone unturned. I had to ditch the jeep a couple of miles back. I stashed the equipment about a mile from here, then circled back and tried to make it look like I'd lost the jeep down a ravine off the main road. I don't know how convincing it'll be."

"Won't matter," Bolan replied. "Even if they don't think we knew about the church, they'll search it just to be sure." A short-horned goat with long blue-gray hair waded through a dozen white chickens pecking industriously at the ground in front of the soldier.

Grimaldi looked around, slung his rifle over his shoulder and shoved his hands into his back pockets. "This isn't what I'd call an ideal place for a confrontation. There's a lot of innocent people here who could get killed."

"I know. That's why we're going to make sure Ortega knows we're not here before they ever reach the church."

"I hope you've got something in mind," Grimaldi said, "because I'm beat."

"I do. Drop your gear and take ten, then we're moving out."

Grimaldi nodded and headed for the well, uncapping his canteen. Bolan walked to the church to join the priest, who stood in the doorway, looking at Tito and his mother, reunited at last. "He'll need to be moved," Bolan stated.

Father Lazaro nodded. "He will be. There's a room under the church, built there in harder times than these, which was used to hide the women and children when the bandits came. They'll be safe there."

"What about you?"

"Costanza won't let any of his men do anything to me or the sisters as long as he believes there's a chance of my blessing on the things he does. He won't admit that chance doesn't exist. At least not yet. Finding the boy here, or perhaps any of the others associated with the caravan, that might prove to be another matter." The priest looked back at the mother and son. "This is a good thing you have done." He glanced up at the warrior. "I don't even know your name."

"It's better that way for now."

The priest nodded. "When will you be leaving?"

"Now, but I need something first."

"Anything I have."

"I need some fishing line."

Father Lazaro started to say something, then changed his mind. "This way." He led the way down the narrow hall to an even smaller room than his office. It held a bed, shelves with more books and clay figurines that had been shaped by the hands of children. A wire rack held more black garments, and there were two extra collars. A twelve-inch black-and-white television sat on a small table at the foot of the bed. The wavering screen glowed gray and showed people as gray ghosts in darker gray suits. The priest shook his head in embarrassment as he reached for the on/off switch. "My one vice," he said. "I do like to see other parts of the world. Not with covetous thoughts, but to see how truly large and magnificent the world is."

"Wait."

The priest dropped his hand.

The screen showed a Colombian male in his early thirties surrounded by Medellín police officers. A few sharp explosions of gunfire flared across the screen, revealing that despite the grayness it was a picture of the night. The caption at the bottom of the screen was almost illegible, but Bolan made it out. The dateline was the same time he and Grimaldi had been hitting Costanza's airstrip north of Medellín.

Shifting perspective, the television camera zoomed in on the Colombian male. He was thin, regal-looking, with an aquiline nose that held more than a hint of the predator. He spoke with passion and vigor, condemning the cartel members who had fought it out in the streets of Medellín, a confrontation that had resulted in the loss of eighteen innocent lives.

"Who is he?" Bolan asked as the man on television demanded justice.

"His name is Benito Franco," the priest said. "He's the new justice minister of Colombia. As you can see, he's violently opposed to the drug trade in our country. But there's not much support for him. These are fearful times for the young. They don't remember La Violencia, nor do they imagine how bad things can become. They would rather hide their heads in the sand and hope things go away."

"But Franco isn't satisfied with that?"

"No. Some of his campaigns against cartel members have met with success, and he speaks often of using the extradition of cartel people to America. There are many who fear for his life."

Considering the wealth and power of the people Franco was setting himself up against, Bolan could understand that, at the same time wondering how hard and how far Colombia's justice minister would be willing to push.

MCCARTER SLIPPED the Browning Hi-Power from his waistband as a second discharge from the shotgun in the hallway blew another hole in Armand Kingston's door. He squeezed off seven shots of the pistol's 14-round capacity at chest level across the door and the walls on either side, spacing them roughly six inches apart. There was no doubt in his mind they'd been set up by Caseros' guardsmen after finding the body.

He was rewarded by a cry of pain, then he was racing backward, following Encizo toward the bedroom. "That little discouragement won't hold them long, mate," he said.

Encizo shrugged out of his sport jacket and ripped his shirt open, revealing the shoulder leather holding his Beretta 92-F and a thin coil of knotted nylon around his waist. He jerked at a knot over his hip and the cord slipped to his feet. "Break out the window," he directed as he affixed a collapsible grappling hook from his jacket pocket to one end of the cord.

The Briton ripped a drawer from a nearby chest and smashed it into the window. Glass, drawer and contents sailed outward, scattering like confetti. "It's gonna be a tight fit, mate." He stuck his head out the broken window and looked eight floors down. "And no way in bloody hell have you got enough cord to reach the street." He stepped back out of the other man's way.

"We can't go down," Encizo said. "They have that covered. Listen to the gunfire coming from the street. I'd say Katz and Manning have their hands full about now, too. We're going up. Maybe we can get through on another building and buy ourselves some time."

McCarter nodded grimly, looking at the height again. It didn't bother him when he was in a plane. A man had equipment he knew and could trust surrounding him, and enough height to use a parachute in case all else failed. But it didn't even compare to dangling eight stories above terra firma by something constructed of the same material that went into women's stockings. "Get started as soon as you can, and I'll slow these joes down a tad."

Encizo made his first cast as he leaned out the window. The slack line and the grappling hook came spinning back down a heartbeat later.

Knowing he couldn't bear to watch, McCarter retreated to the door, slipping a spare magazine for the Browning from his hip pocket. A pair of arms holding a crowbar smashed through the door and shattered the lock. The door flew open.

Using his arm as a brace, McCarter shot the man with the crowbar through the elbow. The force of the 9 mm parabellum spun the man around and dropped him onto the carpeted floor of the hallway. The Briton squeezed off two more shots before the man could get to his feet, driving the corpse back to the floor. He smiled grimly. None of the other men in the hallway seemed eager to join in the festivities. He fired the last four shots in the clip into the walls to weed out any would-be heroes in the bunch, then stepped back inside the doorway as he changed clips.

Encizo looked at him and yanked on the cord. "It's set."

McCarter nodded. "You go on ahead. I'll just stay behind and tidy up a few things here, then I'll nip right along."

"Calvin said there's some action on the rooftop, too," Encizo said. "We could be jumping from the frying pan into the fire."

McCarter winced at his teammate's choice of words. Eight stories up, the last thing he wanted to think about was jumping. "I'd rather take my chances in the open. Keeps everybody honest."

"See you up top."

"Bet on it." McCarter moved back into the doorway just as a guardsman charged through the door screaming defiance. The shotgun in the man's hands roared, blasting a chunk of Sheetrock and acoustic tile from the ceiling.

McCarter stood his ground and shot the man through his open mouth. He brushed the falling body aside as another man started through the door. He squeezed off four rounds in quick succession, following the guardsman's move with reflex rather than intentional tracking. The man went down. Reaching into a pocket of his windbreaker, McCarter pulled out a stun grenade. They'd called them flash-bangs during his tenure with the SAS. He armed the orb and flipped it into the hall, emptying the clip into the walls and corridor. The detonation of the grenade took away all sound and flooded the immediate vicinity with smoke and light.

Slipping his last spare clip into the Browning, McCarter ran for the window. The nylon cord twisted in the breeze. He breathed a silent prayer as he put the safety on the Hi-Power, grabbed the cord and stepped out into the open space.

McCarter put all thoughts of falling from his mind as he hauled himself up the rope. It was only two stories to the top, something over nine yards. Encizo was nowhere to be seen. He remembered the Cuban's comment that Calvin James had reported action atop their building. An image of the collapsible grappling hook flashed through his mind and he tried not to remember he was something over 180 pounds hanging from perhaps only one of those small metal arms. The soreness of his body ate at him with fish hooks. Gravity pulled at the other end of the line, sucking him toward the street.

A man stuck his head through the window of Kingston's apartment just as McCarter threw his arm over the edge of the roof. The gunner lined up his CAR-15.

McCarter twisted and drew the Browning, flicking off the safety. He put two shots into the man's chest just as a line of 5.56 tumblers chewed brick splinters from the wall and into his face. The guardsman fell out the window, screaming his death as he hurtled toward the street.

Not waiting to watch the impact, McCarter threw his gun arm over the roof and hauled himself up. Encizo had taken cover behind an air-conditioning unit, his Beretta braced on the corner.

At first McCarter didn't know what the problem was. A sniper lay stretched out beside the unit, but the man was definitely going nowhere. James's shot had been right on the money, driving through both ends of the scope and into the eye and brain behind it. McCarter wondered if James was aware of how close it had been. Then he felt the backwash of rotors as the sound of a helicopter engine penetrated his numbed ears.

He ducked behind the edge of the roof and hauled up the grappling hook and nylon cord. The helicopter came by on a low pass. A man holding an H&K G-11 caseless assault rifle leaned out the passenger door and sprayed the rooftop.

McCarter didn't waste time returning fire. He looked at Encizo and waved toward the rooftop door as the helicopter flew past. Encizo nodded and shifted so that he could cover the door. Pulling his walkie-talkie from his pocket, McCarter said, "Katz."

"Out of commission," James called back. "He and Manning caught some flanker action and ended up in the water."

McCarter leaned over the rooftop and looked out at the ocean. A line of military jeeps filled the end of one dock as gunners ran to take up positions. "Are they all right?"

"I don't know. I had to sit here and watch."

The Briton glanced up and saw the helicopter attempting another pass. "We need a way out of here, mate."

"Don't I know it," James replied.

"You did a pip of a job on the sniper they had over here," McCarter said as he shifted and coiled up the nylon cord with one hand.

"Don't even tell me how close it was."

McCarter grinned in spite of the desperate situation. The helicopter had leveled off, and the gunner was standing down in position again. "You're pretty good on stationary targets, mate, but how good are you on moving ones?"

"Try me."

McCarter gathered his feet under him, staying under the shelter of the roof. Encizo's pistol drummed out a rapid tattoo, letting him know the odds against their survival were increasing. ''When I pop up, I want you to take out the gunner and leave the pilot intact. Can you do that?''

''You planning on acting as bait?''

''Something like that,'' McCarter replied. ''I promise he'll definitely be interested in me.''

'':You might keep an eye peeled for any other bastards aboard that chopper. I'm going to be busy for a few minutes, and Rafael's got his hands full pinning down the ground team.''

''Can do.''

McCarter sincerely hoped so. He put the walkie-talkie on the rooftop. He didn't need the extra weight. His maneuver would be hard enough as it was. Still, he couldn't keep the grin off his face. He inventoried his personal assets as the helicopter closed in on the building. There were eleven rounds left in the Hi-Power, plus the knife leathered to his leg.

The helicopter gunner chewed hell out of the roof with the 4.7 mm rounds. McCarter stood up, twirling the grappling hook high above his head. As the Briton made his cast, the door gunner tried to track back on him, then froze and tumbled from the helicopter, spiraling out with flailing arms and legs.

The grappling hook sailed true, wrapping around one of the helicopter's skids only seven yards above his head. McCarter ran with the helicopter's forward momentum to lessen the shock he was expecting when the nylon cord grew taut. He took up slack, gritting his teeth as he expected the pain from his wounds to flare into new life.

Then he ran out of roof, his tennis shoes suddenly encountering nothing but ten stories of air.

CHAPTER SIX

"Have you seen my balls?" Alexander Constantine asked. He peered beneath the sofa, wondering if they might have rolled under there. It bothered him that they were missing. He was usually so organized with everything.

Sheila came out of the yacht's bedroom naked, dripping from the shower. "As a matter of fact," she said with a wicked grin, "I did only a few minutes ago."

Still on his knees, Constantine held up his tennis racket. "Not those balls. These balls."

"No, but now that you mention it, maybe Day-Glo orange would look good on you."

"Shit." Constantine stood. He was dressed, wearing tailored white tennis shorts, a green polo shirt with the current appropriate animal over his pocket, and designer tennis shoes. The bronze tan was provided by the health club he was a founding member of, backed by the hours he spent on the yacht in harbor and out. The toothpaste-white smile had been expensive, but he owned it now, even if most of the material wasn't original equipment. His natural hair was blond, but his hairstylist colored it to get rid of the premature gray and give it the highlights that looked so good on television and in the newspapers.

"Come on, Alex, it's not like you don't have the money to buy a few more tennis balls."

He shook his head. "Sheila, do you know why I have the money I do?"

She went into her kitten act, and he knew she was aware she'd irritated him. She tickled him under his clean-shaven chin. "Because you're Miami's hottest lawyer, ducks."

He stepped away from her hand, for once finding her attempted British accent unamusing. She covered her breasts protectively, a confused look on her face. "No, it's because I work hard at what I do. I make the deals. I set myself up in business. I work all the time, always thinking of ways to protect what I have and capitalize on whatever comes my way. I don't take it for granted that my life is going to be smooth sailing and figure tomorrow will take care of itself."

"Hey, I'm sorry."

He glared at her for a moment, then checked his gold Rolex with the oversize face. The narrower, more refined one, he saved for court. Seeing that he was going to be late if he didn't hurry, he started looking for his balls again.

"Is there anything I can do?" she asked.

Her voice was anxious, making him think she was more concerned about the meal ticket she'd found in him than in helping him. "Sure, find my balls for me."

They found them in the fruit bowl a few minutes later, smaller than the navel oranges he had delivered. Constantine knew he hadn't put them there. The woman had already started exercising domesticity, and he hadn't even realized it. The thought chilled him. He shoved the balls into his pockets, then took Sheila by the shoulders, giving her one of the smiles he'd practiced in mirrors until he'd perfected them.

"How long have we been seeing each other?" he asked.

She traced the smile lines of his face with her forefinger the way he used to find so diverting. "About a month."

"Look, I'm sorry. I didn't mean to snap at you. It's just that I've got this case coming up in the next few days, and it's real important to me."

"It's okay. Really, it's okay. I understand. Sometimes, when I'm transcribing testimonies during trials, I get the same way."

He sighed one of the sighs he'd practiced for the courtroom. He'd learned a long time ago that he was always on trial, always prepping for an audience. "Sheila, I think maybe we just need some time away from each other. A few days. Until this blows over."

He knew he'd hurt her, but he didn't really care. He was more concerned that he'd let her develop those territorial feelings without noticing. The last thing he needed was some lovesick female hanging around and fouling up his plans.

Tears glinted in her eyes, and she turned away from him. He watched her go, her buttocks swishing and creating desire within him. He would miss that ass. He shook his head and went topside after tucking a pair of Foster Grants in place, jogging from his slip to his bright red convertible, knowing there were dozens of bikinied young women watching him. He would miss

Sheila, but the woman wasn't irreplaceable. None of them were.

The cellular phone rang as he slid behind the wheel, and he answered it at once. Like the special lines in the yacht and his penthouse, this phone only rang when it was important business.

"Constantine," he said into the mouthpiece. He recognized Luis Costanza's voice immediately.

"There's a problem," Costanza informed him, "and I want you active on it now."

"Yes, sir," Constantine replied, keeping the irritability from his voice, "but there are some things I have to do this afternoon."

"None of them are as important as this, *sí?*"

Constantine looked at the yacht, knowing he'd never have owned it or any of the other things in his life without Costanza's patronage. "Of course." He tossed the tennis racket onto the floorboard on the passenger side.

"Maria Teresina is missing, and none of my people has been able to find her. I want you to handle the matter stateside. If you run into something you can't handle through regular channels, call me. I'll have someone tend to it. She must be found at all costs, amigo. La Araña is sitting on much of the product. With things that have been happening in Colombia, control of that product has become of primary importance."

"I understand. There's been some mention of your problems in the news here, but no special emphasis on your activities."

"Believe me, Alex, the special attention is being paid here. In spades." Costanza exhaled evenly. "There was a man, Chad Lewis, who was with the DEA when the recent attempt on Teresina's life was made."

Panic filled Constantine, and he wondered if he took all the money he could get his hands on and started to run now who would catch him first—Costanza or the Feds? He squelched the impulse because he knew it would be Costanza. It would be better to take his chances with the American legal system. At least there were loopholes in it. Costanza's justice was quick and merciless, with no chance for appeal.

"Find out about this Chad Lewis."

"You think the DEA is onto Teresina's connection to you?"

"At this point I don't know. The people who attempted to assassinate Teresina have links to the Mercado and Rodriguez factions. I'm still examining those."

"I don't want to get caught in the middle of this." Constantine's voice sounded hollow.

Costanza laughed softly. "Alex, Alex, you should have thought of that when you started taking my money so long ago."

Gripping the steering wheel tightly, Constantine kept his anger in check. "I thought we were business partners."

"We are. I just want you to know how serious this business is. Much more important than a tennis game." Costanza laughed again, but it sounded forced.

Constantine looked over his shoulder to see if he could spot whoever was watching him. He couldn't.

"And a further piece of advice," Costanza added. "If you lose the woman, you're a fool. She's been of help to you before, and she has those occasions when she's very creative in bed. You just need to manage her better, not cut her loose."

"You bugged my yacht." Constantine was outraged, and his words were tempered with anger. But it felt futile.

"*Sí,*" Costanza admitted. "And your apartment, as well. It helps make sure no one else plants bugs there. I own you, Alex. I want to keep this friendly, business between friends, you see, but when you get to the bottom line, I own you. The only reason I mention this now is so you'll know how important this is to me. How important it is to both of us."

Constantine remained silent.

"Call me the minute you find out anything." Costanza broke the connection.

Replacing the dead receiver, Constantine looked up in time to see Sheila leave the yacht. She wore a patterned halter dress, sunglasses, and went barefoot, carrying her sleep-over bag and shoes. He figured the sad look on her face was only a drop in the bucket compared to the emotions coursing through him. He waited until her car was lost in the distance, then returned to the yacht to change into his working clothes.

CALVIN JAMES WAS so astonished to see McCarter stepping off the building he forgot what he was doing for a moment. He tracked his Phoenix Force teammate with the scope. The Briton swung like a pendulum under the helicopter, buffeted by the winds of the slipstream, then started up the cord hand over hand.

Realizing he was limiting his field of vision, James opened his other eye in time to see another guardsman start to climb into the passenger seat, unlimbering a handgun of some sort. James closed his eye, peered through the scope, centered the cross hairs over the man's chest, let out half a breath and squeezed the trigger. The .308 Winchester round threw the man back into the pilot as the bullet tore ragged cracks in the Plexiglas bubble.

Jerking to the pilot's side, the helicopter lost altitude, plunging dangerously close to a building before recovering. McCarter stopped climbing long enough to take the brunt of the building on one leg.

For one precarious moment James was sure the man was going to be torn from the slender cord. He let out his breath as McCarter started climbing again. Glancing over his shoulder, he saw that the national guardsmen were still intent on finding Manning and Katz. He shifted his attention back to McCarter because whatever help they could give lay in that direction. McCarter had a hand on one of the skids now. No one else appeared to be moving inside the aircraft.

James squinted through the scope as McCarter drew himself up to a standing position. The pilot held a MAC-10 in one hand, waiting for the stowaway. The helicopter spun in place, buzzing noisily as it climbed steadily upward. For a moment James lost it against the morning sun. Pain filled his eye, but he didn't blink. A tear coursed down his cheek from the sunlight. The subgun shuddered in the pilot's hand,

McCarter ducking out of the way as bullets tore through the thin sheet metal skin. Hoping the Briton would realize what had happened, James squeezed the trigger and put a round through the pilot's face.

The helicopter jerked out of control. James tracked it as McCarter pulled himself inside and fisted the yoke. He sighed with relief as the chopper came into line and hovered over Encizo's position. The pilot's body thumped onto the pebbled rooftop, followed a few seconds later by a rope ladder. The Cuban paused long enough to toss a grenade at the door of the roof, then grabbed the ladder. McCarter took off immediately.

Turning his attention back to the dock situation, James scouted the water. There was no sign of Manning or Katz except for the floating beret and the oil scum starting to form rainbows on the ocean. He blinked to clear his vision. The helicopter was flying over the dock area and drawing attention. The crowd broke and ran along the boat slips. The staccato sounds of autofire ripped through the distance.

McCarter dropped the helicopter and presented the passenger side to the crowd. Encizo stepped out onto the skid with the pilot's MAC-10. The guardsmen, those hit and those unharmed, fell back in a wave.

Knowing that Katz or Manning—or both—had to be in the vicinity, James calibrated the six hundred yards to the dock and leaned into the scope. He laid down a withering blast directed at anything in Panamanian military colors. The guardsmen didn't waste time taking cover.

Under McCarter's sure hand, the helicopter dropped to within four feet of the ocean surface, spreading concentric circles of white foam. Manning clambered aboard, followed by Katz.

"All right," James breathed as he changed magazines. He picked off three would-be sharpshooters as the helicopter climbed skyward.

"Aye, mate," McCarter's voice came over the walkie-talkie. "Better plan on making your ride the first time round, 'cause this bus won't be coming back."

James smiled and picked up the walkie-talkie. "You just get somewhere close and don't worry about me." He ran through the 20-round magazine as the helicopter came closer, making sure the ante was raised high enough to keep most of the guardsmen intent on their own survival. A scattered dozen or so bullets whined off the side of the building.

Slinging the M-21 over his shoulder, James caught the trailing rope ladder and was reeled in by Encizo and Katz. Once he was aboard, McCarter headed for the outskirts of Panama City, aiming for the thick, verdant jungle. "They were waiting on us," James commented as he hunkered down.

"It was a chance we knew we were taking when we decided to pursue Kingston's involvement," Katz said. He shook a cigarette from a watertight container and lit up.

James shook his head. "So we came out of it empty-handed."

"Not quite," Encizo said in his calm voice. He sat in the passenger seat, holding a record album. "Do you know what this is?"

James looked at it. "Buddy Holly. So what? Damn, Rafael, between you and your partner, I don't know who makes less sense. He's lassoing helicopters and jumping off buildings and you're playing *Jeopardy* with golden oldies."

Enciso smiled and tapped the album cover. "Collector's item. Kingston was a music lover, yet he had a collector's item like this little gem in with a stack of regular albums. Made me curious, so I looked inside." He held up mimeographed sheets of paper. "Guess what I found?"

"A copy of Howard Hughes's last will and testament," McCarter answered.

Enciso shook his head. "Wrong." He held the sheaf up for inspection. "How does the location and layout of Caseros's safehouse for Colombian drug dealers grab you?"

"No kidding," Manning said.

"No kidding," Enciso replied.

Katz reached for the sheets, and the Cuban handed them over. "This puts things in a different light," the Israeli said as he flipped through the pages.

"Guess Kingston was figuring on parlaying a larger advance through his CIA buddies," James said.

"Or keeping a little something for a rainy day," Enciso agreed.

Katz folded the papers and put them inside his shirt. "Either way we have our next target. And it's one Caseros won't be expecting us to strike." He looked up at McCarter. "You'd better put us down as soon as possible. Caseros will have other aerial militia up within minutes."

McCarter nodded. ''Already got a spot picked out. Course, what with Gary wrecking the microbus, you blokes realize we're going to be walking.''

''Give it a rest,'' Manning replied. ''It's not like we could have picked it up and brought it with us.''

''THEY'RE COMING now, Sarge.''

Mack Bolan steadied his position, breathing evenly. He'd chosen to use Grimaldi's Galil to lead off the action instead of the M-16 he'd liberated from Costanza's shock troops because he'd sighted in their equipment himself. With the time they'd allowed for the recovery and sting operation, everything had to fall by the numbers. There would be precious little space for recovery if things went wrong.

The first distant rumblings of the jeeps reached his ears. The ''road'' was worn through the jungle, and the trip to the church was made so infrequently that tall clumps of growth dotted the twin tracks. He lay on a rocky ledge fifteen feet above the road. The Galil rested on the bipod, man and weapon part of the scenery.

He didn't touch the transmit button—Grimaldi knew he was there. Things would go down as they'd planned or they wouldn't go down at all. The Executioner had hoped Ortega would be in the lead jeep. Taking out Costanza's second-in-command would have been a nice coup in addition to the cocaine caravan. Instead, the two men in the jeep making its appearance less than a hundred yards away were faceless soldiers in the ranks of the cartel.

Sighting on the passenger first, Bolan drove two shots through the man's head a heartbeat apart, counting on the effect to confuse the driver. Instead of making a run for it, the driver hit the brakes and looked over at the corpse in the passenger seat. Bolan put a double-tap of 7.62 mm rounds over the man's heart, knocking the guy back from the steering wheel.

Grimaldi broke cover at once, yanking the body from the seat and sliding behind the wheel. The Executioner had put three men down in the next jeep before someone noticed Grimaldi making off with the lead vehicle. Flicking the assault rifle to burst mode, he fanned the rest of the clip over the bunched jeeps, aiming for the tires. He changed magazines as he rolled from his position and met the Stony Man pilot, throwing himself aboard as Grimaldi slowed down.

The way was bumpy, filled with low-hanging branches and brush. Grimaldi made a hard left at the tree they'd marked earlier when they'd prepped for the attack. Bullets chased them into the trees. Bolan saw some of the jeeps peel off, cutting cross-country in an effort to head them off. He counted eight. Evidently Costanza had placed a high priority on the mission. Then he reconsidered. Manpower wasn't a problem for Costanza. The man had armies at his beck and call.

"Coming up on the ridge," Grimaldi announced. He shifted into four-wheel-drive and the jeep climbed over broken ground. Small trees went down before them like falling dominoes.

"They know where we're headed," Bolan replied.

Grimaldi turned again, sliding for a moment as the jeep slammed into a tree. Then he was hell-bent for leather down the rugged, loose incline, maneuvering through a controlled fall. At the foot of the incline was the edge of a deep canyon and a narrow bridge just wide enough for a jeep to cross. "Goddamn it, I wish we'd had a jeep to make a trial run across that thing before we did it for real."

Bolan arched an eyebrow. "Father Lazaro said it could take the weight. Don't you want to take the word of a priest?"

Grimacing, Grimaldi steered for the bridge. "Thing's put together with rope. Probably rotten rope. That's got to be a four-hundred-foot drop."

"Four hundred seventy-five feet, according to the stats I've got."

"Shit. If the first four hundred feet don't kill you, what's another seventy-five?"

"It's not the fall," Bolan said, "it's that sudden stop at the end." He peered over his shoulder. The first of the jeeps had cleared the incline, followed by two others. All of them skated down sideways.

"Here goes nothing," Grimaldi grumbled, slowing. The front wheels shivered as they pulled onto the wooden bridge, which swayed sickeningly with the weight.

Bolan shifted in his seat and aimed point-blank at the approaching jeeps. He still didn't see Ortega. Another jeep topped the ridge and spilled over. The Executioner squeezed the trigger.

Bullets chewed at the bridge. A strand of rope parted, the two ends vibrating with the passage of the vehicle. One of the pursuers got up enough courage to try the bridge, realigning himself to drive onto it.

"There goes the fishing line," Grimaldi said as they pulled up onto solid ground.

Bolan counted down three seconds, then the grenades they'd tied under the bridge exploded—the fishing line had been tied to the pins. Wooden planks and ropes fragmented. The venturesome jeep was out in the middle when there was suddenly no bridge. It dropped like a stone, spinning end over end slowly. Another jeep hovered with indecision on the edge of the canyon until the men aboard it jumped out. Then it, too, went over. A curve took Bolan out of sight of the canyon and the small army trapped on the other side.

Grimaldi checked his compass as they topped a rise.

"Four miles from here until we find a main road," Bolan said as he put the Galil beside his seat. "Then it's straight into Medellín."

Relaxing behind the wheel, Grimaldi said, "You never have told me what we're going to do once we get there."

Bolan opened his pack and took out granola bars. He handed one to Grimaldi. "We've put pressure on Costanza through bullets, and now we're going to try politics as a change of pace." He pulled out the war journal and started to explain.

CHAPTER SEVEN

"Do you know the kind of danger you're going to be exposing yourself to?"

Benito Franco flicked ashes from his cigar and watched them fall to the covered rear deck of the deuce-and-a-half. The truck's transmission whined horribly, and the vehicle shook every time it hit a pothole with enough force to rattle the metal ribs holding up the canvas. The Colombian justice minister was dressed for the night as well as the public. He wore a dark gray suit and a royal blue oxford shirt. He looked up at the DEA agent who had spoken. His voice was soft despite the rattlings and whinings from the big truck. "Señor Rodesney, it might amaze you to learn that I know more of my country than you do. After all, I have been here years, all of my life, when you have only been here for months."

The DEA section chief loosened his tie, perspiration streaming down his lean face. "Look, sir, if I've offended you, I didn't mean to. My job here is to keep you as secure as possible. You're a very important man in my country."

Franco shook his head and smiled. He was thirty-one years old, and doubted if three years separated his age from the young agent's. Still, tonight he found the other man's civility nauseating. Or, he had to admit, it might have been his own nerves. "I'm a very important man to me, as well, amigo, and I'm no fool. I know the value of the work I'm attempting to do. That's why I'm coming along tonight. Select members of the press have been alerted that something is going to happen tonight, but they don't know where or when. That's why they've been riding in national police cars since eight o'clock waiting for our call. It's just past midnight now. No one knows where we're going or what we're doing."

"You realize you might be on your way to a trap."

"*Sí,* and tonight I might return home to find a cartel assassin waiting for me in my closet when I hang up my coat." Franco flicked ashes again and examined the glowing orange coal at the end of his cigar.

There were several other men in the vehicle—three others, like Rodesney, were DEA, Lico represented F-2 intelligence, Colombia's national police, and Sigfrido was a high-ranking member of the Department of Administrative Security. Where Lico was a young man, even younger than Bart Rodesney, Sigfrido was an old trooper with gray in his hair and mustache. He chewed tobacco incessantly, spit it on the metal flooring and never released the CAR-15 standing butt down before him.

"Are you saying you want us to beef up your home security?" Rodesney asked. He leaned forward with an intent expression.

Franco expelled a cloud of blue smoke and waved it away. "No, that's not what I'm saying."

The deuce-and-a-half took a wide corner, making the occupants grab for the metal ribs as they slid across the bench seats. Sigfrido kept his position, leaning and hanging on to the assault rifle. A faint smile touched his lips, but it passed quickly.

Rodesney leaned forward again. "If you want more people working security on your house, all you have to do is ask. I know if I had a wife and daughter and I was in your position, I'd want to be sure they were well cared for."

"They're more cared for now than they want to be," Franco replied. "What I'm saying is that I live with thoughts of death every day of my life. My predecessors in this position haven't had the fortune to grow old in it. I'm aware that I was appointed despite my youth because the president truly believes I'm an honest man." He smiled. "That makes me a dangerous individual in this country, my friend."

"Then why are you going? This is a relatively simple bust for your people. You know who you're looking for, you know the amount of cocaine involved, and you know when and where it's going to be. You don't have to be there."

"I think I do." Franco sighed. "I want to make a statement to these cartel bastards. I want them to know I won't back down before them. One of us, either they or I, will break before this is over."

"Bravo, Benito," Sigfrido said softly. The old man looked into his eyes. "Your father would be most proud."

"Thank you, Sigfrido." Franco felt his face burn. In some ways he was so old; in others still a young man.

"And you," Rodesney said, pointing at Sigfrido, "you shouldn't be encouraging him like this."

The DAS man spit a glob of tobacco juice near the DEA man's feet.

Rodesney tucked his Italian loafers under the bench seat, which left him off balance for the next turn the big truck took.

"I've held this position for six months," Franco said. "Every day I've listened to the promises your country has made mine. Cocaine is a blight here just as it is in the United States. Instead of telling us how to conduct our affairs here and worrying about international legalities restraining your different agencies, maybe your time would be better spent training American youth to seek other thrills than cocaine and crack."

"That takes time."

"So does routing the cartels. They're firmly entrenched in every aspect of our society. The cartels provide jobs, a chance at something better, and a semblance of security."

"As long as you can overlook the mass killings that go hand in glove with them," Rodesney replied.

"Colombia has been overlooking violent death for over forty years. This is nothing new." Franco dropped his cigar butt and crushed it beneath his heel. "My father was one of those dreamers who hoped nothing but the best for this country."

"God rest his soul," Sigfrido said, touching the small cross that hung at the open throat of his khaki shirt.

"He was a policeman," Franco went on. "A member of the DAS. He began fighting the cocaine barons in the seventies before the United States realized the extent of the problem here. He was an honest man, a man with values. He taught them to me. My mother and he lived without simple pleasures so that they could afford to send me to university. I was their only child. They saw their future in me, something better than they'd had.''

"Every parent sees that in their children," Rodesney replied. "Mine did the same thing."

Franco leaned back against the canvas-covered metal ribs. "And how did they feel when you joined the DEA?''

"They weren't happy about it. I dropped out of law school." Rodesney looked uncomfortable.

"And you? How do you feel about your decision?''

Rodesney shrugged. "I did what was right for me."

"What do your parents think now?''

"We don't talk about it much."

Franco nodded. "The day I returned to Colombia I broke my parents' hearts. I started working in the justice department in Medellín five years ago, and some of the people I took down were associated with the cartel members. Justice isn't a thing easily found here, as your people have discovered. My father pressed me to leave, to take up other work. But you see, I idolized my father. I wanted to share his struggle. My rise through the levels of the justice department was meteoric. No one wanted promotions. Other people were quitting or dying all the time. And with every new appointment I expected my father to share my good fortune with me."

Rodesney remained silent.

"Instead, with every gain I made he seemed to draw away from me. I felt like I had somehow failed him or shamed him. Three years ago the first attempt was made on my life. My father was there in the court-room as a bodyguard assigned by the DAS. The bullets meant for me struck him when he pulled me out of the way." Franco released a short, tight breath. "The man we were trying to convict was able to escape during the confusion, and he's never been seen since. I held my father in my arms. Before he died he told me how proud he was of me."

"He was very proud," Sigfrido said. "We talked many times of it while we were partners. But he feared for you."

"I know." Franco looked back at the DEA agent. "So don't try to tell me the danger of what I'm doing as if I'm some child or a politician only out to capture glory. I believe in what I'm doing, and I can see no other way to do it."

Rodesney nodded.

Franco started to reach for another cigar, then decided against it. They were almost there now. He checked the watch on his wrist—12:27 a.m.

"Benito," Sigfrido said.

"Yes?"

"The watch, my friend. Take it off. It glows in the dark."

"All right." Franco tucked it carefully into an inner pocket of his jacket. It had been a gift from his father.

The deuce-and-a-half eased to a squeaking stop in a dark alley. Sigfrido jumped out, followed by two men, then came Franco. He adjusted his lapels and mopped his forehead with his handkerchief. He mouthed the practiced words of his speech and wondered if he would remember them when the action was over. Their target was the warehouse two blocks over.

Envigado was a suburb of Medellín. The residents were *paisanos,* peasants, and being such, were tough-minded, blue-collar workers for the most part. *Paisanos,* being the butt of Colombian humor, told their children to go out in the world and make something of themselves. If they did, they were supposed to send money home. If they weren't successful, they weren't supposed to come back.

Franco's family had been peasants. He knew the mentality, and it had made him successful in his court dealings.

The young justice minister felt fear creep along his spine when the warehouse came into view. He fought it down until there seemed to be no feelings left in him, only a numbness that felt so right.

He followed behind the rush of men invading the warehouse. There was a brief crackle of gunfire. He drew his Taurus PT 99, but he didn't have to use it. A solid phalanx of DAS, F-2 and DEA agents stood between him and the cocaine dealers. The warehouse was dimly lighted, but the tables holding the football-shape bundles of cocaine were the center of attention. There had been reports that the street value of the product being readied for shipment was nearly two and a half million dollars. Franco believed it after seeing the bundles.

He got Sigfrido's attention. "Outside," he instructed. "Take all of it outside. The men and the cocaine. I want the American, British and Canadian journalists—along with our own people—to be able to see what we've accomplished tonight."

Then he led the way out to the street, walking through the now-open double doors of the warehouse. His throat felt dry and his hands shook. He wondered if his voice would fail him or if he would forget the words.

"THE PLACE LOOKS LIKE something out of an Anthony Quinn movie," Calvin James commented.

Staring through his own pair of night vision glasses, Yakov Katzenelenbogen had to agree. Caseros's hideaway ranch for Colombian drug kingpins was spread over nearly two hundred acres along the Gulf of Panama. The outer perimeters were marked by guards and electric fences that cut through the surrounding jungle. The guards didn't wear the military dress Caseros usually insisted on.

The main house was three stories high and painted white. The landscape was carefully manicured and featured an assortment of beautiful flowers and trees. A nine-foot-high wall ran around the ranch house grounds proper, enclosing the main house, a half-dozen guest houses, three regulation-size tennis courts, a nine-hole golf course and a swimming pool. Security lights splashed the wall regularly, and the guards maintained a vigilance that impressed the Phoenix Force members.

Katz's lips quirked into a rare smile as he remembered Manning's suggestion that the guards were cut in on a percentage basis. Maybe it was closer to the truth than they'd realized.

"Party's beginning to heat up," James whispered.

Katz shifted his attention back to the swimming pool, where almost three dozen people frolicked. More than half of them were women. As he watched, a woman wearing only the bottom half of a gold-colored bikini dived from the high platform. She hit the green-lit water cleanly, emerging a few seconds later twirling the bikini bottoms over her head. She threw them at a man sitting on the edge of the pool, who promptly dived in after her.

Moving on, the Israeli swept his gaze across the umbrella-equipped tables gathered around the pool. He recognized a number of lesser cartel members, people the Justice Department had files and paper on, but no one as big as Costanza, Mercado or Rodriguez, the main targets of the Stony Man scramble. There was also no sign of Caseros, Phoenix's personal objective.

Katz put the NVGs away and glanced at his watch—12:29 a.m. "Manning, Encizo and McCarter should be in position now," he said softly. Radio contact was out of the question with all the electronic defenses set up around the ranch house.

"They got the back door," James replied. "Leaves us the front. I'm ready when you are."

Katz nodded. There was no question of being ready in his mind. The operation had been planned and re-planned. Now was the time to do it.

He moved out, a quiet, thick-bodied shadow skimming the ground. His face was blackened with combat cosmetics, and a black watchcap covered his head. The hook that took the place of his right hand was of black alloy, as well. He carried a Galil Model 332 in 7.62 mm as his lead weapon, complete with sniperscope. His backup weapons included the .45-caliber Ingram slung over his shoulder and the H&K 9 mm squeeze-cocker. A Ka-bar fighting knife was sheathed in his left boot, and various incendiaries were attached to his combat harness.

Their plan wasn't to confront the enemy head-on, but to provide a diversion that would allow Gary Manning to ply his trade as demolitions man on the team. The mock attack would be a classic pincer movement designed to force the ranch house residents into motion. Choosing between fight or flight, he felt certain most of the people inside would make the right choice.

At his side, Calvin James carried an M-16A1/M-203 over-and-under combo, plus a selection of deadly little devices. Conscious of the clock winding down inside his head, Katz waved James into the landscaped foliage and approached the first outer perimeter guard. He counted to four, allowing his companion to get into position, then stepped out into full view of the man, holding the Ingram instead of the assault rifle. The guard started to lift his own weapon as three silenced rounds from the MAC-10 knocked dust from his shirt. James moved out from the shadows long enough to grab a fistful of collar and drag the body from sight.

Moments later they stood in front of the massive electronically controlled gates that opened onto the ranch house courtyard. Katz took a fragmentation grenade from his harness and waited, knowing James was doing the same.

Autofire cut loose at the back of the ranch house, followed immediately by a series of explosions. The Phoenix team leader knew that would be Manning's opener. Pyrotechnics lit up the sky, more deadly than regular fireworks because Encizo and McCarter would be directing sniper fire at preselected targets lounging around the pool.

Katz ripped the pin from the grenade and pitched it toward the two guards emerging from the gate house. The deadly sphere landed less than a yard from the men, followed immediately by James's grenade, which fell to the ground near the first. The guards saw what had hit the ground and tried to run. The explosions caught them in a flash of thunder and lightning that beat them to the earth.

James stepped forward and unlimbered the M-203, firing a 40 mm high-explosive round that connected with the wrought-iron bars of the gate and left them warped and smoking.

Katz took point, unslinging the Galil and switching the weapon to full-auto. At the moment he wanted to make more noise than anything. Manning had drawn parallels of the plan to the way the North American Indian tribes had hunted buffalo—get the herd moving and pick off the ones the hunters wanted during the melee.

The Israeli squirmed through the hot, twisted metal of the gates, pausing halfway to rake a withering figure eight across a trio of gunners rushing toward him. They went down after firing only a few rounds. Two bullets struck Katz. One punched like a giant fist into his Kevlar jacket, and the other caught his metal prothesis a glancing blow that created a brief spark in the darkness.

Pandemonium erupted around the swimming pool. Men and women panicked, overrunning Caseros's guards trying to wade through them. Single shots rang out, the guards dying as soon as they entered the field of fire. A moment later something landed in the pool. There was a dull pop, then flames spread across the surface of the water and threw wavering shadows on the overturned umbrella tables and chairs.

Lights audibly snapped on in all four corners of the walls surrounding the ranch house. Guards swept them across the landscaped grounds, playing more on the running people than anything else.

"I've got the northeast quarter," Katz said as he hoisted the Galil to his shoulder and fitted his eye to the Startron scope.

"Consider the southeast quarter history," James replied. The M-203 thundered and was followed by an explosion. The lights in the southeast quarter winked out.

Katz didn't go for headshots, sticking with the widest part of the targets he had available. He tagged the klieg lights first, then used the Startron to pick off the guards, knocking them both over the wall. When he looked up from the scope, the remaining two security posts were smoking wrecks.

"Manning's for damn sure not messing around with this one," James said in appreciation as he reloaded the grenade launcher.

Katz nodded as he booted a fresh magazine into the Galil. He swung it across his back when he'd finished, opting for the MAC-10 now that the action had moved to closer quarters. As planned, they moved immediately for the garage, housed separately from the main house. Five more guards crossed their path along the way. They left the bodies where they fell.

The garage doors opened when they arrived, spilling yellow light across the lawn. Katz signaled James back into cover as a Mercedes roared out of the garage and crashed through what remained of the gates. James rounded the corner with the M-16 at waist level, leaving Katz a clear killing field. A door at the other end of the immense garage rattled slightly, so Katz squeezed off a burst that shook the walls. "Grenade."

James nodded and touched off the M-203. Fire and smoke filled the other end of the building as the 40 mm warhead ripped the top from a silver Ferrari. Ten cars, all expensive and all imported, sat in a row under the fluorescent lighting. Slinging his weapon, James moved on the second in line, a pearl-gray Cadillac with a sunroof.

Katz was satisfied. The vehicle suitably passed as a tank, and the way it sat on its tires told him it was armored. He lifted his walkie-talkie. "Manning. Report."

"Five more minutes, Katz, then I'll bring this place down around their ears. It's just like you thought. Place this big, this far out, they keep their own propane gas tanks and generators. And the broiler was right where we thought it was."

"Get it done. McCarter?"

"Here."

"Caseros?"

"Negative."

"Rafael?"

"Negative."

Katz breathed a silent curse as he reached for the Ingram. Caseros had been an elusive quarry for years. The Panamanian president had luck and an animal cunning that had seen him through several close encounters. There was no reason to believe the status quo would change now. Unless they forcibly changed it. One of those forcible changes was going to be limitations of where the quarry could run.

The Caddy roared to life and backed out of the garage with squealing tires. James was smiling as the electric window glided down. "You're going to love it, Katz. There's even a bar in the back for an after-the-blitz party."

A burst of autofire spiderwebbed the bulletproof glass on the passenger side.

After letting loose a line of .45-caliber rounds that knocked the gunner to the ground, Katz dropped the Ingram long enough to open the rear door and slip inside. The smell of fresh leather was almost overpowering. "Give me the sunroof."

The rear section slid back noiselessly as James executed a 180-degree turn that sent the Caddy hurtling across the grounds like a pale gray ghost. The right corner caught a lawn sculpture and shattered it into a thousand pieces, creating a miniature hail that marred the paint job.

"Let the others know what we're in," Katz directed.

James nodded and reached for his walkie-talkie.

Standing up, Katz braced himself in the opening of the sunroof and tracked shadowy figures through the darkness. He was sure only of two members of the opposition and killed them both.

McCarter joined them first, dropping from the wall and sprinting over to take the passenger seat as James slowed. He thumbed the window down and poked out the barrel of his Uzi.

"Got a problem," James said, holding up his walkie-talkie. "Rafael said he just saw a C-130 unload a whole lot of parachutes overhead."

"Bloody hell!" McCarter snarled as he stuck his head out the window. "You think Caseros could have called in reinforcements this quick?"

Katz pulled himself through the sunroof. Dozens of black parachutes were scattered across the night. He lifted his NVG to his eyes. He identified the uniforms and armament quickly and dropped into the back seat.

Calvin James had stopped the Caddy and was looking through his own NVG. "Katz, did you see what I see?" His voice was filled with disbelief.

"Yes," Katz said. "Somebody's called in the United States Marine Corps."

"'When you care enough to send the very best,'" McCarter quoted.

"THE MAN KNOWS how to draw a crowd," Grimaldi commented.

"And how to work it," Bolan added. He stepped aside as a minicam operator and a reporter elbowed past him. The logo on the minicam was of an American network.

They stood across the street from where Benito Franco addressed the clustered reporters and citizens. The justice minister spoke in Spanish, then repeated himself in English. More than a dozen police cars and other assorted vehicles blocked both ends of the street. Blue and red cherries threw garish shadows over the low buildings. The khaki uniforms of the national police stood out in sharp relief in the darkness. Less than a handful, though, were in view of the cameras. Franco's orders on that must have been very clear.

A flatbed paused at one end of the street. Police cars pulled away, letting it through, then quickly filled the gap. The flatbed ground gears and backfired noisily as it crept up the street. The sea of people parted before it.

Franco was in motion even as the truck pulled to a halt in front of the warehouse. The cameras stayed on him. Two men from the cab of the flatbed sorted out a PA system as members of the national police kept the crowd back. Franco clambered aboard, straightening his suit as he accepted a microphone. He listened to one of the men working the PA system, then tapped the mike experimentally. A hollow thump came from the four huge speakers facing the crowd, followed immediately by an intense electronic squeal. One of the electronics technicians moved levers on the control board, and the squeal died away. Franco tapped the mike again, then held up his hands to silence the crowd. "Can you hear me?" he asked.

The crowd mumbled a collective affirmative.

"I could of used another cup of coffee or five," Grimaldi grumbled, stifling a yawn.

Bolan nodded, then stepped off the curb. "I'm going in for a closer look at our boy."

"If you need me, that's me at your shoulder."

Bolan made his way through the crowd, letting his size do most of the work. He was dressed in jeans, boots, a black T-shirt and a short-waisted denim jacket. With his dark hair and dark complexion—and given the time of night—he knew he'd pass cursory inspection as a Medellín native.

Making clenched fists of his hands, Franco lifted his arms above his head and began speaking. "For too long we've been gripped by death in our country. For too long our families, our friends, our neighbors have been forced into lives without hope." His words rolled outward.

Bolan could feel the emotion in the young justice minister's voice touch him. He gazed at the crowd surrounding the flatbed, saw the whispered conversations drift away as attention was focused on Franco.

The justice minister made a motion with his hand, and members of the national police began to throw packages of cocaine onto the flatbed in front of him. He pointed toward the growing pile. "In the streets some call this the White Lady. I call it what it is—death. I want no romance with cocaine. This powder is spilling over into our lives, strangling any chance we might have for a future. If we continue to sit back and let the cartel barons run our lives, *this* is the heritage we'll leave our children." He paused. "If any of them survive to take it up. Is this what you want?"

The crowd whispered a collective no.

"Is this what you want for your children?"

They responded louder now.

Franco waved them down. "I don't want this for my child, either. She's four years old. A baby. I want her to have a good future. I want her to have a new Colombia to call home, a Colombia where our children don't have to die working in the coca fields or pushing cocaine on the streets."

The crowd roared its approval.

The American and English reporters looked nervous. Bolan figured the absence of the traditional question-and-answer format had thrown them off balance.

"I need your help to do this thing," Franco shouted to the crowd. "No! I *demand* your help to do this thing." He spoke directly to the minicam bearing the logo of a Medellín-based television station. "The drug armies are warring among themselves again, and their violence is coming into our homes. Put an end to it. Together we can do this. If you see something, if you hear something, if you know something, call my offices. Your name will be kept in confidence. These men will be shown that justice exists within these borders, and I'll carry your message to them."

The crowd had swelled to hundreds of people, and their shouts of support swept through the street. The justice minister's face remained grim. Bolan knew there was no joy in declaring war, and that was just what the man had done.

Vibrations running the length of the narrow street drew the Executioner's attention to his left. He stared at the line of police cars. An expectant hush fell over the crowd in gradual waves. The basso snorting of a diesel engine in full throttle roared suddenly as a pair of lights rounded the corner a block away from the national police vehicles. The vehicle barreled through the blockade, tossing aside police cars and scattering uniformed men. Autofire erupted from the top of the cab and from the passenger window, raking over the crowd as the people raced for shelter. The driver reaimed the eighteen-wheeler after the initial collision, downshifting and gathering speed again as he drove for the flatbed and Benito Franco.

Bolan drew his .44 Magnum as he broke through the crowd and sprinted toward the big truck.

CHAPTER EIGHT

Metal crunched as the big rig smashed into the line of cars parked at the curbside. Crushed and battered vehicles spilled out into the street like a child's discarded toys.

Bolan pumped his legs as he covered the distance to the driver's door. Bullets skipped over the paved surface in front of him, whining and sparking as they ricocheted. He felt the hot breath of the engine brush his cheek as he dodged the massive bumper and cut back toward the cab. He leaped for the side mirror and caught it, feeling himself yanked from his feet at the same time. The thin metal twisted in his grip but held.

The driver caught sight of the warrior just as the muzzle of the Desert Eagle dropped into shaky target acquisition. Bolan triggered the .44, felt it kick against his palm, then a 240-grain round took the driver's forehead apart. The corpse slewed across the seat, and the truck lurched out of control.

Finding a foothold, Bolan levered his gun arm up and through the window, flailed with his other hand and caught the steering wheel. The eighteen-wheeler pulled sharply to the left, no longer careering toward the crowd, aimed at the blank wall of the warehouse behind the flatbed.

The gunner in the passenger seat had been occupied with shoving the dead body off his lap. He pointed his M-16 toward Bolan, yelling incoherently. Sirens screamed in the background, creating a white noise that almost stripped the world of sound.

Unwilling to release his hold until he was assured of where the truck would go, the warrior shifted and fired two rounds into the shrieking passenger. Seconds later Bolan leaned into the cab for protection as the vehicle struck the exterior wall of the warehouse and smashed through, brick dust catching in his throat as he was thrown free.

Down on one knee in the darkness, he changed magazines and snapped the slide back into place. His chest and lungs ached as he tried to draw a breath, and he tasted blood. Pinwheels of light spun before his eyes. Bolan staggered to his feet and brushed at his face with the back of his hand, which came away bloody.

The Executioner slipped through the jagged hole created by the truck, letting the Desert Eagle take the lead. The sound of gunfire still shattered the night, lancing from the three sleek sedans racing through the hole the eighteen-wheeler had rammed into national police defenses. The lead vehicle came to a screeching turn in the middle of the street as gunners sprayed lead into the few stragglers from the crowd. People went down.

Raising the .44, Bolan shut out the double images and concentrated on the shooter in the rear seat. He kept three shots within the window of the moving car. The man disappeared, his weapon bouncing along the street.

One of the smashed police cars wobbled forward to block the way before the three sedans could escape. The lead car plowed into the police vehicle, the driver reversing quickly. The tires burned, spinning on the street, but the sedan didn't move because the front end was impaled on the ragged bumper of the police car. The national policemen didn't even ask the passengers to surrender. Bullets blazed from their weapons, reducing the windows and interior to bloodstained rubble. The remaining two cars backed away and did 180-degree turns that took them over the curbs and onto the sidewalks.

Bolan stepped forward and trained his weapon on the driver's side of the lead sedan. He triggered the remaining rounds in rapid fire, watching holes open up in the windshield. The car veered out of control and slammed into the flatbed. The explosion came a heartbeat later, licking up from the pavement and climbing the chassis. The flatbed was thrown onto its side and slid across the street, windows shattering from the concussion.

The Executioner ejected the empty clip and shoved another home. Out on the street a gray-haired, mustached man stepped in front of the last car and coolly sighted down the barrel of his CAR-15 as the sedan rocketed toward him. He squeezed off three controlled bursts. A fist-size hole appeared over the driver's side of the windshield an instant before both front tires were punctured. The sedan slewed sideways and rammed into the overturned flatbed. Three men clambered out of the vehicle, carrying weapons. They tried to shoot on the run, pointing in the general direction of the gray-haired man. The CAR-15 spit three single shots, and three corpses tumbled into the street.

Bolan looked for Grimaldi, wondering if he'd managed to clear the area. At least two dozen people were scattered across the street.

"Amigo." The address wasn't a call for attention; it was a command.

Bolan glanced up into the face of the gray-haired man, who held the sights of the CAR-15 centered squarely over his heart. The eye at the other end of the barrel was as bright and unflinching as a laser sight.

"The pistol," the man said, "put it on the ground. Gently. Now."

The Executioner deposited the Desert Eagle on the pavement, raised his hands behind his head and backed away.

BARBARA PRICE LOOKED at Aaron Kurtzman in disbelief. "We just did what?" They were alone in Bear's command post, surrounded by computer equipment.

The big man repeated himself, forcing the words out as if he couldn't believe it, either. "We just invaded Panama. They're calling it Operation Just Cause. God, Barb, we airlifted almost seven thousand troops into that country tonight, and they're talking about more tomorrow."

"What about Phoenix?"

Kurtzman shook his head. "They're down somewhere in that mess. According to the coordinates Katz sent a few hours ago, they're in the same area as Task Force Semper Fidelis."

"The Marines?" Price looked at the screen where Kurtzman had been coloring in sections of a map. The outlines of Panama were all too familiar to her.

"And a light armored infantry company. These people are doing some serious business tonight."

Price clenched a fist but refrained from slamming it against something.

"They've got Marines, Navy SEALs, the Eighty-second Airborne Division, the Green Berets, the Army Rangers and the Seventh Light Infantry Division in there seizing targets."

"And their objectives?" Price made herself forget the emotional issue of the stakes involved, focusing on the physical side of them. That was what Brognola had shifted her into the driver's seat to do. And she, by God, didn't intend to let the man down no matter how many United States military units stood in the way.

"They're shutting the country down," Kurtzman said, "starting with Panama City. Military personnel are engaged to put down the Panama Defense Forces that are loyal to Caseros."

"At this stage of the game it's going to be hard to tell who's who."

"Yeah, I know."

"Do they have Caseros in custody?"

"Not according to the last field report I intercepted. There was a Delta Force team grounded early to snatch Caseros, but the guy was gone from where they thought he'd be."

Price exhaled in relief and crossed her arms over her chest. "Then it's possible Katz had time to move his people out of there."

"That's the least of your worries. Phoenix alone can get out of there. What scares the hell out of me is if they were successful and *they* have Caseros. You can bet the Joint Chiefs of Staff aren't going to be crazy about a covert team as small as Phoenix walking off with the brass ring when they've gone to the trouble and expense of throwing a party this big. And you know Katz wouldn't be willing to part with a Kewpie doll the size of Caseros."

"Shit," Price said. "If no one has Caseros, it's possible he'll make a run for Colombia and drag the action farther south."

"He'll have to walk, then," Kurtzman said confidently, "because the United States owns airspace into and out of Panama."

"That means Phoenix is grounded, too."

"Unless we cut through some red tape somewhere."

"Start working on getting a call through to the chairman of the Joint Chiefs for me."

"I already kicked the ball in motion before I called you."

"Keep me posted."

"You know it." Kurtzman paused, his big hands hanging above the computer keyboard. "Things don't look so good for the home team this time, do they?"

"Scattered across Panama, Colombia and Florida, we're not exactly the home team this time out." Price rubbed her eyes as she left the room. She felt frustrated. And scared, God, yes, definitely scared. She could imagine what it must be like in the country even now, and the images were too sharp, too clear. She could almost smell the gunsmoke.

She found Brognola in the kitchen, wearing a fresh shirt and tie, and his cheeks glistening from a fresh shave. He shook instant coffee crystals into a cup of hot tap water. "Want some?" he asked without turning around.

"You knew, didn't you?" Her tone was pure accusation even though she hadn't meant it to come out that way.

"About the invasion of Panama?"

"Yes, damn it."

Brognola turned to face her. His features were a topographical map of tiredness and near-exhaustion. "I knew it was a possibility."

"That's why you put me on as controller over this operation instead of taking it yourself."

"That's one of the reasons."

"You've got five men down in the middle of that shitstorm right now who are depending on you to cover their asses, or at least let them know if something like this was going to happen."

"Wrong." Brognola's voice cracked like thunder in the kitchen. "*You've* got five men in Panama who are depending on you to coordinate their activities."

"Fine. *I've* got five men in Panama."

"Don't ever make the mistake of thinking this doesn't depend on you, Barb. You're too damn good to be that green. And, yeah, you're going to feel the squeeze on this play until we get something worked out. But we'll work it out. Believe that."

She exhaled with effort, trying to loosen the hard knot in the pit of her stomach.

"We knew this wasn't going to be a cakewalk from the git-go," Brognola said in a softer voice. "Everyone from the President on down has been talking about doing something with Caseros since the busted coup attempt in October. Nobody expected something like an invasion."

"You did. That's why you put me in the hot seat."

"The hot seat at Stony Man, yeah, I sure did. But I'm taking a flight up to Wonderland in just a few minutes, and I'm going to start yelling in every ear I can bend until we get Phoenix out of Panama."

She looked at him as understanding flooded through her. "You didn't tell anyone about this, did you? No one knows Stony Man even has an operation in the area."

"No, this was my call from the beginning. I'd been talking to some people, putting feelers out, but initiating hands-on contact wasn't something these people wanted to talk about. I wanted to do more than talk about it in any case."

She shook her head. "Once this gets around your whole career could go down the tubes."

"I didn't take this job for the glory." Brognola gave her a weak smile. "I took it on because I'm a guy who likes to see things get done, and I was told I could get it done here. I don't mind getting my hands dirty in the doing. Neither do the people I work with. Those are sharp people you're overseeing, lady, and don't you ever sell them short on guts, intelligence or the willingness to do the right thing."

She didn't say anything. Nothing seemed right.

"On the off chance that I do get sandbagged over this, even if only temporarily, I wanted you in charge. I trust you to get the job done and get our guys back home in one piece. Anybody stepping into the operation is going to have to deal with you before they start any string-pulling. You can run interference until you can tell them which way the wind's going to blow. You know the teams involved. You know what they can and will handle. Somebody new wouldn't, and he or she would end up getting our guys killed. You'll take care of them."

"Yes," she replied when she realized there was a question in his words.

Brognola lifted his jacket from the back of a chair. "I'll be in touch as soon as I know something, but experience tells me I'll have to go to the mat to get anything out of the Joint Chiefs or anyone else who's horned in on this piece of action. Still, I have a few favors owed me, and I know where more than one body is buried."

She looked at him as he shrugged into his jacket. "I shouldn't have doubted you."

"Sure you should have. I've been doubting me for four days now. I haven't let up on me yet."

"This one isn't going to go down easy for any of us."

"I don't think so, either." He returned her gaze full measure. "One thing I can tell you, though—there's no one else I'd rather leave this operation in the hands of."

"Thanks."

Brognola leaned over and kissed her lightly on the forehead. "I'll be thinking about you."

"Me, and about a dozen other people I could name offhand."

He smiled for the first time. "Never promised I'd be true."

"Take care of yourself."

He paused in the doorway to give her one last smile of encouragement. "Don't worry."

Then he was gone, leaving Price with her thoughts, confusion and responsibilities.

CHAPTER NINE

Luis Costanza stood in the darkness of one of the recreation rooms of his home, watching a large-screen television that occupied most of the opposite wall. The pictures being relayed were actual footage from news teams in Panama. He flicked through the channels mechanically with the remote control.

Sheridan tanks rolled through the dark streets, accompanied by military jeeps and infantrymen. The scene shifted, showing an Apache combat helicopter sweeping a section of Panama City bordering on the jungle. Brief flurries of gunfire marked the presence of hostile ground troops. The Apache tipped, then green tracer fire from the chain guns slashed through the dark jungle, followed by twin rockets.

Costanza turned away from the television and crossed the room to one of the three wet bars.

"Another drink, sir?" the bartender, Eduardo, asked. He was dressed in a black tux that had been tailored not to show the shoulder holster. Even when entertaining people in his home, Costanza felt the need for protection these days.

"Yes," Costanza said, leaning his forearms on the bar.

The bartender mixed a double margarita with practiced hands, which Costanza accepted with curt thanks.

He licked the salt from the rim of the glass and took a big drink. It burned all the way down.

"This thing in Panama," Eduardo said as he wiped his hands on a white bar towel, "it is bad for business?"

"Very bad."

"And President Caseros?"

"He still has his freedom." Costanza took one of the seats in front of the bar and watched the television again. The scene showed another shot of more American equipment descending from the sky on black mushroom-shaped parachutes. Soldiers moved to take it up immediately. The news reporter narrated the events, saying the primary concern for American military at this point was the freeing of American hostages and locating Caseros.

"It sounds as if President Caseros may not have his freedom long," Eduardo commented.

"Yes, especially if that fool continues broadcasting on that radio station he's been using. He still has delusions that his people love him in spite of the American intervention." Costanza shook his head. "The man has been stupid about his wealth. He had more than he could ever hope to spend in his lifetime, yet he tried to hoard it instead of spreading it around to make sure his people realized his worth. Let this be a lesson to you, Eduardo, should you ever find yourself in this man's position. When you have the power and the money, you should work to make things better for all those around you, not just yourself and your favorites."

"I'll keep that in mind, sir, should I ever be so fortunate."

Costanza flashed him a gentle smile. "It's very possible in your lifetime. You're young and Colombia is a country of opportunities."

"Yes. I'll just remember how you've treated the people you're responsible for."

"Fix yourself a drink, Eduardo, and join me in a toast to our futures."

The young bartender gave him a white smile and eagerly reached for the liquor.

Costanza glared at the still photograph of Caseros in his military uniform displayed on the television screen. The man had been a fool, and Costanza realized he'd be paying for some of the man's foolish ways himself for months to come as new ports were opened for his product. But the market was there. The project would be dangerous, yes, but not impossible—never impossible as long as the American hunger was there.

"Sir."

Turning, Costanza raised his glass with the younger man's. "To our futures."

"And may our successes pass onto our children, whether we know them or not," Eduardo added.

Costanza drained the glass and plunked it onto the bar. "Another, my friend. I have many things on my mind tonight. And join me. I no longer wish to drink alone." He gathered up his fresh drink and crossed the room to the white sectionals that had the illusion of creating a separate room all by themselves. He ran his fingers through the long fibers, then smoothed them as if the fabric were the fur of some favorite beast. He stared at the footage of the Panama invasion with unseeing eyes, thoughts and plans churning through the alcoholic haze of freedom the drinks had given him.

"Sir?"

He recognized Ortega's voice and answered without looking up, still stroking the material. "Yes."

"There's been a problem."

"With the meeting between myself, Mercado and Rodriguez?"

"No. That's arranged."

"Where?"

"At Don Manolon's ranch tomorrow."

Costanza stopped stroking the material. "This was Mercado's idea?"

"I wasn't told, but I gathered that from what was said. Isn't the arrangement satisfactory with you? I can pull together something else, but I know Don Manolon is a respected man."

Costanza waved the suggestion away. "No, It's very satisfactory... just surprising. It isn't often we feel the bite of ghosts from our pasts."

"No, sir."

"This only tells me Mercado wanted to select a place where we could all be secure and talk freely. I feel that this was a most honest decision."

"He also said no guards would be allowed. I wanted to talk with you before I argued the point. Personally I don't feel that this is wise in view of everything that's been happening."

"The absence of guards wasn't Mercado's idea," Costanza said. "It would be at Don Manolon's insistence. To attempt any subterfuge would treat a very dangerous old man with disrespect."

"You know Don Manolon?"

Costanza favored his second-in-command with a grin. "Yes. There are things you don't know about me, Esteban, things that lay in my past. Things I thought had passed away into my boyhood. Evidently Mercado seeks to resurrect these things. And now, I wonder why he wishes to shadow our lives with them again. Of course, I must be suspicious of him, but not of Don Manolon. Never of Don Manolon."

"As you wish."

"What's this problem you wish to speak of?" Costanza gestured toward the television screen. "Already I'm faced with finding new routes for the product."

"Pitin's warehouse was raided tonight, and all of his cocaine was confiscated."

"Who did this thing?" Costanza clamped down on the irritation that stung him.

"The justice minister, Benito Franco. He had the American DEA, the DAS and F-2 with him. There was also a conspicuous number of journalists at the scene."

"Are you saying he staged the attack on the warehouse?"

"Yes, I am."

"And what did Pitin do in return?"

"He attempted to break through the police blockade with one of his trucks and some cars and kill Franco."

"Was he successful?"

"I don't know. There were a number of deaths, but my sources are unable to confirm if Franco was among them."

Costanza was silent, watching as a group of Marines worked their way into a public building. Sporadic gunfire kept them hunkered down. He pressed the mute button, and the sound of gunfire drained away, leaving only the flashes. "What evidence can Franco have in his possession that will lead him to me?"

"None. Pitin doesn't keep records in the warehouse. The accounting's done at different facilities. He knows better than to keep anything with your name on it."

"But Franco will still know even if he can't prove it."

"Yes, I think so, too."

"If Pitin was unsuccessful in his attempt to kill our zealous justice minister, it might be time for us to consider rectifying his error. Franco has begun to overstep his boundaries. It's time someone brought this to his attention. If he doesn't heed our warnings, Esteban, I expect you to take care of this thing for me."

"If you wish it, it will be done."

Costanza nodded toward the screen. "It's curious, isn't it, how my organization and those of Mercado and Rodriguez are being hit at the same time La Araña can't be found in Miami and Caseros is being driven from his country?"

"It is."

"Check into these things for me, as well. I want La Araña found, and I want to know if there's a tie between the American invasion of Panama and what's happening here."

"My ears are yours, sir."

"I want Auerbach to return to Colombia. Caseros can deal with his own problems. I want my people here, with me, where they belong."

Although Costanza couldn't hear Ortega leave, he knew on a primitive level that his second-in-command had vacated the room. He switched the television to a local channel and waited to see the latest piece of the puzzle taking shape around him. Memory of the words of the man who'd promised to put him out of business gusted across his mind like a cold wind from a graveyard. For the first time in a handful of years he reflected on his own mortality. Then he called for another drink.

"GO," KATZ ORDERED as he took his position again in the Caddy's sunroof. He stroked the trigger of the MAC-10 and drove three ranch house guards to cover behind a fountain. McCarter's Uzi stuttered to quick life and ripped one of the men from cover, the guard spinning into the trickling water.

The rear wheels of the big luxury car spun in the grass, then fishtailed as the Detroit engine powered it forward. Katz kept rounds cycling through the Ingram in strategic bursts. With the Marines already touching ground not far from their present position, the few minutes allowed for the hit-and-git strike had suddenly counted down to a precious few seconds.

"Coming up on Rafael's position," James called. "He's going to need covering fire. He's bringing a guest."

"East or west?" Katz asked.

"From the east."

"McCarter, help Rafael with his guest."

"You got it."

Katz stroked the trigger and three .45-caliber bullets struck a partially concealed guard atop the wall in the face, and punched the corpse over the other side. The Phoenix leader changed magazines as the Caddy started to slow.

Encizo broke cover to the right. A man stumbled before him, pushed on by the smaller Phoenix Force member. The prisoner fell only a few yards from the open door of the Caddy. Encizo dropped beside him for a moment, knotted a hand in the man's shirt collar and dragged him toward the luxury vehicle. McCarter helped lift the prisoner into the rear seat.

Feeling the man's fingers close around his ankle, Katz kicked out with a foot. There was a satisfying thud.

"We need this guy alive," Encizo said as he took the rear seat.

"He's alive," Katz replied. He glanced up. Most of the parachutes had cleared from the sky. The possibility of a firefight with American Forces loomed closer. As a government entity, Phoenix Force and Stony Man were unknown. Their presence at the ranch house would be questionable at best. Considering the probable youth and inexperience of most of the troops involved, remaining in the area was an impossibility.

"This guy is one of Caseros's aides here," Encizo said as he cranked down his window. "He also knows where El Presidente has holed up."

"I'm more interested in how El Presidente knew to hole himself up," McCarter replied. His Uzi rattled briefly, and return fire sparked against the sides of the Caddy, leaving tinny rings of ricochets.

"We didn't have time to discuss it," Encizo said, leaning out his window. "That's why I thought we'd schedule a one-on-one later."

"Calvin," Katz said calmly as he tipped a grenade from his harness and lobbed it toward the sculpted pine tree at the southeast corner of the ranch house, "tell Gary to get out of there and blow it now. What we don't finish, the Marines surely will." The grenade blew with a thunderclap.

"He's en route," James yelled.

Katz braced himself in the sunroof as the Caddy slewed sideways. Dark chunks of expensive lawn spit out behind them.

A window on the second story exploded. Shards of glass spun around a human body that flailed for balance, then dropped into a roll. Manning broke into a serpentine run when he got his feet under him.

Katz raked the side of the ranch house as James brought the car around in a sliding 180. He dropped the empty magazine and rammed home another.

"The hood, Gary," James yelled as he got the car in motion again.

Manning didn't hesitate. He launched himself into a flying tackle that left him sliding across the long hood. His fingers became curved talons that gripped the sheet of metal near the windshield. The sudden acceleration pressed his face into the glass, mashing and distorting his features for a moment until James cut left to avoid a tree.

Katz dropped into the rear seat. ''The gate, Calvin. It will be your best bet.''

James nodded. ''Gonna be kind of rough on Gary.''

''It'll be a lot rougher on him if he gets left here.''

''I hear you.'' James tromped the accelerator harder as they roared around the ranch house and aimed the Caddy at the main gate.

McCarter leaned out the window and bellowed, ''Are you going to blow the frigging dump or not, Manning?''

In response, the Canadian rolled onto his side, pulled an electronic detonator from inside his fatigue shirt and depressed the switch. An eruption of noise shattered the night. Katz looked over his shoulder in time to see fire and force demolish the ranch house. Manning threw the detonator away. His mouth moved, but the sound didn't penetrate the glass. Katz read his lips. *Satisfied?*

''It'll do, mate,'' McCarter said as he leaned out the passenger window.

James barreled the wrecked gates and took the first dirt road he came to, then plunged the Caddy through the brush until it could proceed no farther.

Katz got out of the vehicle and reached for his map case. They'd had some maps of the area, but none that covered the immediate vicinity. He'd drawn those himself during their earlier soft probe. ''Penflash,'' he called as he spread out the eighteen-by-eighteen-inch sheet across the trunk of the luxury car. Encizo stepped into position behind him, holding a 9 mm pistol to their prisoner's jaw. A moment later a brief pool of yellow light splashed against the map.

"Goddamn," Manning groaned as he climbed from his position on the car. "What's the deal, Calvin? You didn't think you had enough time to let me ride first-class like everyone else?"

"Katz's idea," James replied as he joined the Phoenix Force leader. "Figured it would save time."

"Oh. Yeah. Good idea, Katz."

McCarter snorted. "Think about the bright side, mate. You ever get tired of the life you're leading now, you can always hire yourself out as a hood ornament. You're experienced."

"Quiet," Katz said softly.

The group fell into order at once.

"I don't have to tell you we're behind enemy lines on two counts," the Israeli stated. "Caseros's people are one kind of danger, American military forces are quite another." He looked around at his men. He'd led them into battle before, into situations where not all of them had come back. Thoughts of Keio Ohara still haunted him in the quiet moments of his life, and there were others who dated back to the Six Day War and his Mossad career. "We can't fire on American forces, but they won't be operating under the same constraints. Our mission here wasn't sanctioned, and covert activity on our part tonight seems to have put us in the jaws of some type of pincer movement."

"What are you talking about?" Manning asked.

McCarter quickly filled him in on the arrival of the Marines.

"Why didn't Brognola tell us about this?" Manning asked.

"Because he didn't know for sure," Katz replied. "The chance of this happening is why he placed Barbara Price in charge of coordinating the three separate teams instead of keeping himself at the head. Hal will be helping us all he can."

James looked grim. "Like my granny used to say when I was a boy, the Lord helps them who helps themselves."

Katz permitted himself a small smile. "My sentiments exactly. Maneuvering through the jungle without alerting the Marine contingent in this area will be difficult, but not impossible. However, getting past the air guard that will be supporting this invasion is another matter entirely. Here, I think, we'll need to make our own luck." He pointed toward Encizo's prisoner. "Rafael found a man who knows where our target is hiding out. Provided the United States hasn't taken El Presidente into custody by now, Caseros remains our priority."

They met his measuring gaze and returned it.

"Good enough," Katz said as he folded his map and returned it to the case. "Then let's get the hell out of here. James, you've got point. Manning, you're rear guard. McCarter, help Rafael make sure our prisoner remains secure."

Phoenix Force moved out to avoid a potential enemy they dared not face, trekking across a country that had suddenly become more dangerous than they could have anticipated.

CHAPTER TEN

The muzzle of the CAR-15 in the gray-haired man's hands never wavered. Bolan kept his hands laced behind his head and searched through the crowd for Grimaldi.

"That was a very brave, very heroic thing you did back there," the Colombian said. "If you hadn't moved as you did, a greater number of people might have died or been injured beneath the wheels of the truck."

"Then why am I on the other end of your rifle now?" Bolan asked.

Other uniformed policemen came over to join the man. They held their weapons in their hands, but most of them seemed uncertain about what they were supposed to do.

"Because I don't know you, *señor*. Because I'm a man who looks a gift horse in the mouth. Very carefully."

Battered police cars backed out of the way of ambulances. Flames crackled and spit as they twisted in orange and black spirals toward the sky. More than a dozen lights in the surrounding buildings had been switched on as occupants came to the windows to gawk at the carnage below.

"You'll come toward me, *señor,*" the gray-haired man instructed, "and leave your hands on top of your head."

Bolan moved. At this point there was nothing to lose. He'd come here looking for allies of a sort, but he'd figured on coming to an arrangement on a more even footing.

"Stop there." The muzzle of the CAR-15 was still over three feet away. "You know push-ups?"

"Yes."

"Assume the position. Quickly."

Bolan lay prone with his hands out to either side.

"Now push up and remain so. Don't move or you'll be shot." A burst of rapid Spanish followed.

A man separated from the group and began frisking the warrior. He was relieved of the Cold Steel Tanto in short order, as well as the doctored passport under the Mike McKay name.

"Now you can get up. Hands on your head."

Bolan regained his feet as memories of drill training in boot camp came back to his mind, incongruous with the situation.

"It says here that you're an American journalist," the gray-haired man said.

"Yes."

"Yet you have no camera."

"No."

"Sigfrido."

The man turned at the sound of the name. "Yes?"

"Release him. He means us no harm."

Bolan looked in the direction of the voice.

Benito Franco stood on the outside perimeter of the crowd looking worse for the wear. His suit was torn and covered with dirt. The justice minister watched ambulance crews sorting through the bodies strewn across the street, separating the injured from the dead.

"You don't know this man, Benito," Sigfrido protested. "He could be anyone. An assassin sent by your enemies."

"An assassin who would risk his life to save all these people?" Franco shook his head. "No. Your time will be better spent having your men round up the cocaine that spilled from the flatbed and finding out if any of our attackers remain alive."

Sigfrido lowered his weapon. "I'll be watching you, *señor*."

Bolan nodded. "My weapons?"

At Sigfrido's instruction a uniformed policeman handed back the Executioner's knife and the Desert Eagle. Bolan tucked them away.

"Will you walk with me?" Franco asked.

"Yes."

The justice minister brushed absently at a torn pocket of his jacket. He walked around the emergency area, his gaze lighting on the ambulance workers, the wounded, the dead. "I saw you in the crowd before the attack."

An old woman pulled her shawl more tightly around her shoulders as she hunkered down on her knees and cried at the side of a young man who was being covered by a white sheet.

"You didn't seem to be a man who fit," Franco went on.

"I came here tonight looking for you," Bolan stated.

"Why?"

"We share a common enemy," Bolan replied.

"Who?"

"The cartel."

"You have picked a large enough enemy, amigo."

"It picked me."

Franco considered that. "You're an American?"

"Yes."

"CIA or DEA?"

"Neither."

"An American agent of some other alphabet agency that dares not show its face in the light of day?" The justice minister's tone was lightly sarcastic.

"I'm a representative of people who care about the situation down here."

"And whose interests do you represent?"

"Those who have suffered at the hands of the narcobarons in the past and those who will suffer at them in the future. You can't assign a nationality to the harm those people do. It's enough that something is being done about the problem without wondering whose hand is offering the help."

"What do you propose to do about our situation? Would you suggest more violence, more death? Look around you at the dead. Sure, we have killed some of their people this time, but how many more of ours have died?"

Bolan looked the justice minister in the eye. "The losses hurt," he said softly, "and they'll never be just numbers to people who care. But you're talking about more losses than just on a mortal plane. You had people excited about what you were doing here tonight. You touched something inside them that couldn't be repressed or frightened away forever. If you let this shake you, if you back down now, there are going to be even more deaths than you can count. You shouldered a lot of responsibility tonight, and you can't just walk away from it. The news agencies gathered here will string your story across the world. People are going to be watching you.''

"Including the narcobarons."

"Yes." Bolan didn't want to pull any punches with a guy shaping up for a place on the front line.

"I didn't know so many would be killed," Franco said in a hoarse voice.

"People fall in war. Good people as well as bad."

Franco looked at Bolan. "I want so desperately to leave this street and this horror, but I can't."

"I know."

"You've seen war?"

"Yes."

"Do you ever get used to it?"

"Not if you remain a person who loves life."

The justice minister nodded. "My father, he used to speak the same way. I saw him change over the years. He was a policeman. He stopped wearing the hurt on the outside, but you could still see it on the inside if you knew where to look.

"I took this position partly in memory of my father. He was killed by cartel guns. I wanted to avenge him. I made this struggle against the narcobarons my own personal war. Only, instead of success, I've been greeted with a series of hollow victories and defeats that have crushed many men working in my office. Tonight I have to ask myself if these people are dead because of my need for vengeance."

"I've had to ask myself the same question before," Bolan replied. "I don't think I've ever answered that satisfactorily for myself. It's something you have to live with. If you hadn't made this decision to act tonight, there would have been a different set of questions you'd have to live with. And their weight would have been no easier to bear."

Franco sighed. "I know you're right. My head listens, but my heart is deaf."

"I learned a long time ago there are some people who can take the initiative and push the fight back into an aggressor's corner, others who can't fight until they themselves are cornered, and still others who can't fight back at all. I choose to fight for people, to take the fight back where it belongs instead of drawing battle lines. If you let the enemy too close, you're going to lose something no matter what you do. I cross their lines first. I fight to lose nothing at all."

"That isn't possible."

"It helps to have that kind of attitude, keeps me from setting goals for acceptable losses."

Franco appeared to consider that. "And you're suggesting that's what I need to do now?"

"I'm not suggesting anything," Bolan replied. "What you decide to do is going to have to come from you, not me."

"Where do you fit into this?"

Bolan avoided a direct answer. He studied the carnage around them.

"Who do you think is responsible for this?" he asked.

"A man named Pitin."

"Do you have him in custody?"

"No. He's among the dead," Franco replied.

"Who's his boss?"

"Luis Costanza, but I can't prove it." Franco studied the warrior. "You knew that already."

Bolan nodded.

"Without proof there's no way I can strike back at Costanza."

"I have some information you could use," Bolan said. "How you use it is up to you."

"What kind of information?"

Bolan removed a manila envelope from inside the denim jacket. "Here are maps to three of Costanza's jungle labs where the coca leaves are processed into cocaine base. If you move fast enough, you can close down all three of them tonight."

Franco took the packet and shook out the contents. "How did you come by this?"

Remembering Father Lazaro, Bolan gave the justice minister a grim smile. "From a very trustworthy source who wants to see Costanza driven from his castle, as well."

"If these are real..."

"They are. I scouted them out myself. My observations are on the back. Go over them before you make any plans. Also, I wouldn't be too free with the information. Costanza's got plenty of taps into every organization in this country. Keep in mind that a small group of dedicated individuals can move faster and hit harder than a large group of uncertain soldiers. Your security will be tighter, too."

Franco tucked the papers away in an inside pocket of his jacket. "You know I can't ignore this."

"I didn't think you could. In fact, I was counting on it."

"What's in it for you?"

Bolan faced the man. "Most of the same things you're finding in yourself at this moment. I've lost loved ones to people like Costanza. That hurt never goes away if you believe there's something you can do about it. And, like you, I believe that I can. Responsibility figures in there, too, a call to duty that neither one of us can ignore."

"You presume a lot to claim to know my mind."

"Tell me if I'm wrong."

Franco shook his head. "You're not." He tapped his jacket over the papers. "So is this where your involvement ends?"

"No. I'll be around." Bolan stuck out his hand and the other man took it. "Good hunting."

"Take care, amigo."

Bolan threaded through the crowd, searching for Grimaldi's face.

"Hey, buddy." The Stony Man pilot stepped out of the shadows.

"Thought for a while there that I'd lost you," Bolan commented as they continued through the throng gathered on the sidewalk.

An ambulance, evidently filled to capacity, pulled away from the scene of the attack. A woman, flanked by two men who were trying to console her, stumbled after the vehicle.

"It was touch and go," the pilot replied. "I was busy trying to hustle people out of the way when you derailed the truck. Then I got lost in the confusion. Didn't find you again until I saw you with Franco. Did he go for it?"

"He will," Bolan said, tucking his hands into the pockets of his jacket.

"You don't sound too happy, guy."

"Maybe I'm not. I'm not used to having civilians involved, and that's exactly what Franco is. I looked into his eyes and saw an ordinary guy trying to find a way to conduct a war in humane terms. The problem is, he's the same guy who has the clout I need to get the job done."

Grimaldi nodded. "The thing you need to remember is that he wouldn't go for it unless he wanted to. You don't make joiners, you find them."

"Yeah," Bolan said, "but he wouldn't be able to get so close to the fire if I didn't show him the way."

"It'll work out for the best."

"That's what I keep telling myself."

"BENITO, what's going on?"

Franco placed his hands on his wife's slim shoulders. He looked at her in the darkness of their bedroom, knowing she couldn't understand the emotions coursing through him. She wore a short, diaphanous nightgown, letting him know she had planned on celebrating his successes tonight in a more intimate way. Her dark hair was loose and hung well below her shoulders, framing a heart-shaped face. He pulled her to him and pressed his lips to her forehead.

"Benito?"

Her voice was a warm whisper in his ear, her perfume gentle and intoxicating. "Ah, my love, I've missed you so much today."

"As I have missed you, love, but that does not explain the presence of so many men in my house."

Franco cupped her face in his hands, tilted her chin and kissed her lips. He had to force himself to release her. He wished so badly that she could take him in her arms and tell him everything was going to be all right. But the manila envelope in his pocket was a weight and a responsibility that wouldn't be wished away. Nor would the memory of the twenty-seven dead men, women and children who had been removed from the street.

He pulled her to the cushion-covered trunk at the foot of their bed and knelt in front of her, holding her hands in his. "There was a tragedy tonight, Dominga. People were killed." He knew she was unaware of the killing. Since he'd taken the justice minister position, she rarely watched television. During one of their infrequent arguments, she'd said it was because she was afraid of seeing him die in front of her eyes.

"Oh, Benito, no." She gazed at him quickly, as if searching for wounds. "Are you all right?"

"Yes, but there are many who aren't."

She touched his brow. "What's wrong?"

He made himself look into her eyes. "I have to do something tonight."

She didn't say anything.

Somehow her silence seemed even harder to deal with. "I don't want to leave you and Andeana here, but I must go."

"Where?"

"Into the jungle. There are men there who I can bring to justice if I move quickly enough."

"What will this do?"

"Perhaps it will even the scales in some way."

"For the people who died tonight, or for your own sense of justice?"

He faced her as honestly as he could. "Tonight they are both the same thing."

She slipped her hands from his and looked away.

Franco stood up. "You and Andeana will be well protected while I am gone."

"And will you be protected?"

"Of course." He was glad she was looking away. She could always tell when he was lying. Then he realized she might have looked away in order to free him to lie, for both their sakes.

He tried to touch her and couldn't. He would only crumble the small amount of control she still possessed and strip from her the dignity she struggled to maintain. "I do this because I want a better future for Andeana. And for us."

"Do you have to be the one to reach for the future for the whole country?"

"I'm not the only one," he disagreed softly.

"You reach harder than most."

He paused. "That was one of the things about me that attracted you, my love."

She smiled at him, her eyes hard and bright under the layer of unshed tears.

He hugged her briefly, then stepped out into the hall and closed the door behind him. He walked through the narrow hallway until he reached his daughter's, kissed her forehead, then joined the men waiting for him in the living room.

Sigfrido stood near the fireplace, staring at the black-and-white pictures of Franco's father. Rodesney was a flurry of agitation, pacing back and forth in front of the small breakfast bar that Dominga had already set up for their morning meal.

Connors, the other DEA agent acting as Rodesney's aide and partner, sat in an easy chair with heavy-lidded eyes and smoked. He seemed more interested in the curling patterns of the smoke than in why the meeting had been called. The other three were men Franco knew only slightly. But Sigfrido knew them intimately and trusted them, or they wouldn't have been there.

Franco dragged the coffee table to the middle of the floor, catching Rodesney's attention at once. The DEA man's face was creased and worn. "So when do you plan on springing your big secret?"

Ignoring the suspicion and anger in the agent's voice, Franco knelt and waved Sigfrido over. "Now."

Sigfrido sat cross-legged at the table as the papers containing the detailed drawings were spread out.

"What's this?" Rodesney demanded as he came to a stop at the edge of the coffee table.

"Maps," the justice minister replied, "containing the locations of three jungle labs Costanza maintains near Medellín."

"Where did you get these?" Sigfrido asked. His eyes were sharp with hawklike intensity.

Franco grinned. "From a friend."

The old man looked up. "Your friend from tonight?"

"Yes."

"Are you talking about the guy who shut the truck down tonight?" Rodesney asked.

Franco nodded.

"We don't even know who he is, for Christ's sake. This could be a trap."

The justice minister rubbed his hand over his lower jaw as he turned to look at the agent. "Is this what they train you to do in the DEA, Señor Rodesney? Find traps in everything that goes on around you? You don't get victories handed to you without taking chances."

"Don't expect me to involve my people in an operation as half-assed as this," Rodesney growled. "We've got better things to do than wander around in the middle of the night chasing ghosts."

"I don't expect you or your men to involve yourselves. I tell you this now only as a courtesy, and because if I don't tell you, members of your team will attempt to follow me as they always do and perhaps give our efforts away."

"This is insane. You don't even know who this guy is, do you?"

Franco shook his head. "Not who, but I know what he is. I knew that from the moment he diverted the truck and risked his life."

"You're taking too many chances," Rodesney protested.

"And your people don't." Franco felt hot anger color his face. "For months I've listened to the promises **your** agency has made to me. Promises aren't going to change the way my people are forced to live. We're fighting for our survival here."

"What do you think we're doing?"

"I don't know."

Rodesney broke the stare and walked away.

Franco released a pent-up breath. He didn't want to become unfavorable to the United States. It could still be a powerful ally, but the fight had to begin here, and it had to begin in the hands of the Colombians who wanted peace for their families. It dawned on him with cold certainty that the big man who'd given him the locations of the jungle labs had known that. Cocaine was a many-headed hydra in Colombia. Even if one head were to be severed, another would surely grow in its place. The roots lay in the minds of the people, as deep and as spread out as the coca plants themselves. He glanced at Sigfrido. "Can this be done?"

"How many of them?"

"All three. There are notes. They say all three positions can be taken tonight with a small force."

The older man sighed. "I will tell you this, Benito. If these notes and drawings are correct, this thing can be done successfully. But a military mind put this together. There can be no marginal allowances for the letter of the law, no repeated demands for anyone involved in this to come peaceably. They come when they're given the opportunity, or they're shot where they stand."

Franco remembered the bodies littering the street not so far away. It went against the principles he was forced to play by, but this was a matter of survival, of snatching victory from the jaws of defeat. "Then we will do it."

"Okay." Sigfrido rose to his feet. "How long until you want to leave?"

Franco handed him the penciled maps. "We're late already, my friend."

BOLAN WATCHED the rain fall as he waited for the connection to be made. He used another credit card from the supply Kurtzman had sent with him. None of the numbers were supposed to be used more than once. It would make tracking the calls made out of the country impossible. The numbers were assigned to different American companies who regularly did business in Colombia, but a computer program through AT&T would basket all the calls back to a special department in Mount Pilot, South Carolina, where Stony Man would cover the charges without them ever hitting one of the corporations' P&Ls. The destination of each call was different, too. The one the soldier was placing now was rerouted through Nashville, Indiana, and kicked back to Stony Man via computers and satellites.

He stood outside a small grocery store near the warehouse district. Grimaldi sat at the curb in the Ford Falcon they'd purchased since hitting town.

"Mack?" Barbara Price's voice sounded strained.

"Something wrong?" Bolan asked. His thoughts turned to Able Team. The last he'd heard, the mission in Miami had taken a turn for the worse. Pol, Gadgets and Ironman were all old friends. His words to Franco came back to haunt him as he remembered that good people sometimes fell with the bad.

"It would be easier to tell you what's going right. What's your situation down there?"

"Still alive and kicking down some walls. I'm starting to think we might choke on this one, though. It's bigger than we'd thought."

"We might already be choking on it. Lyons has turned up missing, along with Able's target."

"What about Pol and Gadgets?" Bolan kept the concern out of his voice.

"They're pursuing it. Leo's linked up with them."

"They'll find him."

A group of youths wearing gang colors rounded the corner at the far end of the street. They seemed to argue among themselves for a while, then turned toward the grocery store.

"Phoenix might be grounded in Panama," Price said.

"Why?"

The woman hesitated. "The U.S. invaded Panama a couple of hours ago. I'm surprised you didn't know. It's all over television."

"Jack and I haven't exactly had time to play the Nielsen ratings game. How are Katz and the others?"

"Mobile, but we don't have a way of getting them out of the country without a lot of embarrassing questions being asked. Hal's trying to leverage some affirmative action on the Hill now. He isn't expecting much. Our involvement wasn't directly sanctioned, and with it on the verge of blowing up in our faces, no one's going to want to get their hands dirty with us."

"It'll work out," Bolan said. "We haven't lost one yet."

"Phoenix lost Keio Ohara before I came on board, Mack. We've already proved you guys aren't invincible. Lyons's prospects at this point for damn sure don't look good."

"Right now we've got no choice but to weather the storm," Bolan replied. "I've set some things in motion here that I can't walk away from without leaving people high and dry."

"I understand. Brief me."

The soldier gave her the details of enlisting Franco's aid in his assault against Costanza's forces.

"Is there anything I can do from this end?"

"Not yet. I'll keep in touch."

Bolan broke the connection and walked back toward the Falcon. Price was a friend, a soldier warring on a common ground. It would never be more than that, and they both knew it. But he could understand her feeling tonight. She was locked into a coordinating position as the separate teams served the cartels prime cuts of the Stony Man Doctrine. It wasn't an enviable position. The Executioner knew. He'd pushed an innocent man into the fires of hell himself tonight. A willing man, sure, but definitely a guy who would be out of his depth as Costanza retaliated.

He slid into the passenger seat as the youths spread out around the vehicle. The oldest and the largest of them approached Grimaldi's side of the car. The pilot flashed the guy a grin. Bolan tucked the fingers of his right hand inside his denim jacket.

"Something I can do for you guys?" Grimaldi asked. The car engine idled unevenly.

The big youth smiled, showing broken teeth. He was over six feet tall, gangly, but carried a roll of baby fat around his waist. He looked about nineteen or twenty years old. "I don't know, amigo," he said in halting English as he bent down to peer through the window. "We thought maybe there was something we could do for you."

"Like what?" Grimaldi asked.

"We know you *norteamericanos* like the nose candy. We were wondering if you might be interested in buying some."

Grimaldi leaned forward, roping his arms around the steering wheel. "Look, kid, do I look like some gringo who just fell off the banana boat today? I came down here to purchase *la merca,* not buy powdered sugar from a bunch of babies."

The youth waved a hand, and one of the other boys approached. His jacket bulged from hidden contents. The leader reached inside the jacket and pulled out a football-shape package. "Cocaine, my friend. Very good stuff." He opened the package to display the contents. "Try it for yourself."

"And take a chance on strychnine poisoning? No way, José."

"This is good stuff," the youth protested, looking upset and angry.

"Where did you get it?" Bolan asked.

"That's none of your business."

"It is if you want to get paid. Otherwise you can keep skipping on down the street waiting for the police to pick you up."

The youth looked troubled.

"That's from the warehouse bust, isn't it?" Bolan asked. "Over half the product confiscated there disappeared into the crowd when the guns started going off."

"What if it is?"

"It tells me you don't have much of an investment in it," Bolan said. "So, if I buy, I shouldn't have to pay market value."

The youth shrugged. "What are you offering?"

"How much have you got?"

"Three packages."

"Let's see them."

The youth reached into his friend's jacket and produced the other two. He held them in his arms. "So what do you think, amigos? Do we play *Let's Make a Deal?*"

Bolan looked at Grimaldi. "What do you think?"

The pilot nodded. "Sure. Let's give him what's behind door number one." He looked back at the youth. "That sound okay with you, kid? You want what's behind door number one?"

"*Sí, sí.*"

Grimaldi opened the door suddenly, catching the youth off guard. The three packages hit the ground as the youth skidded across the street on his butt.

Bolan drew the Desert Eagle and stopped all forward motion on the part of the other youths. Leaning out the open door, Grimaldi gathered the three packages into the seat, then peeled away from the curb. The Executioner used the Cold Steel Tanto to slice the bindings of the packages, then emptied each one out the window as they sped down the street. "What about Franco?"

"They're going for it," Grimaldi said as he drove. He tapped the electronic bugging device with attached microrecorder that lay beside him. "It's all right here."

"Did they mention in what order they were going to be hitting the labs?"

"Just the way you called it."

"That's something at least."

"Guy's going to be drawing a lot of heat damn quick, Sarge."

The Executioner nodded. "That's why we're giving him our full support."

Grimaldi grinned. "Maybe we need to come up with a snappy slogan. Better Politics through Superior Gunplay. Or business cards. Bolan and Grimaldi— Political Support Group—Have Ballot, Will Travel."

"Jack."

"Yeah."

"Just drive."

"Right."

CHAPTER ELEVEN

"They've seen us," Sigfrido's voice crackled over the radio.

Franco looked down from the helicopter bay at the hidden camp as lights started to come on along the outer perimeters. His throat was dry, and his ears hurt from sustained use of the headphones. The gun at his waist felt like a rock in his stomach. The wind tore at his flak jacket as the helicopter rocketed along just above the treetops. A dark green and black panorama spread out below him, a sea of unmoving life forced into full throttle.

Bright sparks flashed around dark hulks below that could barely be recognized as buildings. Dull pops sounded within the helicopter. One of them hit near Franco's hand, and he gazed at a hole that hadn't been there a heartbeat before. He moved his hand and whispered a quick prayer.

Abruptly the lead helicopter carrying Sigfrido and his team dipped, skimming with their landing gear scarce inches above the treetops. The dull roar of the mounted chain gun filled the night, and green tracers darted through the trees.

Franco thought he saw a body fall and be swallowed up by the shadows. He closed his eyes involuntarily before he could be certain. He glanced to his left and saw the reporter assigned to his aircraft leaning out the bay, held by the back of his shirt by one of the dozen soldiers crowded together. The reporter was young and lean, totally involved in the action his minicam was recording.

"Sir."

The justice minister stepped away from the bay opening so that the wind wouldn't whisper across the microphone in front of his mouth. "Yes?"

"I await your direction," the helicopter pilot said.

"Put us down wherever Sigfrido has instructed you."

Franco tried to swallow but couldn't. He touched the butt of the Taurus 9 mm pistol holstered at his side and couldn't bring himself to unleather it. As a boy he'd been fascinated by American cowboys and had practiced his fast draw religiously in front of mirrors. When his father had found him, the elder Franco had placed a real gun in his hand and let him fire it. Somehow it had never seemed the same since. The romance was gone. Now, with his fingers brushing against the cold metal, there was only a tight fear in his chest. His father had taught him to shoot, but killing was another matter.

The helicopter dropped suddenly, feeling like an elevator that had gone out of control. He willed his eyes to remain open, counting his heartbeats as the ground rushed up at them. Only the reassuring throb of the rotors overhead kept him from screaming. The aircraft touched down with a jarring thump.

The reporter was the first to leap through the opening and move toward the camp, seemingly led by the minicam. Franco dropped the headset, and the harsh crackle of gunfire ripped into his hearing. A young policeman came up behind him, carrying an assault rifle.

"I'm Nelo, sir," the policeman said. "The commander assigned me to be your communications officer."

"Nelo, if you have any thoughts as we go along, I want to hear them. I want to see everything of this setup that I can, but I don't want to be responsible for getting us killed. I've never been involved in anything like this before."

"Neither have I."

Franco nodded, realizing the same was probably true of a number of the other policemen beating the brush at the moment. He tried not to think of how many of them might not live to see the morning. When he remembered there were two more such camps marked for destruction within the next few hours, he shuddered. Autofire crashed sporadically through the clapboard buildings.

"A word of advice, draw your weapon," Nelo said. "You might have to use it."

Franco did so, but his hand felt too warm and too slick to grip it properly. The pistol seemed awkward. He shelved the feelings and forced himself into motion. It was important that he see the camp for himself.

An airstrip had been bulldozed through the heart of the camp, bisecting the area into definite east and west. A dozen clapboard sheds with raised floors and sheet metal roofs with some type of plastic covering faced the east, with several more toward the west.

The justice minister advanced cautiously, taking care to remain within cover. He reached the first of the sheds without incident and clambered up on the raised floor. The door stood ajar and he peered inside. Only darkness greeted him.

"Sir, stand aside," Nelo said. "Cover me when I go in." He took up a position on one side of the door, flicked on the flashlight taped to the end of his rifle barrel and ducked inside.

Franco followed, the pistol seeming to move too slowly in his hands. A startled yelp drew his attention. He felt the pistol raise almost of its own volition as his breath caught in his throat. His finger tightened on the trigger.

The yellow beam of the taped flashlight bathed a scrawny old woman dressed in rags. She was on her knees, her thin arms stretched out to them in supplication. "Don't shoot, for the love of God, don't shoot!"

Arms trembling with the effort it took to remove his finger from the trigger without firing, Franco turned away and walked farther into the building.

"Lavaperros," Nelo said in disgust as he switched off the flashlight and followed.

Franco knew the young policeman's feelings summed up how most of the law-enforcement people felt about the Antioqueños. The northern Medellín street people had earned the slang name "dog washers" by hiring out to cartel members for every crime from courier to assassin. In his heart, however, he felt the *lavaperros* were as much at the mercy of the Colombian economy as anyone else.

He slipped the safety back on his pistol. He'd come too close to shooting first and looking second. He realized he didn't belong out here. He was better in a courtroom, with rules he knew. Life and death hung in the balance there, as well, but he knew the territory.

"Sir."

Franco looked back over his shoulder and took the walkie-talkie Nelo held out. He hit the transmit button and breathed his name into it.

"Sigfrido," the old man said in his recognizable voice. "It looks like your friend was right about the size of this lab. It's bigger than anything the DAS has taken down since Tranquilandia. I've counted three airplanes and four helicopters so far, all tucked away under netting that would make them invisible from the air."

A grunting sound came from the side of the building. Sighting down the barrel of the Taurus, Franco saw three pigs come into view, snorting as they snuffled through the piles of garbage stacked there. A black plastic bag ripped and spilled trash as the pigs shoved into one another trying to be the first to discover whatever was to be had.

"Benito?"

"Here."

"Are you all right?"

"Yes. Just had a scare, that's all. A group of pigs. I hadn't expected that."

"You'll find pigs, turkeys, rabbits and chickens here. This is a very complete setup, and it'll hurt them to lose this place. The cartel had at least eighty Antioqueños living here processing the cocaine, and they were provided with generators, showers, washers and dryers, foodstuffs, entertainment and clothing. At last count we've taken more than sixty people prisoner. Only the cartel security force does any fighting. The Antioqueños don't even pick up weapons. But have a care when you come this **way**, Benito. Some of the security team has gotten away, and we think they might overrun your position in their efforts to get away."

"Thanks, Sigfrido." Franco cleared the channel and handed the walkie-talkie back to Nelo. He took the lead, letting the policeman cover their backs.

The moonlight was uncertain in the trees. He skirted the edge of the airstrip, perspiring profusely. A crackle of autofire directly ahead of him sent Franco and the policeman to the ground.

The sound of running feet came from the airstrip. Seconds later the video journalist who had accompanied Franco on the helicopter broke through the brush and into view. The man dropped to one knee and directed his minicam back the way he'd come. Autofire thundered again. The reporter's head jerked backward, his silver-rimmed glasses spinning through the air. His body crashed to the ground as the camera dropped from nerveless fingers.

Without thinking of the consequences, only of the man who had been shot, Franco pushed himself to his feet and ran out into the airstrip. Even as he reached the reporter, three men carrying assault weapons raced into view. He raised his Taurus in one fist, aiming at the lead figure, then found he couldn't pull the trigger.

They didn't have any hesitation at all.

MACK BOLAN LAY prone and concealed on a hillside three hundred yards from the cocaine lab. The butt of the big Barrett Model 82A1 pressed against his shoulder, the thirty-three-inch barrel resting on its bipod. He peered through the Mark-700 Series Startron scope at the three men standing in front of Benito Franco. He laid the cross hairs over the heart of each man, squeezing the trigger and moving on without checking to see the effects. The Barrett kicked into him relentlessly.

He kept the Startron on the third man. The 12.7 mm round, leaving the barrel at 2,848 feet per second, crashed into the man and threw him backward. The Executioner raised his head from the scope and checked the area. All three of Franco's attackers sprawled lifelessly across the grass airstrip.

The justice minister holstered his weapon and moved toward the wounded cameraman. A moment later Franco threw the man's arm across his shoulders and helped him to cover. Nelo raced forward and recovered the minicam.

The Executioner rested the butt of the Barrett on the ground as he lifted the night glasses at his side. The walkie-talkie, monitoring the frequency the national police assault force was using, kept up a continuous stream of voices that were shocked and surprised over what was being found.

A helicopter, which had yet to touch down, circled overhead. Bolan knew it carried the DEA agents. The jungle lab assault was out of their present field of operations, but they were under orders to stay with Franco.

Other helicopters took off at the DAS commander's instruction, high-intensity spotter lights mounted on their bellies lighting up the night. Sporadic autofire followed, but it quickly faded. The throbbing sound of the rotors of a half-dozen choppers filled the air. A large group of the khaki uniforms surrounded Franco at the airstrip. Most of them moved on after the area was secured.

Bolan touched the transmit button on the throat/ear receiver he and Grimaldi were using. "Jack."

"Yeah."

"Ready to move out?"

"Been ready ever since we stopped here."

Bolan stood and lifted the heavy Barrett by the handle.

"Our boy froze out there," Grimaldi pointed out.

"I saw."

"He had the shot and didn't take it."

"I know."

"Now isn't the time to find out if he has the heart to follow this thing through."

"Franco has the heart," Bolan replied. "He's got too much heart. That's why he didn't drop the hammer." The uphill grade to where the pilot sat with the jeep was steep and tortuous, overgrown with vines, brush and gnarled roots.

"It's going to be hard running interference for a guy who won't lift a gun to protect himself."

"When the time comes, and the stakes are high enough, Franco will use a gun if he has to."

Grimaldi's grunt was noncommittal.

Bolan topped the hill. He put the Barrett on the rear deck of the jeep, slipped the throat/ear receiver off and dropped into the passenger seat. "You remember the first man you ever killed?"

"Yeah. He was just a face on the ground, a VC in a sector where we were laying down napalm. I put part of the load down almost on top of him. I've never been able to forget it."

"That's where Franco's head is right now. He knows he won't be able to forget, either." Bolan glanced at the circling helicopters overhead. Somewhere down there he knew Franco was going through some serious decision-making. The soldier didn't doubt the justice minister would make the right choices because the right choices were the only ones the man's heart and soul would allow him to make. He sighed and braced his right foot against the floorboard as Grimaldi engaged the transmission. The Colombian cartel was the crucible, and the Executioner was the heat that would forge the young justice minister into something more than he had been—or break him. And Bolan knew he wouldn't be able to deny his share of responsibility.

"You were a very lucky man, Benito."

Franco looked up from the trio of dead men. Sigfrido stood with his CAR-15 canted off one hip. "Luck had nothing to do with it," he replied, surprised at how calm his voice sounded. "It was him."

"The man who gave you the location of the labs?"

"Yes."

"You saw him?"

Franco shook his head. "I just know."

Sigfrido knelt, grabbed a fistful of one of the dead men's shirts and yanked the body from the ground. The hole in the corpse's chest looked big enough to shove a fist through. "Your friend doesn't believe in halfway measures."

Only the sound of the hovering helicopters drifted around them.

"The maps he drew and the observations he made told you that."

Sigfrido let the body drop from his fingers. "That's true. The man is very organized." His smoldering eyes locked onto the younger man's. "This man is also using you as a staked goat, Benito. He knows the cartel will focus on you as a result of tonight's actions." The DAS man's voice was soft. "You serve his purposes as well as your own."

"Our own," Franco said automatically.

"Yes, our own. But it's a dangerous game he plays with your life. I wouldn't want to see Dominga made into a widow while so young."

Armed men continued to file around them, herding the prisoners like cattle. There was no more resistance.

"She won't be," Franco promised. "I intend to live for a long time. I have much to do for my country, and Andeana wants a little brother."

Sigfrido grinned widely. He spit a stream of tobacco juice onto the ground, then covered it with his foot. "Then you'll truly be a busy man, Benito. I just want to make sure you stay alive to do all these wonderful things that are in your head. I promised this to your father."

"I know."

The walkie-talkie on Sigfrido's hip called for attention. He spoke into it briefly, then put it away. "There, watch the fruits of your labors tonight." He pointed toward the western edge of the camp.

Jets of fire screamed skyward, bouncing yellow glints off the circling helicopters. The explosion trailed slightly, sounding like a sonic boom as it roiled through the valley. More explosions followed.

"By the time the fires stop burning," the DAS man said, "there'll be nothing left of the cocaine, ether or any of the other chemicals stored here. We'll confiscate the planes, helicopters and weapons. I have men among our force who can fly and will see to the retrieval of whatever ordnance we can use. They'll meet us at the site of the third lab we hit before morning. That way we'll be at eighty percent strength at all times."

"Just the way the plans suggested."

"Yes. The man is a good tactician." Sigfrido shrugged and spit more tobacco juice. "I give him that gladly, but I question his motives."

"If you had looked into his eyes as he spoke, you wouldn't."

Sigfrido shrugged again. "Maybe."

"How many casualties did we take?"

"Only three. There are some wounded, of course, but none requiring immediate medical attention."

"We take our dead with us."

"Of course. They have already been loaded."

Franco made himself move, hypnotized by the death that seemed to surround him. Besides the men he saw before him, there were others he'd have to view, as well. "They'll be buried with full honors."

"Of course."

A chill worked its way up Franco's spine as he walked through the brush. Sigfrido followed, giving new orders over the walkie-talkie. The justice minister couldn't get the sights out of his mind. He could almost smell the gun oil covering the pistol in his hand as he stared down the barrel of the Taurus at the three men running toward him. His finger had refused to pull the trigger despite knowing they intended to kill him. Then there had been the three thunderclaps that had smashed the men to the ground in quick order. He'd been watched over, and he'd been watched over just like the staked goat Sigfrido had mentioned. The chill flushed through him again. Thoughts of Andeana and Dominga crowded into his mind, reminding him that despite all the death he walked through, he had to remain alive for their sakes. He knew that next time he wouldn't hesitate to fire. Part of him was saddened at the realization of how easily the animal side of a man's nature could overtake him.

He didn't intend to remain a staked goat. If he was going to be bait for the predators, he wasn't going to solely depend on the hunters for his deliverance. He drew the Taurus and walked on. He would learn to hunt, as well.

CHAPTER TWELVE

"It's lovely, isn't it?"

Bolan glanced over his shoulder, knowing Father Lazaro was there because he'd heard the man's approach. "Yes, it is."

Dawn crept over the tree line, painting the sky a dozen variations of purple and red.

"I've lived most of my life here and I never get tired of seeing the sun rise over this part of the land," the priest said.

Bolan cranked the bucket up from the well, pouring water into a bowl, then carried the water bowl and placed it at the foot of the tree he'd chosen. He'd used the Cold Steel Tanto to hang a small steel mirror from his kit at eye level on the tree. Naked to the waist, he draped a borrowed towel over his shoulder, splashed his face with water, lathered with bar soap and took the straight razor from his pocket. He shaved with quick, firm strokes, then rinsed the blade.

Lazaro was reflected in the mirror, a thin figure in black. The priest wore his hat and kept his hands tucked inside his sleeves. Gray pain shadowed his face, but the soldier kept the observation to himself. Lazaro was a private man.

"You handle the straight razor well," the priest observed. "You don't often find people with hands steady enough to use one. Sister Yanett finds herself being asked to assist men in their shaving nearly every morning.''

"My father taught me,'' Bolan replied as he rinsed the blade.

"It's a good thing to hear of a father handing down knowledge to a son.''

Bolan rinsed the razor again, then started on the other side. "He taught me a lot of things that children tend to take for granted as they get older.''

Lazaro nodded. "Was your father a soldier, too?''

"No, he was a steelworker.''

"A builder. That's a fine trade.''

"I suppose it was.''

"Did he have dreams of your joining him someday?''

Bolan whisked away the growth on his upper lip. "I don't know. We never had the chance to talk about it. But knowing my old man, I'd say he probably did.''

"Did you ever think about it?''

"I never had the chance. He...died sometime ago.'' Bolan nicked his cheek at the memory. He watched the blood trickle down, then went back to shaving. "I was away when it happened, fighting a war nobody wanted to claim.''

"Vietnam.''

"Yes.''

"Your family?''

"Gone, too.''

"I'm sorry. I didn't mean to bring up such painful memories. I was unsure how to get around to the subject of your mission last night. I was awake when you came in this morning, but I knew you needed your rest."

"The mission went well. The three jungle labs I reconned and alerted Medellín police forces about were taken down last night."

"What of the people working there?"

"They were released. There was no need for the DAS to take them into custody. The important thing was destroying the drugs and equipment found at the camps."

"How much damage will this do to Costanza's holdings?"

"Depends on how much he needed the cocaine that was destroyed last night. I've hit him in other areas, destroyed other shipments. It's got to be hurting his operation. Part of Costanza's credibility as a businessman depends on being able to get the product from one place to another on time. Never get the idea that this isn't business."

"Yes, I understand that."

"His losses aren't going to end there," Bolan went on. "As long as I'm getting some cooperation through the justice minister's office, we're going to hit every one of those jungle labs you told me about."

"What do you think you can accomplish by doing that?"

"I'll put Costanza on the defensive, and I'll definitely throw a monkey wrench into the machine he's got pumping cocaine onto American streets. By working with Franco and the Medellín police teams, Colombian interests wanting to end the cartels will have their day to stand and be counted."

"Your country's Ernest Hemingway wrote of bull-fights," Lazaro said.

The warrior smiled mirthlessly. "Maybe you could call it that."

"Judging from the scars on your body, you've come close to the bulls on several occasions."

"Yeah, but at the moment I'm operating as an unknown quantity. Franco's in the hot seat as far as the raids go, and he runs the most direct risk of any retaliation on Costanza's part."

"I can see by your face that you're not comfortable with that."

"No, but it's what needs to be done to give us a chance of pulling this off. All I can do at this point is try to get Franco to continue to see things my way and ride shotgun on everything he does that takes him away from his security." Bolan patted his face dry. "You and this church aren't sitting in an enviable position, either. Costanza's intelligent. After these strikes continue, he'll pinpoint you and the church as a possible source for the information I've been using. I think you should consider leaving here for a while."

Lazaro spread his hands. "There's nowhere else for us to go. And to flee now..." He shook his head. "That's why I gave you the information, so we wouldn't be chased from our home."

"Do you understand the risks you're taking?"

"As surely as you understand the ones you're taking." The priest smiled slightly. "We're both experts in our chosen field, and this country is my home, known to me as surely as those who would declare me an enemy."

One of the nuns stepped out of the church to motion them inside.

"Breakfast is ready," Lazaro announced. "The sisters have worked very hard to prepare you and your friend a good meal."

Bolan nodded. "It'll be appreciated. Let me get dressed and I'll join you inside." He walked toward the small barn he and Grimaldi had used as a bunkhouse and hiding place for the jeep. As he entered, the pilot came awake at once, rolling over on the tarp-covered floor and coming up with his Beretta clenched in his fist. The warrior grinned. "Morning, Jack."

"Already?"

"You missed reveille. If you don't shake a leg, you're going to miss breakfast, too."

The pilot yawned and scrubbed at his face with a palm. "God, three hours' sleep all at one time. The next thing I know, you're going to have a valet service for us on this little expedition through hell."

"Hardly. But you'll find a shower behind the church. You have to draw your own water." Bolan pulled on an olive-green T-shirt and tucked it into the denim pants. He didn't feel comfortable about sitting down armed to a table the nuns had prepared, but he felt less comfortable about sitting down unarmed. He donned the 93-R's shoulder holster, then shrugged into a white cowboy shirt and left the tails out so that the material wouldn't hug the outlines of the pistol. He rolled the sleeves up to midforearm.

"So what's on tap after breakfast?" Grimaldi asked as he got to his feet.

"We do some solo activity," the Executioner said. "I'm planning an excursion into downtown Medellín for another one-on-one with Franco. I need you to scare up a plane. If you find it, I'll help you get it. After that, I'm going to contact Barb and have her start watching chemical buying in the States, as well as find out about Phoenix. With the way we're going to be taking down Costanza's jungle labs, he's going to need supplies to make up new product. To do that, he's going to have to surface bits and pieces of his operation to make his connections. It'll enable us to get a better feel for everything he's got his hooks into. Aaron can cut through the red tape on the invoices and let us know what import-export companies he's subsidizing in the United States and Colombia."

"And Operation Shutdown kicks into high gear all over again."

Bolan nodded. "On all fronts. I want Costanza to know this one's for all the marbles."

"No, SERIOUSLY," Orrin Tyler said as he ran his hands through his gray hair, "despite everything you hear on the news, this post is nothing but sucking hind tit."

Jeremy Hitch shook his head as he stopped the car at the curb in front of the small restaurant the older agent had suggested for breakfast. Medellín was in full swing around them. The sights, sounds and smells were still new to him, filled with mystery and more than a little danger.

Tyler slammed the door shut and leaned across the car. "Goddamn it, I'm serious, kid," the big man said good-naturedly. "This is a peach. You need to lighten up and enjoy yourself a little."

Shading his eyes with his hand, Hitch glanced at the three-story buildings on both sides of the street. The restaurant squatted under newer businesses like an orphaned child. Green paint colored the walls. The daily specials were painted on the windows, letting him know they weren't changed often, if ever.

"For three days I've been listening to you quote DEA codes and regs at me," Tyler complained. "Today I want you to do things my way. Rodesney runs a loose operation here. He's a stand-up guy and won't tolerate any slacking, but he knows operating by the book won't cut jackshit out here in this hick country. I'm going to take you to breakfast today at one of my favorite places to eat, my treat, and I want you to crawl out of that Johnny Cool, Secret Agent mode of thinking you're in."

Hitch didn't say anything as he slipped off his Foster Grants and tucked them into a pocket.

"These people already know who we are," Tyler continued. "They've learned how to smell the DEA coming down on them. Trust me on this. If they wanted us dead, we would be. We haven't given them any reason to in a long time."

Hitch looked at the other man in disbelief. "Didn't you hear anything about what happened last night?"

Tyler waved it away. "The jungle raids? Wasn't us, kid. That was the DAS playing cowboy again. They do that every so often. More so now that Franco is justice minister. Rodesney's been trying to get him to cool his jets for months, but the guy won't listen. There'll come a day, though, when he'll wish he had."

Straightening his jacket over the holstered side arm at his waist, Hitch said, "What makes you sure we didn't have anything to do with those raids?"

"We'd have been told," Tyler said. "God, you sound like a veteran, Jerry, already thinking the Administration has its head up its ass here in Colombia."

Hitch didn't say anything. It wasn't a matter of thinking. He believed.

"Take my word for it, kid. The cartel people know better than to fuck with the DEA and the United States. Phelps straightened out those asswipes on that score a long time ago. And they know we can't do shit without cooperation on the part of the Colombian government, which is harder than finding a virgin over the age of eighteen back home in L.A. We're safe as houses. Come on."

A sudden screech of rubber drew Hitch's attention. He whirled around, deliberately not going for his pistol in case it proved to be nothing. The last thing he wanted this morning was Tyler on his ass about overreacting. When he saw the motorcycle roar up over the curb and thump to a landing only a few yards behind them, he went for the gun, anyway. His fingers closed around the pistol butt just as .45-caliber rounds from the passenger's Ingram knocked Tyler to the ground. The pistol cleared leather as the redirected stream of bullets dug into his chest. He died before he could pull the trigger.

CHAPTER THIRTEEN

"This is Sam Waterston reporting live from Medellín, Colombia, where daring midnight raids coordinated through Justice Minister Benito Franco's office have resulted in a successful strike against the cocaine cartels plaguing this country.

"However, that success may be short-lived. Unconfirmed reports are filtering in that the special strike force teams used last night didn't go without casualties. Authorities are tight with concrete information at this point, pending release from the justice minister's secretary and notification of the families.

"On that same note it appears that two DEA agents were gunned down in the street early this morning at a restaurant not far from where I am now. Sources indicate this was a direct response from unknown cartel members regarding possible DEA involvement in the strikes carried out last night. This station has been unable to confirm Drug Enforcement Agency cooperation. Section Chief Bart Rodesney has been unavailable for comment.

"Behind me you can see the Justice Ministry building, looking grim and foreboding now with the uniformed guards keeping everyone out except those people who have business within its walls today. A large crowd has gathered before the steps. If you look closely—can we get that camera on those people?—you'll see men, women and children standing there awaiting official word of what has happened.

"Tension seems to be the key emotion at this point. For many years cocaine has been king in this country. I could go on about programs instituted by both the United States and Colombia for some time. It appears Justice Minister Franco is no longer content to merely talk about it. I've been told he left with the strike force teams after a drug raid ended in tragedy last night, and that the jungle raids weren't planned at all before then.

"However, like everyone else, we're waiting on the real story. Despite the U.S. invasion of Panama last night, which may or may not be linked to what is currently happening here, Colombia's attention is rooted on Justice Minister Franco and his efforts. We can only guess how long it will be before the cartel members responsible for the deaths of the DEA agents will strike at the man who called the operation into being.

"Here comes Minister Franco's helicopter now. It's landing on top of the Justice Ministry. I'm going in now to see if I can get a word with him. If so, there'll be another special broadcast.

"This is Sam Waterston, bringing the story to you live from Medellín, Colombia."

FRANCO STEPPED from the helicopter onto the roof of the Justice building and stared at the crowd gathered before it in helpless fascination. He felt tired, and he looked at Sigfrido, who appeared undaunted by the night's activities. "It appears the news travels quickly."

The DAS man nodded and pulled his long-billed cap lower over his eyes. "Yes. And you'd make a good target up here."

A chill settled over Franco's heart as he realized the truth of the man's words. He followed the line of men through the rooftop door and down into the building. Even though he'd been working inside the structure for years, somehow it all seemed like unexplored territory to him this morning.

Under Sigfrido's supervision the strike team formed a flying wedge around Franco when they hit the floor his office was on. People in the hallway, primarily reporters and lesser bureaucrats from the Colombian congress, stepped back before the show of force, although some of the minicam operators had to be moved bodily.

Sigfrido closed the door behind them as they entered the office. "I took the precaution of stationing people I trusted here overnight," the DAS man said. "There's no need to think bombs have been planted before our arrival."

Collapsing into the swivel chair behind his desk, Franco looked at the man and said, "I hadn't even considered the possibility."

"Perhaps, my friend, if I do my job right, you'll never have to think of them."

Franco managed a small grin. "If you should ever fail, rest assured I'll hold you accountable for whatever happens." He lifted the phone receiver from his desk and punched in his home number. Dominga answered on the first ring.

"Benito, it's been all over the television this morning. Are you all right?"

"Yes. Just tired. Spiritually I feel better than I've felt in months." He wanted to convey the satisfaction that was his primary emotion, but guilt got in the way when he heard the anxiety in her voice.

"The television said that some men had been killed."

"Yes, some were." He faltered, unsure of what to say next. The losses were still too high to say that they had been worth it.

"I want you home."

"I know. I want to be home, too. But there are things here that must be taken care of first."

"You'll be home soon?"

"As soon as I am able."

She hesitated. "I love you, Benito."

"And I love you, Dominga. Give my love to Andeana." He held on to the receiver until he heard the click of the broken connection, unable to break it himself.

Sigfrido placed his CAR-15 against the wall and rummaged through the cabinet space behind the desk. He straightened up a moment later, holding a bottle of whiskey in one hand and two glasses in the other. "Join me in a drink, Benito."

"Where did you find that?"

The DAS man winked at him. "You aren't the first justice minister I've known to sit in that chair." He shrugged. "These things have been passed on. Now, perhaps you'll find yourself in occasional need of its medicinal purposes." He splashed liquor into both glasses and slid one across the empty desktop. "To your health."

"And yours." Franco lifted the glass and drank the contents in one swallow. The explosion hit his stomach and triggered a fit of coughing. He groped through the desk drawers for the supply of fresh handkerchiefs he stored there.

"More?" Sigfrido asked.

"No," he replied in a hoarse voice. He waved the hand holding the handkerchief, realized it looked like he was surrendering, then laughed in a scratchy wheeze.

The DAS man poured more whiskey into his own glass. "You find something amusing?"

Franco explained the handkerchief, then shook his head, knowing part of the emotion came from exhaustion. "I'll need to talk to the reporters," he said when the moment passed. "They need to be told of what has happened."

"Are you ready?"

"Yes."

Sigfrido moved to the phone, spoke briefly, then hung up. "My men will have the pressroom secured within the hour to make sure there are no assassins among their number. It'll give you time to prepare your speech."

"That will be fine, but I want extra guards posted over Dominga and Andeana."

"It has already been taken care of."

"Good."

"So what happens next?" Sigfrido asked.

"We wait." Franco leaned back in the swivel chair as the alcohol worked to relax him.

"For your mysterious friend to reappear?"

"Yes. He will."

"I know." Sigfrido finished his drink, then drew a plug of tobacco from his pocket and cut off a chunk, which he chewed with gusto. "These are dangerous games you're playing, Benito. I won't pull punches with you."

"If we don't face the danger," Franco said softly, "there'll be no way for us to save a future for our families at all."

"The cartel probably has a price out on your head at this moment."

The words chilled Franco. "It would not surprise me. Where's Rodesney?"

"He has problems of his own. Two of his men were shot down in the street this morning."

"Why?"

"To make a statement to the Americans."

Franco looked away from the older man. The responsibilities and repercussions of his actions seemed to know no bounds.

"The United States invaded Panama last night," Sigfrido went on. "It's my belief that the cartel people believed them to be behind the raids on the jungle labs, as well."

"But we did that on our own."

Sigfrido nodded. "They'll find that out soon enough."

"Am I doing the right thing?" Franco asked. "The warehouse raid cost lives last night. So did the strikes against the labs."

"You have made them stand for something. Before, without the actions we have taken, they would have merely been numbers. Now they are a rallying point."

"You make it sound so callous."

Sigfrido's eyes narrowed. "This is war, Benito. You learn quickly that there's no time for sentiment during the fighting of it."

"Perhaps, then, I'm the wrong man for this job. I can't escape the feelings that accompany everything I have caused to be done."

"No. You are exactly the right man for the job." The DAS man's voice was soft and compelling. "Your friend, whoever he really turns out to be, couldn't have selected better. You're still an innocent in many ways. Even the death of your father at the hands of your enemies didn't rip this away from you. There's a willingness in you to fight the cartel people, and a belief that the fight against them can be won."

"You make it sound like you don't believe that."

"I don't."

"Then why do you follow me? It can't be just because my father and you were friends."

Sigfrido shook his head. "I follow you because you have a special gift. You make me *want* to believe again. When I'm around you, I feel that very strongly."

Uncomfortable with the other man's honesty, Franco felt relieved when someone knocked at the door. "Enter."

Luis Costanza walked into the office with two policemen following him. He wore an expensively cut blue-green three-piece suit and carried his hat in his hands. His sunglasses were dark and allowed no hint of his eyes.

Franco stood up behind his desk and waved to a chair before the desk. "To what do I owe this unexpected honor?"

Costanza sat in the chair and crossed his legs, perching his hat on his knee. Gold glittered across his fingers from the light of the goosenecked lamp. "I came to see you both as a concerned citizen as well as a member of congress."

Franco leaned forward, quelling his impulse to challenge Costanza's claim to being a concerned citizen as he rested his elbows on the desk. "I see. Concerning what matters?"

"Let's not be coy," Costanza said. "I'm speaking of your recent successes against the cocaine traffickers in Colombia."

"As I remember, in the talks you've given in congress, you've never believed the problems of cocaine to be worth the time they've taken up during our sessions."

"I still think there are other things more deserving of discussion. Things that would be more to the benefit of our country instead of to its detriment."

"I don't consider stopping the flow of drugs through Colombia to be a detriment."

"I don't wish to argue or quibble."

"I don't feel that I'm doing either."

Costanza spread his hands, palms up. "Can we speak privately?"

"I have no secrets from Captain Sigfrido."

Costanza hesitated only a heartbeat. He smiled and got to his feet. "Perhaps I'm taking up too much of your time. You're a very busy man, Minister Franco." He walked toward the door.

Franco watched him go with the same sick fascination he would have given a poisonous snake.

Costanza paused at the door. "One word of caution, my friend."

"Yes?"

"As the American slang goes, don't bite off more than you can chew." Costanza closed the door after him.

Franco sighed and settled back in the swivel chair. His hands shook as he splashed more whiskey into his glass. He drank it quickly without thinking.

"You have made a very powerful enemy there," Sigfrido observed.

"In this business," the justice minister said as he stood and gathered his notes, "I've learned there's no other kind."

"NOT A VERY HEALTHY situation if you ask me, mate," David McCarter commented. He studied the target area through the binoculars again.

"Isaac Auerbach and Chaim Feldman may be there," Yakov Katzenelenbogen stated in a dry voice. McCarter didn't comment. He already knew of the tension between the ex-Mossad agents. "According to the information Encizo's snitch gave us, Caseros should be holed up in the second house.''

Phoenix Force's leader nodded.

The target house was a standard two-story, white-washed, American-style dwelling in the Canal Zone. A wide stairway led up to the second floor on the outside. A thirty-year-old sedan with cracked and peeling paint sat almost concealed under the attached carport. Dozens of houses just like it lay in all directions. The only thing that set it apart was the radio antenna bolted to the red-tiled roof.

McCarter shifted to tuck the binoculars under his arm out of sight as a man hurried past them.

Amador Road was representative of the chaos Panama City had become. Vehicular traffic was non-existent. American forces had sealed off the metropolitan area with tanks and jeeps, and were in the process of moving to secure the outer edges, as well. Gunfire and explosions had become normal street sounds.

"At least the Special Forces troops haven't started their house-to-house search here for Caseros," McCarter said as he scanned the upper windows of the structure. "How do you want to handle this?"

Katz reached for the butt of the MAC-10 under his windbreaker. "About the way you'd want to do it."

McCarter smiled as he put the binoculars away and slid on the amber-colored aviator sunglasses. "You mean kick in the bloody door and give 'em hell?"

"We don't have the time to tunnel over," Katz replied without humor.

"True, mate. And as an added attraction, this way you know a lot sooner how the plan's going."

Katz spoke briefly into the walkie-talkie and Phoenix Force closed in, taking previously assigned routes.

McCarter took the lead, sprinting across the two-lane street as he tugged his Uzi from under his jacket. Quick blasts from the back of the house told him Encizo and James had already encountered resistance. Glass shattered somewhere, and somebody screamed, followed by more gunfire.

Motion attracted the Briton's attention to the upper-story patio. He brought up the muzzle of the Uzi as a gunner stepped into position halfway out the screened door. The Uzi chattered briefly in McCarter's hands, and 9 mm parabellums chewed through the thin wire mesh and tracked onto the guard, spinning the man around.

Pain from his previous wounds tried to slow McCarter, but he refused to give in. He pounded his way up the straight staircase, slamming his hip into the railing as he twisted to fire at another man.

Knowing the burst had failed to reach its target, McCarter threw himself flat through the hole the dead guard had made. He rolled onto his side, extending the Uzi as he continued twisting. His finger locked on the trigger as he rolled, chugging the magazine dry. Splinters flew into his face from near misses digging into the wooden floor. As the 9 mm rounds caught the guard, they drove the man back inside the room.

By the time McCarter gained his feet, he'd shoved a fresh magazine into the pistol grip. He slung the machine pistol over his shoulder and drew the Browning

Hi-Power as he charged into the small bedroom. The Briton had a brief impression of yellow pastels and a child's dolls and stuffed toys, then he was in a narrow hallway leading past other rooms to inside stairs leading down. He pushed off the wall and ran toward the stairs, taking a two-handed grip on the Browning as he whirled around the wall.

At the bottom of the stairs behind the sights of an M-16, Gary Manning smiled up at him.

"Clear?" McCarter asked.

"Clear."

The Briton slid down the banister. "Katz?"

"Basement. With Encizo."

"James?"

"Procuring transportation. He hated giving up the Caddy and was hoping for something as flamboyant."

"Plush style isn't exactly what we're looking for at this point, mate."

"He knows to keep the window-shopping to a minimum."

McCarter took in the carnage—bullets had ripped through pictures, furniture and Sheetrock. Two dead men were sprawled on a threadbare carpet.

Encizo appeared from the basement stairs first, followed by Caseros. The Panamanian president had a bruise starting over one cheekbone that, at a glance, was about the size and shape of Encizo's M-16 buttstock. The man's hands were tied behind his back. Katz brought up the rear, the barrel of the MAC-10 resting lightly between Casero's shoulders.

"I counted two men upstairs, two down here," McCarter said.

"Five more in the back," Encizo informed him. "Calvin and I accounted for them."

"Katz got one on his way in," Manning said. "I bagged another one outside."

"I'd say you got your limit." McCarter gave the Canadian a crooked grin.

McCarter faced Caseros. "I make that eleven men, El Presidente. Surely an important bloke like yourself would rate a far larger guard than that."

Caseros remained silent. He looked small and defeated.

Katz stepped forward, the Ingram still resting on Caseros. "Calvin?"

Manning lifted a curtain with the snout of the M-16. "Outside."

Katz nodded. "Let's go. Rafael, Gary, you've got our prize."

"Couldn't we try to trade him in for something bigger?" Manning asked.

"I intend to," Katz replied without explanation. "David, you're point."

McCarter took the door, checked, then moved out toward the old sedan James had liberated. The engine gave off acrid blue smoke but sounded smooth as it idled. The Briton slid inside, followed immediately by Katz. Encizo and Manning sandwiched Caseros in the back seat.

James put the car in gear and moved away from the curb at a sedate pace. McCarter shook out a cigarette from his pack of Player's, lighted it, then handed his lighter to Katz. He heard the window cranking down on Encizo and Manning's side.

Katz turned in the seat to look at their captive. "Where are Feldman and Auerbach?"

Caseros said nothing.

Katz's voice was chilling when he spoke again. "As you no doubt know from television, you're very much the wanted man in this country. You might look on us as the last hope you have of getting out of this alive. The CIA has probably fielded any number of operatives in Panama City who have orders to kill you as soon as they have you in their sights to save themselves whatever embarrassment you might cause."

Caseros looked up hopefully. "What do you want?"

"I want to know where Auerbach is."

"He was called back to Colombia by Costanza."

"Why?"

"I don't know."

A sudden plume of black smoke followed by the sound of an explosion drew everyone's attention.

"Evidently Striker's warming things up on the home scene," Manning grunted.

"The man probably wasn't invaded by the U.S. Army," James pointed out. "He's had a freer hand to operate."

Katz settled back into the seat and took a deep draw on the cigarette. McCarter knew the Phoenix Force leader was upset and relieved with the turn of events concerning Auerbach. The shared history that had existed between the two men couldn't be erased despite the river of bad blood separating them now. He'd had the same problem with men he'd known. The solutions hadn't been pleasant, nor had they been easy to sleep with during those nights when no one else seemed to be around.

"Where to?" James asked. "There doesn't seem to be a safe harbor for unclaimed spies like us anywhere in the whole damn city."

"Spies like us?" Encizo repeated.

Katz didn't hesitate. "The Vatican embassy." Complete silence, except for the occasional bomb blast and sporadic autofire, filled the sedan.

"I've always heard people get religion when they know the end's in sight," Manning said, "but I certainly didn't expect it of you."

"Offhand," Katz said, "the Vatican embassy is the only neutral territory I can think of where I can use a phone. If we turned up at the American embassy, assuming we could make it there without being shot full of holes, we'd be taken into custody along with Caseros, and all sorts of embarrassing questions would be asked. I'd rather find a way to carry on the war."

"Maybe they can teach us to walk on water," Manning muttered.

McCarter flicked his cigarette out the window. "Still be a long walk, mate, and they do have submersibles, you know."

ANDEANA PAUSED at the back door, not looking at the men in hiding around the house because she knew they'd be watching her. They always watched her. The Americans wore their dark sunglasses, suits and stern looks. Her own people wore the light brown uniforms and always tried to smile at her.

Poised for flight, the four-year-old surrendered to the urge to run. She released the door and heard it slam shut behind her as she pushed off the stone steps. Her mother would chastise her for that, and she'd chastise her for being barefoot when she found out about that, as well. But the backyard was huge. Only her father seemed to understand how it called out to her. He went barefoot with her sometimes.

She ran as hard as she could toward her hiding place in the row of hedges along the back wall. She dropped to her knees and clambered through the worn dirt to the opening. Once inside, she could forget she was watched all the time and enjoy this quiet, secret place.

Then sudden explosions shattered the stillness over the yard.

Andeana cried. She yelled for her mother and father to make the noise stop. She clamped her hands over her ears, but the noise seeped through her fingers.

The birdbath crumbled as something invisible crashed into it, and the explosions seemed to go on forever.

Andeana wondered why her mother didn't come to her. She kicked and screamed in terror, rocking back and forth against the wall.

A man, one of the khaki-clad guards, stumbled in the middle of the yard, then fell. Blood covered his face.

Andeana felt herself trembling, then the noise went away. She continued to hold her hands over her ears just in case. She wanted to shut her eyes when she saw a man's boots stop directly in front of her. She tried to scream and couldn't.

The man dropped slowly to his knees, putting a black pistol away under his jacket. He looked at her. "It's okay, honey," he said in accented Spanish. "No one's going to hurt you." He had black hair and a stern face like the American guards. His features were hard, but he was handsome, like her father. He wore jeans, a T-shirt and a windbreaker despite the warmth of the day. Dark sunglasses covered his eyes.

Andeana cringed when he reached out a palm.

"My name's Mack," the man said. "I'm not here to hurt you. We need to get inside the house before someone else comes. Please, Andeana. I'm a friend of your father's."

She wondered how he knew her name, but she didn't move. Tears ran down her face.

"Andeana." The man removed his sunglasses, showing her eyes that were so blue.

She caught his fingers in one of her hands and allowed him to pull her from the hedge. She held on to him tightly, wrapping her arms around his neck and crying into his shoulder.

"It's okay," he soothed. "Everything's going to be just fine."

His voice sounded so calm and reassuring, the same way her father's did after she'd had a bad dream. She hugged him as he carried her toward the house.

SAM WATERSTON PAID the bartender at the counter and joined the half-dozen TV and newspaper reporters he knew at a back table. He felt tired, restless and

irritable from too much coffee and too many cigarettes. The double bourbon would help take the edge
off those feelings, and if it didn't completely do the job
with the aid of others like it, there was always the local
flora and fauna for a quick roll in the hay.

The bar was a dive by any standards Waterston had
ever known, but it was comfortable. Bars like this had
that little feeling of home that he'd never discovered in
any of the numerous hotel rooms he'd spent time in all
over the world. Evidently the other American and Eu-
ropean reporters agreed with him because it was where
most of them chose to hang out.

Blair Considine, of the *Miami Herald,* scooted over
to make room for him. Her blond hair was in wild dis-
array, and her eyes were enflamed from mascara and
drinking. She looked up at Waterston as he sat down.
"I say the whole country is about ready to go to hell in
a fucking hand basket," she commented.

Waterston raised his glass and gave his peers a smile.
"I'll drink to that." He did.

"Hey, Sammy." Kinsley Thomas, a BBC correspondent, leaned forward with a sly look on his fox-
like face. "I've gotten a new pot together. Would you
like to venture a quid or two?"

"What's it on?" Waterston asked. He signaled an
overworked waitress for another drink. She knew him
well enough to know what he wanted.

"Benito Franco's probable life expectancy," Cora
Clayton told him. She was the oldest of the group and
fought the ravages of advancing age daily. Rumor had
it that the reason she had maintained her roving reporter status for the cable news station she worked for

was through the diligent efforts of a makeup artist and a kind cameraman whom she refused to work without.

"Personally," Considine said as she swirled her drink, "I think anything over four days from now is a losing proposition."

Waterston groaned in mock revulsion. "Quite the callous bunch today, aren't we?"

"Balls," Thomas retorted. He gave them a sneer never captured on camera. "Come on, Sammy, we've all been around the block with this bleedin' country. Announcing your candidacy for any public office means you get your choice of posters. One with your hand out for the bribes that come with the responsibilities, the other with a bull's-eye around your face. Franco's asking for it, and I'm betting he'll bloody well get it."

The waitress set the drink on the table in front of Waterston. The reporter paid her at once from a roll of bills he kept in his shirt pocket. It was an old habit. He paid as he went so the bartender could never haggle with him over the bar tab and delay his departure when a story was breaking. Or, worse yet, overcharge him and forget to give him the receipt.

"What have you got left?" another voice asked.

Waterston glanced over his shoulder and saw Berkley, a radio news correspondent, and Meyer, a freelance stringer for any of a half-dozen international news services.

"I thought you two had stopped talking to each other," Waterston said.

Meyer waved the comment away with a chubby hand. "That was a week ago. Don't you keep up with current events?"

"So what have you got left?" Berkley repeated. He was a darker copy of the fair-haired and heavy Meyer. People in the trade who knew them called them Tweedledee and Tweedledum. Usually one of them was threatening to kill the other for stealing one exclusive or another.

Waterston figured the tension running rampant through the country would be making as many strange bedfellows as Colombia's drug-based economy. He glanced at Blair Considine hopefully.

"I divided each day into hours, twenty-four hours a day," Kinsley said, checking a small notepad. "The first six days are already gone."

"Let me think about it," Berkley said.

Meyer dug out a five-dollar bill and handed it to Waterston, who passed it to Kinsley. "Give me a solid three-hour block that morning, and a two-hour block just before midnight."

Kinsley wrote it down.

"Figuring on a morning execution?" Cora Clayton asked, blotting her lips with a perfumed handkerchief.

"The cartel's gonna want to make a point," Meyer replied. "If they do the job at night, it'll only be because the bribes aren't working and the security's too tight."

Waterston noticed the low rumble of conversation dying away in the bar. He started to look over his shoulder just as Considine gripped his forearm tightly, sinking manicured nails into his flesh.

The reporter got a brief glimpse of a handful of men carrying automatic weapons as they poured through the door. He grabbed Cora Clayton's blouse and pulled her under the table just as the firing started. He stayed there, holding her close, knowing some of the people he'd been drinking with were dead, hoping he wouldn't become one of them.

CHAPTER FOURTEEN

"She's sleeping," Bolan said as Benito Franco entered the bedroom. He moved to one side so that the man could see his daughter more clearly.

Andeana lay on the twin-size bed curled up in a fetal position, covered by a white sheet spotted with pink unicorns that matched the color scheme of the room.

Franco knelt by the bed, his hand trembling as he stroked his fingers across the girl's forehead. "She wasn't injured?"

"No."

"My wife?"

"She went into the kitchen to fix you something to eat as soon as she heard you were coming home." Bolan lifted the curtains covering the window that overlooked the backyard. Emergency teams still labored under the midafternoon sun to remove the corpses littering the nearby area. Neighbors gathered in small clusters, talking among themselves and pointing, held at bay by the police cordon. He let the curtain drop from his fingers. He didn't need to see any more. He'd already counted the dead for himself.

"I was told I have you to thank for her safety," Franco said as he rose to his feet.

"A lot of good men fell out there trying to protect your family."

"I won't forget about them. But it was you who brought Andeana in safely."

"I got lucky. I happened to be in the right place at the right time."

Franco shook his head. "From what I've seen of you, amigo, you make your own luck. You knew they would strike at my family."

"I decided it was a strong possibility."

Turning back to the sleeping child, Franco tucked the purple teddy bear in closer to his daughter. "She's so beautiful when she sleeps."

Bolan agreed.

Franco looked at him. "I still don't even know your name."

Hesitation touched the Executioner for a brief instant, then he brushed it away. The justice minister had every right to know the whole score. If the man pulled out at this point, so be it. The warrior still had to live with himself. "It's Bolan. Mack Bolan."

A nerve jumped in the justice minister's jaw. "That explains why you've chosen to pursue such a bold course in my country."

Someone knocked on the door.

Franco opened it. "Yes?"

DEA Section Chief Bart Rodesney stuck his head into the room, focusing on Bolan immediately. "I'd like a word with you if you have the time."

Franco nodded and stepped out of the bedroom, followed by Bolan.

"Who's he?" Rodesney asked, jerking his chin toward the Executioner.

"A friend," Franco replied.

"Your friend got a name?"

"Doesn't everyone?"

"Well?"

"Why don't you ask him yourself?"

Rodesney shifted his stare to Bolan. "So I'm asking."

"McKay," Bolan replied.

Rodesney leaned toward the living room, where two more American agents stood talking. "Johnny, get in here with that list."

One of the agents came over at once, digging a notepad out of his jacket.

"McKay," Rodesney said. "Tell me about him."

The agent flipped through yellow sheets. "Says here Mike McKay's a writer."

"Who's he working for?"

"Doesn't say. His visa's in order, though, according to the files."

Rodesney considered that. He took off his sunglasses, revealing hard, bright eyes. "You know, it's amazing the things people can do with computers nowadays. I marvel at it myself."

Bolan remained silent.

"You got your visa, pal?"

Bolan grinned. "Not with me."

"Where?"

"With the rest of my things."

"Suppose we go take a look at it?"

"Suppose we don't," Bolan said.

"Who are you working for, McKay?"

"Me. I free-lance, which means I do things on speculation and hope for the best."

"You're packing a lot of heat for a guy hoping for the best."

"Said I was hopeful. Didn't say I was a fool."

Rodesney rocked on his heels. "From the way I hear it you're pretty seasoned with violent situations."

"Firsthand experience lends believability," the warrior replied.

"Not with this audience."

Franco's voice cracked into the conversation. "Enough." He glared at Rodesney. "This man is a guest in my house. He saved my daughter. If you persist in this treatment of him, I'm going to ask you to leave."

Rodesney shut up, releasing a pent-up breath. "I've got three men dead who were helping with the security of your family, Mr. Franco. I still have to go call their families and give them the bad news. On the other hand, you have a new friend I've never heard of who managed to succeed where a half-dozen guards failed. Maybe if you weren't so personally tied up in this, you'd be asking the same questions I am."

"No," Franco replied. "I'm satisfied of his intentions."

"Doesn't mean I have to be."

Bolan met the DEA agent's level stare. He knew Rodesney wouldn't let the situation stand untested. He also knew his presence forced Franco to make a decision.

"I don't want to lose any more men," Rodesney said. "Two more were gunned down this morning, bringing the total to five, all because you've developed some wild hair up your ass and started playing hardball with the cartel. What you've failed to take into consideration is the fact that you're in no position to do that."

"Medellín forces were responsible for the destruction of three labs last night," Franco said.

"And all you've succeeded in doing is getting them stirred up. Your whole family could have been wiped out over this. Did you think about that?"

"Yes, only I thought their target would be me."

"My advice, strictly from me to you, is for you to back off before things get any worse. I don't have the authority to intercede in the territorial wars you're causing, and I don't want to see you lose the goodwill of the United States. Understand?"

"I do." Franco looked at the door meaningfully. "Is there anything further?"

"No. I've got some phone calls to make now." Rodesney shifted his attention to Bolan. "Do you know who organized this hit on his house?"

"No." It was easier to lie to the DEA agent than it would have been to lie to the justice minister. Even with the facts presented before them, either man would have had laws to follow. The warrior had a free hand, and he intended to use it.

Without another word Rodesney left, taking one of the men with him. The other stayed in the house, organizing some of the outside activities over a walkie-talkie.

"Benito?" Dominga stepped around the corner of the kitchen. "Are you ready to eat?"

"Yes, darling. I'll be there in a moment." Franco looked up at Bolan. "Will you dine with us?"

Bolan shook his head. He'd have felt out of place in the familial setting. Even more so after he'd finished his business here.

"There's something else?" Franco asked.

"Yeah." The warrior lifted an envelope from inside his jacket but didn't offer it. "Five more jungle labs. If you want the information."

Sick fascination settled on the justice minister's face as he looked at the envelope. "Last night, in the street, I had the heat of anger burning in me when I accepted your information. This morning I felt very much the hero. Now I feel only the chill of mortality. If Andeana had died, I would have blamed myself."

"I know."

Franco squared his shoulders. "If I don't take that envelope from your hand, will you think any less of me?"

Bolan answered truthfully. "No."

COSTANZA SAT in the back of the white Mercedes limousine and let the memories wash over him as the car nosed through the front gate. Don Manolon's ranchero looked the same as it had twenty years ago, as if nothing had changed. Adobe walls still surrounded the main house, concealing probable advances made in the security measures. The ranch hands dressed in white as always, and went armed. The straw sombreros the men wore still brought a smile to Costanza's lips.

The main house was two stories and lavish inside as well as out. The satellite dish to the east was definitely new, telling him Manolon's taste in viewing had perhaps finally been assuaged. The road leading up to the house was long and dusty. Clouds pursued the limousine and almost obscured any view rearward.

"You never mentioned how you knew Don Manolon," Ortega said. He sat next to Costanza, his elbows resting lightly on his thighs with his fingers interlaced.

"No," the narcobaron replied in deliberation. "I haven't." He looked away from his second-in-command. "You will remain in the car while I speak with Mercado and Rodriguez."

"How will I know if you need me?"

"I won't need you. This is Don Manolon's home. I have nothing to fear at this place. I have you along because we must talk on the way back. If everything goes as I expect it will, there are new plans to be made."

"Yes, sir."

The limousine rocked to a stop in the hard-packed dirt drive before the main house. The clouds of dust swept past.

Costanza adjusted his clothing, making sure everything was perfect. He had chosen the steel-gray pinstriped suit with every intention of impressing his audience. He had allowed himself only one ring, carefully matching the diamond solitaire Rolex on his wrist. "There is one thing I want you to do for me as soon as you get back to Medellín."

"Anything, sir."

"Ruiz, the man who organized the hit on Franco's house."

"Yes?"

"I want him dead before night falls. He can tie the assassination attempt to you and me."

"It will be done."

Costanza opened the door and got out. He'd given his chauffeur strict orders to stay inside the limousine. He breathed in the hot air and immediately wished the meeting could be conducted inside the house.

A gaunt, wrinkled man in a white linen shirt and pants sat in a rocker on the front porch. A black-and-tan coon dog lay asleep at his feet.

Costanza came to a halt before the man. "Don Manolon?"

The old man shot a stream of yellow tobacco juice into the overflowing flower bed just over the edge of the porch. A purple-plumed zinnia bobbed in response. "In the back."

"With the bulls?"

"As always." The old man showed him a tobacco-stained grin.

"Thank you."

Costanza had known Manolon would be with the bulls. Of course, with the satellite dish, it was possible the Don could have been inside the house. Somewhere in the world there was a station playing late, late movies. But nothing, no word, no deed was ever taken for granted at the ranchero. There was respect demanded and given for all things.

He made his way toward the rear of the house, remembering his way now. There were more flowers than he recalled. A fine sheen of perspiration covered him by the time he walked around the final corner of the house. The breeze that met him felt cooling.

The bull pens connected to a large barn and to an open area where a young man in emerald-green-and-yellow matador's clothes taunted a racing black bull with a red cape. The tips of the horns streaked for the young matador's midsection, then ripped through nothing but air as the man sidestepped and furled the cape. The bull snorted angrily, pawing at the ground as it came around for another charge.

Don Manolon lounged against the rail fence. He wore a vaquero's clothing, looking even more plain under the layer of dust that covered them. A wide-brimmed sombrero's chin strap grooved into the loose flesh under the jawline. The man was as brown as a nut, with a salt-and-pepper beard resting on his chest.

Various emotions swelled up in Costanza at the sight of the old man. As he approached, he reached for a hat he wasn't wearing, caught himself and dropped his arm to his side.

The bull cut toward the matador again. There was a furl of red and emerald and yellow, then the big animal pawed loose clods of dirt from the ground again.

"Olé!" Don Manolon yelled between cupped hands. "Olé, Pascual, olé."

The youth in the matador's clothes beamed.

Costanza came to a stop.

"Luis, come on up here and watch this boy." Manolon waved a thick arm.

Costanza wasn't surprised that the old man had heard him. Don Manolon possessed the ears of a fox as well as the wits. He halted at the railing and watched as the boy continued working the bull. "It's good to see you, Don Manolon."

The old man replied without taking his eyes from the boy and the raging animal. "If it's so good, Luis, why haven't you come to see me sooner? Why do I have to wait until José calls you here to meet?''

"I've been busy."

Don Manolon chuckled, the noise rising from his barrel chest. "Yes, very busy building empires. I've heard you're a very successful man. Very wealthy."

"I had a good teacher."

The old man shook his head. "No, I didn't teach you to traffic in the White Lady. This was a thing you would have never learned had you remained under my roof. The product was the reason I retired."

"It's no worse than the alcohol, cigarettes and electrical equipment I used to smuggle while working for you. And it has made me a very wealthy man."

Don Manolon chuckled again, looking at Costanza for the first time. "There are two kinds of coin dealt out for the product. One is money. The other is death. The one never travels with the other. So far you've been fortunate."

"It's no worse now than when we smuggled Scotch."

"In your eyes, Luis. And you have always had such hungry eyes. That's why you listened to me so much. That's why you learned everything you could and why you went out to challenge the world as soon as you were able." The old man shook his head. "You only see the benefits of what you traffick in because that's what you choose to see."

"The coca leaf is also what keeps fresh lifeblood pumped into this country," Costanza said. He felt the heat of emotion rush to his face. "The funds I generate through the empire I control also benefit the cities and the peoples who live there. Without cocaine we'd be totally dependent on nonexistent American generosity and support.''

"Now you're a politician, as well, eh, Luis? And I'm not talking about the congressional seat you hold. Now you not only traffick in cocaine, but you also sell dreams. How many, I ask myself, have you sold yourself?''

"You don't understand.''

"Oh? You think my ways are too old-fashioned to keep me up with the times. Luis, cocaine will bring a new reign of terror upon this country. I won't live to see it, but you will. You're one of the catalysts. You, José and the others like you. You're too greedy, and the profits are too large to allow you the luxury of only small dreams of wealth. You and your kind want it all, and you fight among yourselves to get it. Once, I knew a time when you or José would give your life for the other. Now I'm called upon to act as mediator for the differences you two have.''

Costanza kept quiet with difficulty. Only respect and knowledge of the fact that the old man would have one or two snipers with their sights over his heart at this moment kept his tongue still.

"I think you're more controlled by the White Lady than you control her,'' Don Manolon added.

"If the others are here,'' Costanza said as he glanced at his watch, "we need to get on with the meeting. I had a full schedule today, and I had to postpone many things to be here.''

The old man laughed, throwing his sombrero back as he pointed at the young matador. "That boy is in touch with his world, Luis. See him work the bull? See how narrowly he evades death or injury? It's him against the animal, with each of them relying only on his own abilities. With you, I see cocaine as a white bull. Only, instead of evading it and controlling it, you seek to stay ahead of its horns and, foolishly, you never look at the road before you. You'll trip and fall one day, my friend, and the vultures will strip your bones."

"Perhaps you'd sing a different tune if you were twenty years younger, Don Manolon."

The old man nodded. "Perhaps. But I'm not. I'm an old bandit who's given up his wicked ways for late-night television. I was over my great hunger when cocaine became the profitable export it is now." He put his fingers in his mouth and whistled. A stable hand came forward, leading two saddled horses by their bridles. Don Manolon took the bridles and placed the reins of one into Costanza's hand. "Ride with me, Luis, the way we used to do when you were a boy with big eyes and unfulfilled ambitions."

Costanza was amazed at the ease with which the old man pulled himself into the saddle. "What about José?"

"They wait for us in the old box canyon." Don Manolon snapped his fingers and pointed at the stable hand's sombrero. The man handed it over at once. "Here. For your head. It'll be hot along the way. You are overdressed for the weather."

Costanza gripped the saddle pommel and reins in one hand, then swung a leg over the horse's back. The stirrups fitted well even for the Italian shoes he wore. "I wanted you to see me at my best, Don Manolon."

"I saw you at your best twenty years ago." The old man kicked his horse into motion.

WHIRLING CEILING FANS gave the small restaurant an undercurrent of noise as Bolan entered the west door and removed his sunglasses.

The clientele at this hour of the day was limited to a handful of coffee drinkers. Ernesto Ruiz occupied a corner booth by himself as he ate.

The restaurant was laid out in an even-legged L, with a scarred counter running in both directions. Two waitresses stared at him hopefully, flashing tired smiles. The white-suited cook continued scrubbing his grill.

Ruiz looked up at the warrior's approach. He was a big, balding man with a droopy mustache that threatened to invade his mouth. When he smiled, the mustache almost bisected Ruiz's face.

"Mind if I have a seat?" Bolan asked as he sat down.

"Do I know you?" Ruiz asked.

Bolan glanced out the window at the long sedan at the curb, which contained two of Ruiz's soldiers. "No."

Ruiz started to wipe his fingers on a napkin.

Glancing back at the man, Bolan said, "Keep your hands above the table."

Irritation showed on Ruiz's face. "Why?"

Bolan put on a grin for the two soldiers outside. "If you take them from the tabletop, you'll never live to hear the answer."

Ruiz placed his hands on the table. "I don't know who the hell you think you are, friend, but I have men outside who'll gladly kill you if I tell them to."

"Like the hands, guy, you'll never live to see if they're able to do the job."

One of the waitresses glided over with a coffeepot. "Coffee, sir?"

"No, thanks. Maybe in a moment."

The waitress shuffled away.

"Who are you?" Ruiz asked. "DEA?"

"No. I'm the guy that screwed up the hit on the Franco family for you. I saw you giving directions from that car outside just seconds before the assassination attempt went down. Not changing cars was pretty sloppy, don't you think?"

The Colombian smiled evenly. "This isn't American television. The people I work for own most of this city in one way or another."

"They don't own me, and they don't own the justice minister or his family. And there are a lot of good cops who weren't born with their hands out, either."

"What do you want with me?"

Bolan ignored the question. "You've had a busy morning, Ernesto. I know you organized the hit on the Franco house, and I'm betting you called the shots when the DEA agents and reporters were killed. Ortega is Costanza's second-in-command, so I figure he's the one who gave you the word."

Ruiz sipped from his water glass. "If you had proof of these accusations, you'd try to have me jailed."

Bolan shook his head. "Like I said, I'm not a cop, but I was the guy who carried a frightened four-year-old girl to her house over dead bodies this morning. Her world will never be the same again."

"These things happen in war. You should be glad nothing happened to you."

Bolan gave him a wintery smile. "The terminology fits, but the law keeps the other side from playing by the same rules, doesn't it?"

"I'm getting tired of listening to you. What do you want?"

"To deliver a message to Costanza."

"I'm not a messenger boy."

"That's not how I see it. You put out a message to the DEA this morning. You put out a message to the reporters to back off the story only a little later. You tried to leave a message for Justice Minister Franco. Seems to me you're in the message business."

Ruiz remained silent.

"I want you to tell Costanza that things only get rougher from this point on."

"I'm not going to tell him that," Ruiz growled, reaching under the tabletop.

"Maybe not," the Executioner said as he whipped the 93-R from shoulder leather and shot the man in the face twice, "but he'll get the message all the same."

Ruiz's body followed the backward motion of his head, leaving him curled up in the seat. The two men in the sedan reacted at once, grabbing for their weapons.

The warrior stood by the table and fired through the window, killing both men and sprawling their bodies on the street before they could get off a single round. He changed the empty magazine in the Beretta, holstered it and slid the sunglasses back into place. Then he got out of there, heading for a new spot on the front line. The war was on.

"I APPRECIATE your seeing me on such short notice, General," Hal Brognola said as he stepped into the rear of the bulletproof limousine. A military aide closed the door behind him.

The chauffeur put the big car in motion and pulled away from the Independence Avenue curbside. The flags on the front fenders fluttered and snapped in the breeze. Washington, D.C., stayed in constant motion around them. The driver turned south on Canal Street, bringing the three House Office Buildings into view.

"I didn't really feel like I had much of a choice," General Lew "Ironwood" Arnett replied. "Everybody I owe favors to has been calling me for the past two hours telling me I needed to speak with you." He regarded the Justice man with a critical eye. "Evidently the people I owe favors to owe you favors."

"We work a big world through a handful of people when you get right down to it," Brognola said. "Mind if I smoke?" The tension of the past few days had forced the big Fed to resume his former bad habit.

"Go ahead, just push that flame over this way when you're done with it."

Brognola lit a cigar, then held the lighter for the general's cigarette.

"Now what can I do for you, son?"

Brognola looked at the man, trying to remember the last time anyone had called him son. He expelled smoke. "I've got a team down in Panama."

"Officially?"

"No."

Arnett considered that. "What do you want me to do about it?"

"I want to get them clear of the invasion."

"No can do, son. We got a tight squeeze on that popcorn fart of a country, and we mean to keep it. The last thing we need is press about how we had a covert team in there before the official invasion began. If I cut special orders to get your boys out, you know somebody's going to pick up on it. There's going to be enough bad publicity over this thing when the dust begins to settle as it is."

"You don't have Caseros, though."

Arnett regarded Brognola in a new light. "You got something you want to tell me?"

"I didn't come here to beg a freebie," the big Fed replied. "I'm not much of a bluffer. When I sit down to a table where high stakes are being played, I make sure I'm holding some good cards. In this instance I've got your ace."

"Caseros?"

"Yeah."

"Shit, and we've got teams in there turning that country inside out." Arnett flicked ashes from his cigarette onto the immaculately carpeted floorboard. "When did your people take Caseros down?"

"This morning."

"Explains why he hasn't been broadcasting lately."

Brognola nodded.

Arnett stared out the window. "It might play in our favor to let your people hang on to him for a while.

Give us some more time to hammer the opposition and make sure some other tinhorn doesn't step into Caseros's place."

"My people might get bored playing baby-sitter for the Joint Chiefs of Staff," Brognola said dryly. "They've got a job to do elsewhere, and they know it. If they're kept from it, chances are they'll set up a deal for a television movie or an interview with Geraldo, Donahue or Oprah just to stir the pot a bit."

Arnett chuckled. "That I'd like to see, son."

Brognola blew a smoke ring. "Maybe you'll get the chance. With you heading up the military end of things in Panama, I'm sure they could get you on as a guest speaker. Could mean a whole new career for you. And about that time, when people realize several thousand troops could be sent down to Panama and still miss the man they were sent after, you might be looking for another line of work."

"You like playing hardball, don't you, son?"

"When I have to."

"I like a man who stands by his people."

"So do I."

"Suppose we deal. What are you going to want in return?"

"A Lear jet. One of those in Caseros's private fleet will be fine. All my team needs is a window and enough time to get out of Panamanian airspace."

"And not one word of this to anyone?"

"No, sir."

Arnett held out a steady hand. "Consider it a done deal, son."

Brognola took the hand. "I will."

"I'll get on the horn and put things in motion as soon as I get back to my office."

CHAPTER FIFTEEN

Dressed in a bright orange mechanic's coverall like everyone else at the small airfield, McCarter followed his prey. The guy he trailed was the pilot of the sleek Lear jet on the runway.

The airfield reeked of tension. Orange-suited men ran back and forth from the hangars to the two dozen small craft sitting ready for takeoff. They all knew of Panama City's fall to American forces, but had nowhere to run. The jungle between the airfield and the city was a flimsy buffer zone at best, but so far it had seemed to work in their favor.

McCarter knew the real reason why the airfield hadn't been shut down was due to Brognola's efforts in Washington. The big Fed had come through for them again. The Briton smiled when he thought of the conversation that must have taken place between Arnett and the Stony Man liaison.

He waited until the pilot was about to step up on the stairway leading into the jet, then removed a pipe wrench from his coverall pocket and dropped the man to the hot tarmac. He stepped over the unconscious man, fisting the wrench again in case the Lear wasn't empty as observation had led him to believe. Once inside and sure that he was alone, McCarter tossed the wrench out and pulled the door closed.

Seated in the pilot's seat, he slipped into the headgear, switched the channel to the frequency Phoenix was monitoring, then did an instrumentation check. The fuel tanks were already topped off. He'd checked that earlier.

"Father Goose calling the Ugly Ducklings, over," he said as he primed the ignition.

"Ugly Ducklings standing by, Father Goose, over," Manning replied.

McCarter grinned. He opened the window on the copilot's side, then the one on the pilot's side, drew the Browning Hi-Power from inside the coverall and placed it between the seats after slipping off the safety. "Step lively, Ugly Ducklings," he said into the mike, "because these laddies are definitely one scare short of psychotic at this stage. When I pull out of here, expect all hell to break loose. Over."

"Roger. Out."

McCarter hit the ignition and heard the twin jet turbines kick into violent life. The Lear trembled like a good foxhound straining at the leash to get into the hunt. He enjoyed the feel of the power in his hands. She was a good plane, well taken care of according to his inspection.

The whining aircraft was noticed at once. The Phoenix fighter looked out the window and saw that the airfield mechanics had stopped whatever they were doing. One of them pointed. Evidently the unconscious form of the pilot had been discovered. A half-dozen men started for the aircraft.

Putting the Lear in motion, McCarter headed for the opposite end of the runway where he was supposed to pick up the rest of Phoenix Force. The tarmac shimmered before him in the midafternoon heat, blurring his view of the jungle, clearing just as he whipped through the waves of heat.

He applied the left brake harder than the right as he neared the end of the runway, and the jet swung around obediently. He allowed himself only one look at the small mass of vehicles bearing down on him, then dashed back to open the door. Katz was the first aboard and followed him to the copilot's seat.

McCarter belted himself in and reached for the throttle. Keying the PA system, the Briton said, "Hope you lads have got yourselves tied down, because we don't have time to mess about. If you look forward, you'll see a brief presentation of the in-flight movie, a modern adaptation of *Villa Rides,* starring a cast of dozens." He opened the throttle and the thrust pushed him back into the seat.

The ragged line of jeeps and running men closed in on the jet with unbelievable speed. Gray puffs rippled from automatic weapons.

McCarter cursed, willing the jet to become invulnerable. A hole would limit their flight ceiling and their speed. He didn't fancy the idea of flying a wounded duck, especially an unidentified wounded duck, into Colombia. Other planes moved on the runway now, at least two of them outdated warbirds. But outdated or not, they had guns and he didn't.

"It's going to be close," Katz observed as the jet thundered toward the first of the jeeps.

"Damn right," McCarter returned grimly. The two passengers of the lead jeep abandoned their vehicle after guiding it straight for the Lear. Knowing he didn't have the necessary speed built up for a full jump, McCarter touched the flaps, managing an ungainly hop that took the Lear over the line of men.

"Very good, David," Katz complimented.

"Thanks, but I really didn't know if the old girl could come through for us or not."

Bearing down on the throttle, McCarter kicked the jets into full life. They were airborne heartbeats later. He retracted the landing gear and keyed in the American fighter frequency Brognola had given them.

Katz leaned toward his window. "We have company."

"Friend or foe?" McCarter asked as he dipped a wing and circled for altitude.

"From the airfield."

"Terrific."

"Take a look over your left shoulder," Calvin James said over the headset.

McCarter looked and saw the white burnout identifying the two Navy fighter jets. The three warbirds from the hidden airfield were closer. Even as he watched, the Phoenix pilot saw fiery bursts flare from the Panamanian fighters' cowlings. He banked sharply, rolling over as he vacated threatened airspace. The verdant growth of the jungle below gave way to the rolling blue of the Caribbean Sea. The Panamanian fighters lost altitude and swooped in pursuit.

The headset crackled. "Blue Plate Special, be advised that you have entered American-controlled airspace. Over."

The voice was young and cocky, and it warmed McCarter's soul to hear a kindred spirit. "This is Blue Plate Special. Over."

"Sir, our orders were that you would be given a free pass through our zone. Nothing was said about more than one plane. Over."

"Laddie buck, surely you can see for yourself that those boys back there don't have our best interests at heart. Over."

"Roger. We wanted to ID you for sure before we engaged. Over."

McCarter grinned as he watched the Navy fighter planes stretch for altitude and circle around so that they'd be attacking coming out of the sun.

"Blue Plate Special, be advised you have the Broncobuster and the Snowman flying your back door. Over."

"Roger. Over."

"Blue Plate Special, would you like assistance in flushing your pursuers? Over."

"That's affirmative, Broncobuster, unless you'd like to see us shot down while under your free pass. Over."

"Roger. We're coming in now. Over."

"Good. I'll play decoy for a bit longer. Over." The Navy jets screamed out of the sky. McCarter knew the three Panamanian fighters never saw them until it was too late.

"Blue Plate Special?" Manning repeated. "Makes you wonder what Hal had on his mind when he put this deal together."

Two of the Panamanian fighters turned immediately into fireballs and fell from the sky. The third tried to cut and run. One of the Navy jets flipped over and began pursuit, closing quickly. The tail of a rocket streamed through the air. The Navy fighter pulled up just in time to avoid the wreckage of its target.

"Blue Plate Special, this is Broncobuster. Be advised you are free and clear from this point on. Over."

"Roger that, Broncobuster. Maybe I can return the favor some day. Over."

Encizo broke in. "Ask them if they can stick around for a few bars of 'You've Lost That Loving Feelin'.'"

McCarter relayed the message and was politely declined. The navy fighters flipped over in unison and thundered away. The Briton returned his attention to the Lear's controls, aware that they were hardly out of danger. Phoenix Force's theater of operations might have moved, but the game they played was still going to be just as deadly.

THE CONNECTION from Medellín sounded fuzzy. Barbara Price gave Kurtzman a questioning look. The big man shrugged, signaling that there was nothing he could do about it. The fuzziness didn't come from the scrambling equipment or any of the telemetry devices being used.

"You sound like you're talking from the bottom of a well," Price said. She wore a mobile headpiece that allowed her freedom of movement to check the files she'd accumulated and spread out across the workspace she'd set up in the computer room.

"It's not much better at this end," Bolan replied.

"How are things there?" she asked. His voice sounded tired and strained. She wanted to ask how he was doing, but she knew any weakness like that on her part would alienate him, cause him to withdraw. The soldier was a professional, first and foremost, not devoid of feeling, but sparing of them in the midst of a mission.

"Tense." The Executioner gave her a quick sketch of the events that had unfolded since last night.

"Franco's continuing on despite the attack on his wife and daughter?"

"Yeah, the guy's solid, but he's not used to the blood. Politics is a dirty business and he's accustomed to the dirt, but war is a totally different matter."

"Is there anything I can do to help from this end?"

"I've got to try to move the battle lines back into an arena Franco can handle without stressing himself out. He's getting plenty of press, and I think public support is swelling."

"You're right about that," Kurtzman chimed in. "Franco's declaration of war on the Medellín cartels is overshadowing the Panamanian invasion in some South American areas. CNN and the other news stations are taking regular breaks here to bring the viewers up-to-date on the Colombian situation."

"What do you want to do?" Price asked. She couldn't sit down at the desk. Instead, she paced back and forth, watching the silent images of news footage spill across the large screen at the other end of the room.

"I want to set it up so that Franco can take on Costanza in his own element. A political strike. Costanza's a congressman and he's proud of that seat he has, not to mention the parliamentary immunity that comes with it. I want to give Franco enough ammunition to topple the guy out of congress, then get the minister and his family to a safe port.''

"What do you need from me?''

"Hard copy of everything we've got on Costanza and his people.''

Price hesitated. "Some of that stuff's come from sensitive sources, Mack. If Franco starts breaking it to the press, people are going to know he got it from American sources. And you can bet some of those sources are going to know they didn't give it out. They'll start looking for holes in their organization. If we're not careful, this could lead back to Stony Man.''
There was silence on the line for a moment. Kurtzman looked at her. She bit her lip in silent frustration.

Bolan's voice was quiet when he spoke. "Barb, it's your call from that end. You're in the driver's seat. But I need Franco to make this stand against Costanza. The man's roots run too deep, too crooked through too many strata of Colombian society for me to take him alone. Too many people still believe the guy to be some kind of saint. They don't associate him with cocaine. They know him as the guy footing the bill for free housing for the poor, for churches, for this cause or the other. In order to uproot him and his organization, Franco's going to have to shine the light of truth on those roots until they die and wither away. If you break down Costanza's connections in this city by exposing the corruption that stems from him, people he has on his expense sheet will turn away from him, disrupt the flow of information he's depending on. If I'm seeing it wrong, tell me.''

Price sat on the edge of her desk. "No, you're seeing it right. I'd just hoped Stony Man wouldn't have to come this close to going public."

"We're all taking risks on this one," the soldier said. "I'm backing a man down here who's not only put his life on the line, but the lives of his wife and child, as well. I'm not about to pull support on him."

"I agree." Price searched for a pencil and paper. "When and where do you want this information?"

"Tomorrow morning at nine in Franco's personal office." Bolan read off the number. "Fax it in Spanish and English."

"It'll be there. Anything else?"

"Yeah. Contact Dade County and find out if they're still interested in extraditing Ortega."

"What have you got in mind?"

"With Franco's help I'm going to take out Costanza's congressional seat and number two man in one fell swoop. Give him a taste of being the hunted for a while."

"You got more trouble headed your way, Mack," Kurtzman said.

"Name it."

"Isaac Auerbach and Chaim Feldman are en route to Medellín from Panama City through conventional air traffic from Costa Rica."

"Costanza called them back in?"

"Looks like," Kurtzman agreed.

Shifting topics, Bolan asked, "What about the chemical companies?"

Price grabbed the printout on her desk. "A large shipment has already been sent down to Cartagena from Houston, Texas."

"Costanza didn't waste time."

Price smiled grimly. "No, and neither did we. Phoenix Force is already en route with orders to destroy it."

"They made it out of Panama in one piece?"

"Yes. Hal cut a deal for them on the Hill. Of course, it didn't hurt any that they had Caseros in their pocket at the time Hal sat down at the table to negotiate."

Some of the strain seemed to lighten in the soldier's voice. "What about Miami?"

"Lyons is still MIA. Word on the street is that La Araña's dropped out of sight, as well. A lawyer named Alexander Constantine is digging into Carl's alias pretty heavily, but the cover's standing up."

Bolan was silent for a moment. "Carl could have gone down in a cross fire I engineered from this end between Costanza, Mercado and Rodriguez. A reversed sort of friendly fire."

"You didn't know Teresina was La Araña. None of us did. Carl was closer to the target than we even would have guessed. And don't count him out yet. He has a way of turning up."

"I haven't. Anything else I should know about?"

"No."

Bolan broke the connection without another word.

"Barb?" Kurtzman asked.

"Yeah?"

"How does he sound to you?"

She stripped away the headset and placed it on the desk. "You've known him longer than I have."

"I still want to hear what you think."

She sighed and pushed the papers away from her. "I think he's getting personal with this one. Is that what's on your mind?"

Kurtzman nodded. "With him, the war started out personal. When his family was killed, he couldn't see any other way to act than to go after the people who were responsible. Some people called him a vigilante, but the way Mack looked at it, hell, it was the only professional thing he could do. The job needed doing, and he was a man who measured for the job."

"And now?"

"The thing with the little girl nearly getting killed got to him. The problem is, I don't think he knows how bad it got to him."

"So what are you thinking?"

Kurtzman shook his head. "I don't know, boss. I just wanted to clear my mind. This mission was cobbled together from leftover hopes and broken dreams as a first-class offensive, and we're responsible for sending men who revere life into the heat of battle with every defense we can conjure up. If it had been a simple hit-and-git, an assassination or an extraction, a mission rather than a short, protracted war, I don't think our guys would run the risk of becoming personally involved. As it stands now, Mack's having to mix directly with the locals to get it done."

"We couldn't scrub the mission at this point if we wanted to," Price said. More footage of the violent invasion of Panama streamed across the screen. "And you know Mack wouldn't bow out gracefully now."

"I don't think he could if he tried."

CHAPTER SIXTEEN

Jack Grimaldi had the small airfield all figured out. He knew how many planes were stationed there, approximately how many people were on hand to service them, and how the cargo was handled, both going and coming. What he didn't have figured out was the man watching the airfield from the jungle the way he was.

He settled back on his haunches, trying in vain to find a comfortable position. He kept the binoculars moving slowly, careful to keep the lenses from flashing against the afternoon sun.

The airfield was a small operation, but it was the primary air transportation that José Mercado owned. The hard-packed strip cut a swath through the thick jungle north of Medellín, running east and west. Three tin buildings, covered with camouflaged netting so that they would be harder to see from the air, occupied the south side of the strip. A half-dozen Broncos and military-styled jeeps were parked irregularly in front of them. The dress was casual—everything from white cotton shirts and pants to ones bearing Hawaiian flowers were in evidence. The assault weapons the home team carried looked brutally efficient.

The Stony Man pilot spotted the unidentified man shifting slightly in the underbrush. The guy was good, Grimaldi had to give him that. He wasn't sure how long the man had been there. He'd only picked up on him an hour ago.

The man wore loose camous that had to be uncomfortably hot. A small hat of the same material covered his head, shadowing a face stained by dirt and combat cosmetics.

Grimaldi withdrew from his position slowly. Recon on the airstrip was finished. The pilot figured that he and Bolan wouldn't have any problems as long as a suitable diversion was created. He'd chosen the six-seater Piper Cub for their needs.

He drew the Beretta from its shoulder holster, then moved out to scope the mystery guy. He paused several yards farther on, moving into the open long enough to verify that his target hadn't pulled up stakes. Satisfied the guy wasn't going anywhere and didn't know he was silently being stalked, the pilot tugged down the camou scarf covering his head to blot the perspiration from his eyebrows, then faded back into the jungle.

Beretta up and ready, Grimaldi catfooted to the foliage in back of the hiding man. The guy was still hunkered on his knees, binoculars to his eyes, sweeping the airfield in a practiced side-to-side motion. Noting the absence of weapons, Grimaldi moved in, bracketing the man's chest with a two-handed grip on his pistol. "Hey, buddy," the pilot said quietly. His voice didn't carry far.

The man raised his hands above his head as he turned around. The smile on his face looked entirely out of place. "Been wondering when you'd put in an appearance, friend."

A cold chill darted down Grimaldi's spine. He started to shift in an effort to fade back into the brush. The recognizable feel of a pistol muzzle pressed into his neck just under his skull.

"I wouldn't if I were you," a deep voice advised.

Grimaldi didn't. A big hand reached forward and trimmed the weight of the Beretta from his open palm.

LUIS COSTANZA REINED in beside Don Manolon. The old man leaned forward in the saddle, putting much of his weight on his hands as he stretched his back.

"Sore, Don Manolon?" Costanza asked.

The land rolled away from them in three directions. Ahead of them, less than twenty yards away, the hill they'd climbed ended abruptly. A ragged line of grass whipping in the gentle wind marked the edge.

"I still ride every day," the old man replied, "but every day the ride seems a bit harsher on these old bones."

Costanza's horse snorted and pawed the ground impatiently. He knew the animal smelled the water from the box canyon. He'd smelled it, too, back when his senses were those of a starving boy yearning for some small part of the world that was in constant motion around him. Now he couldn't. He'd been part of that larger existence for too long. He didn't miss it.

Manolon removed his sombrero and mopped the crown of his head with a red handkerchief. Replacing the hat, he narrowed his eyes and nodded toward the box canyon. "José and the other man await you there. I'm going no farther. The business you have to speak of with one another is your own. I want no part of it."

He looked at Costanza. "If not for the relationship I had with the two of you as boys, you wouldn't be here now."

Costanza returned the old man's gaze, realizing more than just his sense of the place had changed.

"As before, when you were two strong-willed boys without purpose in your lives, José has asked me to act as mediator before you destroy each other. I honor his request because I cared for those two boys."

Meaning he cared nothing for the men they had grown into, Costanza realized.

Don Manolon's voice softened. "You weren't the first two boys I took from the streets of Medellín in those days, nor were you the last. I took you in from the gutter, tried to feed you good food, enrich your lives with knowledge, only to find that you have returned to that selfsame gutter that spawned you. If you're not careful, Luis, you'll die in that gutter."

"It's business, Don Manolon, that's all. A businessman always runs certain risks. Even yourself, when we smuggled Scotch—"

"Never." The old man's response was vehement. "Never did I traffic in cocaine. It carries the taint of death with it. Your greed has blinded you, so you can't see this."

Costanza was unable to control his anger any longer. "My greed hasn't blinded me nearly so much as your age has blinded you, old man. You rail against cocaine, yet you don't understand that it has become this country's lifeblood. Without it we'd surely suffer even more poverty or, worse yet, become another of the puppet countries the United States fights to control in fear of Communists."

Don Manolon flushed, then gripped the pommel with a clawlike hand. "Go, Luis, go and have your meeting before I decide to change my mind and kick you the hell off my land."

Stung, Costanza kicked his horse into motion. Memories of the old man, proud and dominant, crumbled in his mind. They could never be rebuilt. He knew he'd never try. The final link to the poverty-stricken youth he'd been had just been sloughed off, like a snake shedding its skin. Even Don Manolon recognized the strength he wielded, and even Don Manolon feared it. He tossed the sombrero onto the ground.

"You were given the courtesy of not being searched when you arrived," the old man called out behind him.

Costanza didn't reply, angling the horse down the steep trail winding its way to the bottom.

"Rest assured, Luis, if you attempt anything against José, I have men in these hills who won't hesitate to bury you where you fall. My word is your bond today."

Concentrating on the horse, leaning back in the saddle, Costanza seethed. He wanted to lash out at something but knew if he did so now, he'd bring injury only to himself. He promised himself there would come a day when the old man showed him the respect he deserved.

The trail was steep, but not dangerously so for a practiced rider. Loose rocks and pebbles bounced from the cliffside and rattled through the brush below. Long, torturous moments later, he made solid ground again.

Mercado and Rodriguez looked out of place in their suits amid the broken rubble and tall brush of the canyon, and neither man looked rested or at ease.

Dismounting, not showing the pain that came with the movement, Costanza tethered his animal to a tree and walked slowly toward his competitors.

"Welcome, Luis," Mercado called, displaying a broad white grin. He didn't offer his hand.

Costanza came to a stop six feet away, hands crossed before him in the pose he habitually adopted when speaking with underlings. He knew Mercado would recognize it.

Mercado did, and failed to mask a scowl of resentment.

"You wished to speak with me?" Costanza asked.

"Yes. I feel there's much we need to discuss." Mercado pulled a white monogrammed handkerchief from inside his jacket and ran it across his face. "It's too damn hot here, but I knew of no other place you'd meet me on even terms."

Costanza nodded. "After today, even this place will no longer exist."

"Because of Don Manolon?"

"He doesn't know his time has passed."

Mercado nodded. "He still thinks of us as ill-mannered children." He put the handkerchief away and squinted up at the canyon wall. "He watches us even now, seeing what we do."

Glancing back up the side of the canyon, Costanza saw the silhouetted figure of the old man and the horse. "He lives as much in the past as the cowboy movies he watches."

"Remember when we were sure we were destined to grow up to be fast pistoleros, Luis?" Mercado asked. He continued staring at the figure on the ridge. "And that old man, he was the father of us all."

"He represents the weakness of Colombia now," Costanza told him. "It takes a strong man to reach out and demand what is rightfully his."

"And is that what it has come to between us, Luis? Do you seek my ruin for your own profit?"

"I haven't lifted my hand against you," Costanza replied.

"Then who robbed my club and Raul's bank?"

Costanza gazed wordlessly from Mercado to Rodriguez, then spoke softly. "What about you, eh? Do you think I had someone rob your bank?"

Rodriguez appeared uncomfortable. "I don't know what to think, Luis. When I look around, I ask myself how many men could afford to have my bank robbed, then burn and scatter the money it contained. There aren't many answers."

Tapping his chest with the finger of both hands, Costanza almost roared his rage. "I'm a businessman. A businessman!" He adjusted his jacket, calming himself. "How would it profit me to rob your bank and not take any of the money, eh?"

Rodriguez was silent.

"Think before you speak." Costanza paced in front of them, confident he could win them over to his side. Or, at the least, neuter the immediate threat they posed. They—even together—weren't the greater of the problems facing him. "If there's a war between us, our war is fought in the marketplace, and our winning hangs on the profit and loss statements. But this, these attacks here in our own homeland, is not of my doing. One of the men responsible for them has contacted me, just after destroying my airfield north of the city.''

"I had heard of this," Rodriguez said. "We were shot at after our establishments were robbed. At first we considered the possibility that you had sent one of the Israelis after us. Then, when we learned of the airstrip strike and the attacks on your caravan and labs, we realized we shared an unknown enemy.''

"We thought if we worked together," Mercado put in, "that we could triumph over whatever new menace has risen to threaten us.''

Costanza didn't reply. He'd learned long ago in negotiations to let time work for him when it could.

"You say this man called you, Luis?" Mercado asked.

"Yes.''

"And he's unknown to you?''

Costanza flicked his fiery gaze over the man. "That's an asinine question. If I knew who this man was or where his forces might be camped, their bones would be bleaching in the sun even as we speak.''

Mercado nodded, taking no offense.

"You know of the invasion of Panama?" Costanza asked.

Both men answered affirmatively.

"I think, beneath the surface, the two events are related in some fashion. Discovering this, we could further confuse the issue by letting the governments fight over their territorial disputes while we regroup and find out who these men are. Once they're known to us and remain within our reach, they're dead men."

"What should we do until then?" Rodriguez asked.

"Use your resources to help me find out the government connection," Costanza replied. "Someone is leading Franco around by the hand on these jungle raids, and more are protecting him in ways the DEA haven't been able to. I'll use my power in congress to seek out this connection and sever it."

"If Franco's their willing tool, why don't we just kill him and have done with it?" Mercado asked. "We could take the pressure from ourselves much faster."

"Wrong. We could only reduce part of the pressure, and then—in the eyes of the public who remain our friends—we become villains. We've spent a lot of money keeping the public's trust. I won't see it squandered so easily because one of us panics. Franco isn't to be touched. Yet." Costanza was acutely aware that he wanted it to be his hand that struck the killing blow, not that he was afraid of the murder coloring his popular support. Franco had made things personal. When the time came, he wanted the man to know that in his last dying thought. Costanza's image with the public as lord protector and philanthropist had been carefully cultivated and paid for. It wouldn't shake easily.

"All right," Mercado agreed.

Rodriguez nodded. "It will be as you say."

Costanza held out his right hand palm up. "Together, my friends, we can defeat whoever has challenged us and send them home like licked puppies."

Mercado put his hand on top of Costanza's, followed by Rodriguez.

Costanza covered them with his remaining hand. "Let this be our vow at this moment," he said in a solemn voice. "Whatever enemy faces one of us, faces all of us. Agreed?"

"Yes."

"Agreed."

He released their hands and stepped back. "Now there are many things I must attend to."

Rodriguez walked away, leaving Mercado behind. "Luis?"

Costanza gazed at the man speculatively. "Yes?"

Mercado clutched a fist to his chest. "This place, at this time of trouble, brings back many memories of the boys we once were."

"That was a long time ago."

"Yes, but standing here now, it doesn't seem so long ago." Mercado fell silent and locked eyes with Costanza. "When our time of trouble is over, things can never be as they once were, can they?"

Costanza gave him a smile filled with artificial warmth. "A writer, José, has said that you can never go home again. Even Don Manolon has told me this today."

"It's sad, though."

Costanza nodded even though he didn't think so. Yesterday had been full of youth and ignorance. He preferred today, when he had the money to buy and dispose of friendships as he wished. Real friendships were dangerous. Only power was an absolute.

"God go with you, Luis."

"And you." Costanza turned, the wistfulness in Mercado's gaze as irritating as a boil. Emotions like that could get a man killed, and no doubt would when the time was right.

He mounted the horse and rode it back up the incline instead of joining the other two men in a more circular and less dangerous way back to the main house. Twice, he thought the horse's hooves were going to slip and topple then down into the canyon. He tried to appear more confident than he felt when he gained the top and rode into Don Manolon's view.

He reined in his horse at the old man's side and smiled. "You're wrong about me, Don Manolon," he stated in a soft voice. "I am in tune with my world every bit as much as is your young matador. Only my world actively seeks my blood instead of playing with a bit of colored cloth. Here, I face bulls that are much, much larger. I've become more man than you're willing to admit."

"You press your idea of self-worth too hard, Luis, to even dream of speaking to me like this on my own land."

"I have nothing to fear from you anymore, old man."

"Only your life."

Costanza grinned. "Would you be willing to sacrifice the lives of your family to take my life from me, Don Manolon?"

The old man stared at him in stony silence.

"Because, I'll tell you now that's what you'd be doing. My men would descend upon you and your family and this ranchero like hungry locusts. There'd be nothing left. Think about that before you *ever* threaten me again." He kicked his horse into motion, never deigning to look over his shoulder to see what the man was doing. His days of fearing anyone were over. Franco and his unknown accomplices would find that out in short order.

CHAPTER SEVENTEEN

"What's on your mind, Marty?"

Martin Flynn turned away from the window. There had been nothing to look at for hours except the cloud layer over the Caribbean Sea. He wiped his damp palms against his slacks. His girlfriend, Sharon Lansing, in all her moussed blond glory, sat beside him with an animated look on her face. "Nothing," he replied.

"Wicked boy," she said in response. "You should know by now I see every dark thought that trickles through your mind."

He smiled despite his inner tension. "Then tell me what I'm thinking at this very minute."

She rolled her blue eyes at him. "No challenge, lover. You're thinking about how much you'd like to steal back to the bathroom with me and become a member of the Mile-High Club."

He shrugged. "Can't hide anything from you."

She reached out and took his hand. Her expression was serious this time. "Look, Marty, everything's going to be all right. Virgil knows how to handle these things."

"Virgil *says* he knows how to handle these things. There's a big difference." Flynn sighed and leaned back into the seat. Years ago, when he'd been just a child, flying had been so interesting to him. It pained him to notice that interest missing. There were so few things that had any life to them these days. Impulsively he leaned forward again and kissed Sharon. She responded immediately, biting his lower lip and breathing hotly through her nostrils.

"Hey, hey, you two, break it up."

Flynn came out of the kiss reluctantly and looked up to see Virgil Bell leaning over the seat in front of them.

"You trying to draw attention to yourselves or what?" Bell asked with a sloppy grin on his face.

Flynn forced himself to return the smile. At times he was enamored of Bell's reckless behavior and flagrant disregard for the pitfalls in life. At others he'd have preferred never to have seen the guy. He supposed that was true of the others in his group, as well.

"I think Marty's getting a case of cold feet," Sharon said.

"Well, then, sounds like you're gonna have to warm them up for him," Bell replied. "You got all night tonight, if you like, but if it was me, I'd take in as many sights around Medellín as I could. God knows when we'll get back this way again. Me, I'm going to find a place that stays open all night, serves chilled beer and Mex food, and has pretty *señoritas* as hot as green peppers. I don't intend to sleep until we get back stateside. But that doesn't mean I won't get to bed sometime." He winked meaningfully, which elicited a giggle from Sharon.

Lifting the pocket-size television from the backpack between his feet, Flynn said, "According to a news station I picked up a few minutes ago, the local police pulled off some kind of coup last night and there's a gang war tearing up the streets.''

Bell waved it away. "Don't hit the panic button, Marty. Those things are always beefed up for TV. Makes you wait longer for the commercials.''

"It showed bodies being picked up out of the streets, Virgil.''

"Probably old footage.'' Bell shook his head. "Relax, pal, you're with me, remember? The name's Virgil, not Virgin. You're getting the best when you hang with me. You keep that in mind while I go hustle this stew. I heard her tell a friend she's getting off in Medellín for a layover. Maybe I'll convince her to lie over me.''

"Oh?'' Sharon said. "Planning to spend this little three-day jaunt with just one woman?''

"Bite your tongue, babe. She's just gonna be an appetizer.'' Bell shuffled down the aisle and struck up a casual conversation with the flight attendant.

"I can't believe everything's so easy for him,'' Flynn said. He looked at Sharon, knowing she could see the envy in him. "I'm serious. Look at how easily he gets to know anyone he wants to know. I wouldn't want to bet anybody that he won't have her in the sack tonight.''

"I'd take that bet, because I know he will. Unless her husband's in town.'' Sharon draped an arm across his shoulders.

He liked the smell of her, and usually it was enough to relax him. But not now. Not when he had a cashier's check for fifty-three thousand dollars in his wallet. The thought of the money set his stomach fluttering again.

Sharon smoothed his forehead with her other hand. "You're worried."

"You're damn right I am. People are getting killed down there. We've got no business going down to that city with Virgil."

"You were the only one the others would trust, baby. And one of your father's export businesses is located in Medellín. Remember, if it wasn't for your father's flight out of there two days from now, we wouldn't have a way home with the cocaine."

"Jesus, Sharon! Would you whisper when you talk about that?"

She giggled at him. "I'm talking into your ear, lover, or hadn't you noticed."

Still angry that she'd taken a chance of compromising them, Flynn said, "Virgil could be wrong, you know."

"And he could be right. That's why the others sent us down here. Look, Marty, they're not fools. They know the street market value of the stuff's going sky-high right now with everything that's been happening. The way Benning's got it figured, Virgil's estimates aren't that far off. With the fifty-three thousand the seven of us were able to scrape together, we should be able to gross a quarter of a million dollars by the time we sell it. That kind of money could go a long way toward getting some of our dreams into motion. Benning wants to set up a computer information service, but his father won't lend him the money to do it. With his share of the money he won't need his father."

"I know." But Flynn also knew his voice didn't sound very convincing, even to him.

"Personally I'm tired of my mother looking over my shoulder. I'm tired of being questioned about where I go, who I'm with and what I'm doing. I'm twenty-three years old, for Christ's sake."

Flynn looked out the window. He could sympathize with her feelings of parental entrapment. Hell, he'd been there himself for too long. He sighed. "I just don't like it."

"Don't like what?"

"The fact that this little excursion was Virgil's idea and the others went along with it so quickly."

"They went along with it because it was good business," Sharon said. "Remember, we're all the brats of good business. It's in our blood. Our homes might be in Miami, but our parents walk the world."

Flynn smiled.

"That's what binds all of us together."

"Except Virgil."

She nipped his earlobe. "So Virgil doesn't get a monthly allotment from his parents like we do. So maybe he works for a living."

"Used to work for a living. He sponges off us now, remember? We're the ones who put him in that little apartment of his, as well as maintain his existence."

"You've been happy with his existence plenty of times before."

Sighing, Flynn said, "Maybe you're right. Maybe I am too uptight about the whole situation."

"I know I'm right. Once this is over with, your sense of adventure will return and you'll be asking yourself why we never did this before. Remember how dull things used to be before we met Virgil?''

Flynn did, but somehow—at the moment—those days were looked back on with an unremembered fondness.

''He didn't introduce any of us to cocaine, but he sure straightened out the supply problems. Just like he's going to do now.'' She smiled at him brightly. ''Only this time we're going to turn a profit at it.''

''Do you realize getting caught with that much stuff will send us to prison?'' he asked. The fear choked him, made him unable to look at her.

''We're not dealers, lover, get that straight in your head if that's what's bothering you. Cocaine is the recreational drug of our crowd. That's all. And Virgil knows where we can parcel off all that we decide not to keep.''

''Yeah, that's what he says.''

''I believe him.''

''Well, nobody believed him enough to send him down here with the money alone.''

''That's different.''

Flynn didn't say anything.

''You know how Virgil is with money. All his pockets have holes in them, and it trickles straight through. That's why Andy does his books for him and pays his bills, and why nobody's ever lent him their Beemer. We're not fools, but we do recognize Virgil's talents. And, like Benning said, we're going to capitalize on them.''

''I wish we weren't here, though.''

"Oh, come on, Marty, this'll be fun. You, me and Virgil, strolling down the streets of Medellín. It'll be like Chevy Chase and Dan Aykroyd in *Spies like Us*. It's going to be fun."

Flynn smiled at her and kissed her to get her to shut up before someone did overhear them. But at the back of his mind those niggling seeds of doubt started to flower.

MACK BOLAN DIDN'T KILL the man when he found him. Instead he tapped the guy's head with the butt of the Desert Eagle and lowered the unconscious body to the ground. Too many times in Vietnam he'd been in situations where he didn't know if he was hiding from enemies or allies. He'd never killed anyone until he positively identified him as an enemy. He used the guy's belt and shoelaces to tie him up, then went on, silent and unseen in the jungle undergrowth.

Even though he hadn't found Grimaldi, he still expected to find the pilot alive because the men hadn't left the area. They stayed for reasons of their own. Grimaldi wouldn't have talked unless tortured, and the proximity to the airfield ruled that out.

Seven minutes later he found guy number two. Like the first, he wore camous suited to the jungle and showed a high degree of professionalism that was lacking in Mercado's men out on the airstrip.

The Executioner slipped through the jungle easily, catching the man just as he turned to face him. The first blow of his fist rocked the guy backward, and the second put out his lights before he found his voice.

Bolan secured the man, checked for ID, found none and went on.

Fourteen minutes and another unidentified player later, Bolan found the hollow where Grimaldi sat with five other men drinking coffee. The pilot's hands weren't bound and nobody had a gun on him.

The group was in the brush, almost a thousand yards back from the airstrip. No one talked. The gear spread out around them clearly spoke of a small armed force. The men were weathered and grimy, their camous stained from having lived in the jungle for more than a few days. Shaving and grooming appeared to have been sporadic at best.

"You've got a friendly in the bush," Bolan advised in a low voice without revealing himself.

The small camp jumped into action as each man sought his weapon and cover. Grimaldi remained seated, his hands on his coffee cup. He grinned from ear to ear. "That you, Sarge?"

"Yeah."

"Come on in."

Bolan leathered the Desert Eagle under the denim jacket and walked into the clearing. The weapons slid away reluctantly.

"You remember that possible Canadian angle our guy mentioned back at the Farm?" Grimaldi asked.

Bolan nodded.

"Well, you're looking at some of the finest Royal Canadian Mounted Police that Canada has to offer."

One of the men stepped forward and offered his hand after slinging his M-16. "Sergeant Charlie Mc-

Pherson,'' he said. "I'm commanding officer of these men."

Bolan took the offered hand. "Mike Belasko."

McPherson nodded. "And who are you with? Your friend there seemed a little evasive."

"Strictly free-lance talent."

The answer didn't sit well with the Mountie. "Yes, well, I suppose we all have our secrets as our governments wish. I'd say we probably haven't got a legitimate passport among the bunch of us."

The warrior gave the man an honest smile. "I'd say you're probably right."

"Coffee?"

"If you've got it."

"We've got it."

"You've got three men out there tied up in the bush."

McPherson looked concerned. "Injured?"

"No. You might pack some aspirin when you send somebody to cut them loose."

"Your friend said you were good."

"Been working at it."

"You've the look of it." McPherson moved his attention to his troops. "Moore, Clark, get your asses up here."

A tall man and a shorter one moved forward.

"If you'll tell them where those men are, I'd appreciate it."

Bolan did and the two Mounties faded into the bush. He joined McPherson, who'd retrieved a thermos.

"Your friend there is an observant man, Sergeant Belasko," McPherson said as he handed Bolan a cup.

"Otherwise we'd never have found a need to come clean with him."

Bolan drank the cool coffee slowly, almost wincing at the taste.

"Apologize for the state of the coffee, but we had a cold camp last night. Had some action go down near our position and didn't want to take any more chances than we had to."

Grimaldi held up his cup. "I figure the coffee's about all the chance you can stand."

"What brings you to Colombia?" Bolan asked.

"Same thing that brings you men, I'm sure. The cocaine traffic. I worked an arms case involving a drug transaction almost a month ago that went sour and got some of our people killed. Usually we stay at home, take care of domestic problems. After our losses, the higher-ups decided this bit of cocaine business was a domestic problem even if it was on foreign soil."

"Who's your target?"

"Likely the same as yours—Costanza."

"Yeah."

"Nothing but the big fish." McPherson smiled, but it was devoid of humor.

Mentally considering his options, Bolan made his decision. The mission seemed to turn a wild card over at every play, but some of them were falling their way. "What are you planning to do with Costanza?"

"This isn't exactly a sanctioned bit of business here," McPherson told him. "The only reason I'm telling you that now is because there was a rumble of information before we came down that we might not be alone. After I heard about the bank and club robberies, and Costanza's airstrip being blown up, I was sure of it."

"You can scratch a caravan of cocaine going north and three drug lab sites, too," Bolan said. He finished off the coffee and threw the dregs into the bush.

"Sounds like you people have been busy. How many of you are there?"

"You're looking at it."

McPherson shook his head. "I thought you Americans had a way of overdoing things like this. Panama, for example."

"Panama had congressional approval," the Executioner said.

"Yes, but two men can hardly expect—"

"Two men have done a lot these past few days."

McPherson nodded. "There is that, of course."

"Suppose we pool our resources."

"I've got twenty men with me, Sergeant, every one of them damn good in the bush despite your introduction to them. And each one of them serious about fracturing Costanza's business going up north. Pardon my bluntness, but what have you got to offer?"

"Intel. I've mapped a lot of this country, drawn up some plans for limited strikes against Costanza's forces, hit-and-git blitzes designed to bleed him dry and cause morale to drop within the ranks. And I'm working real close with the Colombian justice minister on this. I've got five jungle labs set to be razed by the DAS and F-2 tonight. After last night's raids, the guards are going to be expecting trouble. It'll be tougher knocking them down. With your help we could cut the odds by more than half. You can bet they'll be in constant radio contact with each other. When one gets hit, the others will know about it. Costanza may even have set up a mobile force to attempt dealing with the threat of raids. If we give them two targets, chances are we can get them all with less loss of life.''

''You've got this on paper?''

Bolan took out his map case and explained the diagrams as well as the coordinated attacks. When McPherson started asking logistical questions instead of doubting the information, the Executioner knew he'd made his sale. Recruitment was definitely up on this one. And the enlistment office had a tough line straight to hell.

THE ATTACK ON THE AIRSTRIP started at dusk, just before the security lights were switched on. Mack Bolan knew the numbers had already started to fall even as he moved out.

The planted explosives shattered the night in a chorus of thunderclaps. Flames gushed into the tin buildings as men poured out.

Three planes had been singled out before the assault began. Grimaldi opted for the Piper Cub while two RCMP pilots confiscated a matched pair of Beechcraft King Cabs.

Armed with a CAR-15, the warrior led the ground charge to meet the airstrip gunners as they retaliated with a momentary defense. Men fell quickly and were hastily dragged away by their comrades as the reaction turned to retreat. Falling behind a parked jeep to reload and evaluate the situation, Bolan hit the transmit button on his headset. ''McPherson.''

"Here."

"Your position?"

"Solid."

"And your men?"

"All hale and hearty."

"Things couldn't be better, then, I take it."

"That's affirmative. These boys weren't ready to take a hard attack."

"Maybe." Bolan moved on, raising his weapon to fire a 3-round burst at a man skulking along the top of one of the few buildings left standing. The 5.56 mm tumblers drilled their target and punched the man off the tin roof. "Jack." He paused at the side of a hangar with shredded metal sides.

"I'm in the driver's seat now, Sarge."

Bolan glanced over his shoulder and saw the twin props of the Piper Cub kick into life. "I'm on my way."

"I'll be waiting."

"McPherson."

"Copy that," the Mountie's crisp voice replied.

"We'll see you topside."

"Roger."

Bolan ran, taking advantage of the cover he found between him and the Piper. High-velocity whines of ricochets sounded behind him. The breeze blew in gently, bringing a tidal wave of heat from the burning buildings. The sky was full of stars until a dark shape hovered in from the east and blotted part of them out. "Jack, McPherson, we've got a bogey approaching."

"Shit," Grimaldi said with feeling. "That's no bogey. That's a goddamn attack chopper."

McPherson broke in. "They've got ground coverage coming in, too. My communications officer just confirmed transmissions between the helicopter and at least three vehicles moving this way."

Bolan sprinted, pushing his body as hard as it could go, refusing to release the extra weight of the assault rifle. "What about their ETA?" he asked.

A rocket whooshed by overhead, exploding on the tarmac runway. The vibration threw Bolan off-stride, causing him to nearly fall when loose rubble skittered away from underfoot.

"No estimate," McPherson radioed back.

The warrior glanced at the Mounties' end of the airstrip. Smoke curled upward, thick and gray against the ebony sky. Then another rocket impacted against one of the planes, turning it into an eye-searing comet that dropped flaming debris to the ground.

Bolan threw himself onto the wing of the Piper Cub and hoisted himself through the narrow door. Grimaldi fed power into the small aircraft, coaxing it forward. "Come on, baby, don't give up on me now."

Another plane, this one next to the crafts selected by the RCMP, went up in flames. Chain guns rattled, chewing up tarmac in front of the Piper Cub as the helicopter roared by overhead.

"Mercado's pulled out all the stops on this one," Bolan said. "He was expecting someone to come knocking on his door."

Grimaldi nodded as he fought for takeoff speed. "Got a neophyte piloting the chopper, though. Otherwise the guy would've already made mincemeat out of this airstrip to keep us from leaving. That's the only edge we've got to play." He gave the Executioner a tight grin. "That, and the fact that this baby's armed." He indicated the firing setup. "Figure a thousand, maybe two thousand .50-cal rounds in a belly gun. If it's loaded. And I'll be firing on instinct. There're no sights. Probably tooled this baby up for noise and flash only, in case they ran into something that could be scared away. The Coast Guard would whack 'em out of the sky."

The nose of the little six-seater lifted and contact with the ground drifted away.

"Sometimes you have to play the hand you're dealt," Bolan said as he glanced down at the runway. A swirl of men encircled the aircraft chosen by the Mounties. To even attempt takeoff the planes needed to retrace the broken rubble lining the runway.

"Yeah, well, one thing I learned about the sky," Grimaldi stated, "is that there ain't a lot of room for bluffing up here, and it doesn't forgive mistakes. You either got the right stuff or you don't."

"Your target's at ten o'clock."

"I see him," the pilot said grimly. "Film at eleven."

The Piper heeled over as Grimaldi worked the controls. Bolan kept the attack chopper in sight. The craft looked like a praying mantis in the black of night, ribbed and lean and deadly.

As if noticing them for the first time, the helicopter swung around. Muzzle-flashes flared as the chain guns kicked into renewed life.

Bolan buckled his seat belt.

"That's right, you son of a bitch, play follow-me for a while. Give the other guys a minute to catch their breaths.'' Grimaldi nosed the aircraft straight up, gaining altitude at a rate that was impossible for the helicopter to match. A rocket whizzed by them, lost somewhere in the night. "That's right, guy, this isn't a jet. You can't just fire away and depend on heat-seekers to make you a marksman.''

Losing the helicopter somewhere below, Bolan scanned the dark skies, wondering if Mercado had any more aerial surprises in store for them.

"We're gonna lose the engines in a few seconds,'' Grimaldi warned. "When we go into a full stall, we'll drop like a rock. I'm depending on the guy's combat inexperience to put him where we need him on the way down. I'll get just one shot to put him away, and we might end up in the jungle ourselves if I can't get some life back into these engines.'' Even as the Stony Man pilot finished speaking, the right engine shuddered and died, followed immediately by the left.

White-knuckled, Grimaldi held on to the controls, waiting until all acceleration had drained from the Piper. Then, with the pull of gravity once more securely in control, he nosed the plane over, plummeting like a falcon with folded wings.

Keeping one hand on the controls, Grimaldi reached for the firing stud and pressed. Green tracers whipped out before them, sparking slightly below the helicopter.

Grimaldi tugged on the controls as he released the firing button, worked the rudder and added curvature to the dive. When he pressed the firing button again, his aim was dead on target. A white-hot explosion of light filled the night.

Bringing the diving plane under a semblance of control, Grimaldi leveled off in time to catch a wave of flames washing across the nose of the Piper. The sudden thunder of the explosion sounded cataclysmic.

The Piper nosed toward the vast ocean of trees and bush. "Come on, baby," Grimaldi coaxed, thumbing the ignition switches. "Things haven't been nearly as rough on you as they're going to be if you don't show me some kind of life."

Bolan heard the upper branches of the trees below whip into the landing gear, setting up a series of small vibrations. He looked for a place to ditch the aircraft if at all possible, but found none. Reluctantly the engines caught in an uneven buzz saw of noise. The Piper Cub shuddered as power and control returned.

"Yeah," Grimaldi breathed softly. The small airplane responded easily to the pilot's confident touch, circling around to reapproach the airstrip.

Lights from several small, off-road vehicles spilled onto the broken tarmac at one end of the airstrip, but it was too late to stop the Mounties. The RCMP pilots were already airborne, heeling out into the flight path they'd agreed on, staying close to the tree line to avoid friendly and unfriendly radar.

"Looks like we all made it, Sarge."

Bolan nodded, wondering if they'd be so lucky next time.

CLAD IN A SNUG BLACKSUIT, Calvin James slid through the darkness like a greased shadow. He went light, carrying nothing but the deadly little packages in his backpack.

The dock in Cartagna, Colombia, was noisy at this time of night even though most of the dockhands had ceased working. He paused as three drunken sailors marched arm in arm across the wooden planking, singing a Spanish sailing song that wasn't meant for genteel ears.

After the men had passed, James dropped onto the planking, cushioning the noise on bare feet. He carried no weapons except for a Randall survival knife, the kind he'd adopted while in the SEALs. Guns meant noise, and noise meant that part of the mission had been blown. If the mission was blown, he was on full-scale retreat and could only hope to make it back to the rest of Phoenix Force before things turned entirely sour.

The *Lady of Veils* sat apart from the dock, a hundred yards farther out to sea. From an earlier recon he knew that the freighter was heavy with guards. According to the information Barbara Price had given them, the ship was also loaded with ether, acetone and other chemicals.

Staying in the shadows, James moved to the edge of the dock, then lowered himself into the dark, chilly water, released his hold and submerged. The cold ate into him with sharp, jagged teeth. Clamping down on the impulse to gasp for breath when he surfaced, he exhaled shallowly and began the swim for the freighter. He couldn't ignore the cold water. Hypothermia was a problem he'd encountered both as a SEAL warrior and as a hospital corpsman. Instead, he went with it, rolling with the steady drain it made on his physical resources.

Nearing the end of the docked boats, James removed the snorkel from his backpack and bit into it. He'd painted the red ball black with fingernail polish earlier so that it couldn't be detected by casual inspection.

He swam with slow deliberation, staying well within his oxygen abilities with the snorkel and keeping every part of his body beneath the surface. With the moon shining down on him, he knew he'd be all but invisible to the security people on the ship. However, at the same time he'd be blind to everything above the surface himself.

A shadow fell on the water.

James stopped forward motion, willing himself to sink as he took a final deep breath. Seconds later, after affirming he'd reached the freighter, he sunk the snorkel and surfaced only inches from the barnacle-encrusted steel hull. He trod water soundlessly as he shrugged out of the pack.

The shadow drifted across the railing above him. He submerged, keeping only his face above the surface of the water. The shadow went on.

Using care and knowledge, James placed the two shaped charges he'd made after ascertaining the tonnage and class of the freighter from Kurtzman. Then a bright light flicked into life beneath his position. James froze, clinging to the barnacles, his lungs starting to strain for air. A frogman swam into view, carrying an underwater lamp and a spear gun.

The black badass figured the man to be on a routine search. With Costanza having the kind of problems Bolan had been stirring up, it wasn't surprising to learn that the narcobaron had beefed up security. If the enemy had spotted James or overheard him, there would have been more than one frogman.

The Phoenix Force warrior slid forward by using his fingers and toes, carefully watching the frogman. When the guy came to a stop dead in the water, James knew the explosive had been spotted. Denying the screaming need for air buried within his lungs, he launched himself from the hull, drawing the Randall survival knife from its thigh sheath.

The light whipped around in front of him, taking his vision away. Knowing the discharge from the spear gun had to follow, he rolled away, flailing to continue toward his target. He was too close to set off the explosives safely now, and self-sacrifice had always been a last resort for any of the team.

A stream of bubbles erupted to his left, shimmering silver in the light and announcing passage of the spear. The light dropped to the murky bottom as the frogman jettisoned it and the spear gun.

James reached forward in midstroke and clamped his fingers around the man's ankle. He pulled himself up on the man, sinking the Randall between the man's ribs. He repeated the action, felt life leave the body, then released it.

Lungs aching with need, he angled for the surface. Gasping, he cleared his head with one shake as he came up, glancing back toward the *Lady of Veils*. The flat crack of a rifle filled his ears, and a bullet zipped through the water near him. He didn't bother trying to locate the sniper. He dived, reaching for the depths that were both haven and menace.

He stripped the remote control from his belt, gripping it tightly in one clenched fist, unable to keep from reducing his speed. He surfaced, estimated the distance, heard the roar of an outboard keen above the normal dock noises, then dived again, tripping the detonator. He clapped his palms over his ears, screaming into the water to lessen the residual tension from his body.

The explosions were dull roars, and the ensuing concussion tossed him, out of control, through the water. Moments later he surfaced half-conscious, noting the high-pitched whine of the outboard without giving it another thought. The detonator had tumbled from his fingers.

Shots punctured the surface of the roiling water around him. He looked up at the approaching outboard in time to see the muzzle-flashes that signaled bullets spitting straight at him. In the background the *Lady of Veils* had sundered in the center below the waterline. Everything was going down as flames raced to ravage the deck.

James stroked for the dock, knowing he'd never make it before the outboard overtook him or the shooters tracked onto him. Unable to keep his speed up beneath the water, he stroked topside, watching as ruby rays from at least three laser sights bounced erratically around him. Saltwater erupted into the air as bullets sliced nearby.

James's arms and legs churned mechanically. His lungs labored like an overworked bellows pump, burning from the exertion. His ears still rang. Something trailed cold electricity across the calf of his left leg. He took a deep breath and plunged back under the water. The shadow of the outboard streaked over him seconds later. He watched the whirling white spume of the propeller trail behind it, curving gradually as it turned for another pass. He surfaced again, gasping for breath, unable to stay under for very long at the rate he was burning oxygen.

The outboard circled, pitched off balance by the gunners' shift as they tried to bring him into target acquisition. The burning wreckage of the freighter left orange highlights across their faces.

The flat crack of a big-bore rifle reached James's ears a heartbeat after the tillerman pitched over the side. The outboard lost control between two large vessels. Before any of the shooters could move, another man dropped as the crack of the rifle rang out again. Without a helmsman the outboard smashed into one of the freighters and sank.

When James glanced toward the dock, he saw McCarter in a kneeling position with a Beretta M-21 in his hands. He swam for the Briton, knowing the presence of the rifle would keep the curious away. The Cartagena police were another matter.

"Aye, mate," McCarter said with an insouciant grin plastered across his face. "I thought you said this would be a simple in-and-out run for a seasoned pro like yourself."

James took his teammate's hand as he clambered up the wooden ladder built into the dock. He turned to look at the masts of the freighter barely visible above the water. "Yeah, well, the way I look at it, the ship's down and you got the chance to whack a couple of Costanza's boys. Sounds pretty simple to me.''

McCarter shouldered the sniper rifle and pushed his teammate toward the street. "Simple, huh? I'll tell you what's simple—you got the luck of the simple, is what you got, mate.''

James looked at him solemnly. "If it wasn't for simple luck, I'd have no luck at all.''

McCarter rolled his eyes.

"Besides, I have a pure heart.'' James limped to the waiting car in as dignified a manner as possible.

CHAPTER EIGHTEEN

Martin Flynn stood on the patio balcony of the hotel room, worrying about what he'd gotten himself involved in. The bathroom door opened behind him, drawing his attention from the empty street below. Sharon came out, clad only in a large green terry-cloth towel. The vanishing smile on her face told him she'd sensed what was on his mind.

"You're really trying to screw up what could otherwise be a great short vacation," she said. She sat on the edge of the bed and began to dry her hair.

"Didn't mean to."

She sighed. "You sound just like my kid brother when you do that."

"Sorry."

"Oh, Christ." She dried more vigorously.

Flynn was confused. He didn't know if it was anger or regret that he felt more strongly. Turning to look back out over the city, he rested his palms on the stone wall around the patio and felt the dankness of the rock. "It's not everybody who takes a vacation to score cocaine," he said softly.

"Maybe you'd be surprised."

He considered that. Maybe he would be. No one in their group had questioned where the coke came from that they partied with. They'd always just accepted that it would be there for them when they got ready—until their source suddenly dried up and Virgil Bell got his bright idea. The thought of Bell made him remember that the guy was down there somewhere, prowling the dark streets to set up their buy.

"Medellín isn't exactly a vacation spot," Sharon said. "Sure, there's lots of flowers and old buildings to look at, but that isn't the attraction. We're just a few of thousands who come from the States to do what we're here to do."

He wondered what they'd do if Bell didn't come back, how they'd explain it. No answers came to mind. "Have you really realized we could get caught at this?"

"Yes."

He shivered at the silence and the cold.

"What you need to realize is that we have more than a fair chance of getting away with this. Your dad's a respected businessman down here. An investor. If we can get the cocaine onto his private jet, it's a safe bet we won't be bothered at either end of the flight by customs or anyone else."

"What if we get caught with it on the jet?"

She didn't answer.

"Do you realize my dad could go to jail, too? For something he didn't even know he was doing?"

"That's not going to happen, Marty."

"I didn't see anybody handing out guarantees when we agreed to do this."

"Then why did you agree?"

"Looking back on it, I don't really know."

"Then I'll tell you why. You did it because you wanted to prove to yourself how macho you could be.

Especially since Virgil seemed so willing. You don't see him standing around worrying like this."

"That's because he actually thinks he's in control of the situation." Flynn suddenly realized that was the scariest proposition of all. The springs squeaked as Sharon got up from the bed.

He turned to watch her, the full moon streaming into the dark room from over his shoulder. She pulled on one of his white shirts, buttoned it low and rolled up the sleeves.

She came to him and put her arms around his waist. He felt the heat of her, the dampness of her hair against his chin and chest. His body started to respond to her in spite of the doubts clinging to his mind. "You need to relax, lover." She tugged him toward the bed, walking backward to pull him down on top of her.

"You know," she said, placing a painted fingernail against his lips, "if my father knew you had his little girl in a hotel room at this moment, planning to do erotic things to her body, he'd probably consider having you drawn and quartered."

Flynn didn't laugh because he knew it was true.

"And that, Marty, is a thing you should be afraid of."

Despite the tension he felt from his present situation, Flynn demonstrated how unafraid of her father he was, bringing them both to a shuddering climax on the squeaking bed that shrilled with such intensity they couldn't help but laugh. A half hour later he did it again, more tenderly this time because his feelings for her were as real as any he'd ever had. For a moment he wondered if she knew that. Covered with perspiration, he collapsed on the bed beside her, his lungs laboring.

Sharon lay on top of the sheets watching him, her body glistening in the moonlight. "All hail the conquering hero," she teased.

He smiled at her, tracing her features with a forefinger. "I love you, you know."

"I know."

"I've never told you that before."

"I know that, too."

"So what makes tonight so special?"

She bit his finger with enough pressure to make him yank it away. "Because you're living on the edge of danger tonight. Because for the first time in a long time, you're not really sure what tomorrow will bring."

"And that's something to rejoice about? That's crazy, is what it is."

"We aren't sane creatures, lover. I learned that in all those psych classes at college."

There was a brief knock on the door, then it opened. Sharon squeaked in surprise and dived under the sheets. Flynn got to his feet, hand curling around the unlighted lamp.

"Whoops," Virgil Bell said as he closed the door behind him but made no move to leave the room. "Looks like I got back at one of those inopportune moments. Hope you were finished." He grinned lewdly.

"Goddamn it, Bell, what the hell are you doing here?" Flynn set the lamp back on the nightstand. Sharon had the sheets pulled up under her chin. He was acutely aware of standing there bare-assed naked. He reached for his jeans and pulled them on, hopping from one foot to the other.

"Just dropped by to let you know everything's been set up." Bell seated himself on the room's small desk. "You really ought to keep that door locked, my man. You don't know the kind of people who stumble around in the darkness out there."

Sharon sat up in bed, draping herself with the sheets as she put her elbows on her knees. "So when do we do it?"

"Tomorrow evening. We're supposed to meet the guy in a cantina not far from where we are now."

"Do you know this guy we're meeting?" Flynn asked.

Bell shook his head. "I don't know anybody down here, buddy. I'm just working off the names of friends of friends. That's the way you do business down here if you're a little guy. However, I didn't come down here to be taken advantage of." He pulled his hands out of his jacket pockets, withdrawing two oilskin pouches with them. He tossed one to Flynn.

It was solid, heavy and angular. Flynn pulled the drawstring and reached inside. What he brought out was a small pistol that gleamed and smelled of gun oil.

"Smith & Wesson .38s," Bell announced as he opened his bag and revealed a duplicate. "Small and efficient, easy to hide, and they pack a hell of a punch for their size. You do know how to shoot?"

Flynn nodded. The pistol symbolized everything he'd considered was going wrong with their trip.

"Good." Bell dropped his weapon back into the pouch and returned it to his pocket. He smiled. "Why don't we get together for lunch tomorrow? I found a great little café while I was out wandering around. My treat."

Unable to say anything, even to remind Bell that the money he was spending had been given to him, Flynn nodded. He tucked the .38 back into the oilskin pouch and pulled the drawstring tight.

Bell tapped the door as he stood in the doorway. "You might want to lock up before you get back to whatever you were doing." He grinned and shut the door.

Flynn shot the bolt and exhaled. When he looked back at Sharon, he saw that some of the sense of adventure had left her face. He got a beer for each of them from the ice bucket on the desk and hoped she didn't notice the way his hands trembled.

STILL HOLDING his unholstered weapon, Benito Franco stood in the carnage of the lab and watched dark gray smoke spread out against the night-black sky. He was still scared, but the fear had a dull edge to it now, nothing like the razor-sharp and screaming thing that had almost devoured him hours ago when they'd made the first raid. He forced himself to holster the pistol but left the flap unbuttoned.

"Benito."

Recognizing Sigfrido's voice, Franco turned around. "Yes?"

The DAS man waved at the wreckage around them. "It's all like this. The chemicals, the planes, the equipment, they've all been destroyed. I think this was the work of your friend."

"He can't have done this by himself."

"No, I don't think so, either." Sigfrido pushed a fresh chew of tobacco into his cheek with a finger. "Who does he represent?"

"I still don't know for sure." Franco stared in morbid wonder at the still bodies that were in evidence. He had fired his pistol tonight, at people who had fired on him. He wasn't sure if he'd hit anyone, and he was more thankful for that. But, if this continued, he was sure there would come a time when he was forced to take a life knowingly.

"Do you even know his name?"

"Yes, I do." Franco made no effort to lie. As with his father, he'd never been able to lie to Sigfrido.

The walkie-talkie at the DAS man's belt crackled. Sigfrido spoke, then listened intently. He signed off, clipped it back to his belt and looked at Franco. "My spotter craft has just found the next site exactly as this one. I'd say things have changed since you last saw your friend."

"He's gotten help from an unexpected source."

"Maybe."

Franco ignored the sarcasm in the comment. "Otherwise he'd have apprised us of the change in the situation."

"Again I feel I must caution you about prizing this man too highly."

Franco looked at the man and smiled slightly. "And I must remind you about looking a gift horse in the mouth."

"It would have saved a lot of Trojans, Benito."

Taken by surprise by the man's comment, Franco laughed out loud. "I didn't know you read the classics."

"I don't, but your father, he was a great reader, always. Some things he told me have stuck in my head." The walkie-talkie crackled again. Sigfrido answered it, then said, "I must attend to something."

Franco nodded and watched the other man leave, striding purposefully through the accumulated debris. The justice minister kept one hand on the pistol butt as he surveyed the scene and wondered how many men had died tonight.

"Minister Franco."

He turned at the sound of his name, and a dark shadow stepped from the jungle. The justice minister almost pulled his weapon before he recognized Bolan. He let out a short breath. "This is your doing?" He indicated the lab.

Bolan nodded. His face was stained by cosmetics and smoke. The eyes were volcanic blue, piercing. He had looked big by daylight and in the street the night they had first met. Tonight, with the jungle framing him and the moonlight frosting him, he looked like a small giant carved from the shadows.

"You weren't alone?"

"No. I found others looking for the same thing we are."

"Costanza's defeat."

"Yes."

"They must be experienced men."

"Yes."

"Why are you here now?"

"To let you know the other three labs have already been destroyed."

"Sigfrido has already guessed that."

"He's a good man."

Franco nodded, aware now of the way death and isolation seemed to cling to the man. He wondered how much of it was visceral and how much of it had been conjured up by remembered news stories concerning the Executioner's personal war against the Mafia.

"I also wanted you to know we're moving the theater of operations for a while," Bolan said. "If you're willing."

"To where?"

"The congressional floor."

The prospect chilled Franco, recalling the image of Costanza as the man had been earlier that day in his office. "Why?"

The warrior seemed hesitant to answer for a couple of seconds, then said, "I want to get you out of the blood for a while. You could never find a home here."

"And you have?"

"I survive. My talents put me on the front line every time I go out to do battle. Yours were honed for the courtroom and for the trappings of politics. It's time we gave you a chance to excel. The media is behind you already. After tonight you'll be able to choose whatever headlines you want to make."

Franco considered that. "What have you got in mind?"

"I'm having information faxed to me that should enable you to take Costanza's congressional seat away from him. Names, dates, places, everything you'll need to tie him to this country's drug trade."

"And if I'm unable to do that?"

"You'll be able to. Public sympathy's on your side. Many people are starting to talk again. I've heard them. It won't be long before they decide it's time to dream again, and plan for the future. If they reach for that, the cancer of the cartels and Costanza is going to have to be cut."

"You're eloquent, my friend. Maybe you should take up politics yourself."

The warrior's smile was wan.

Franco felt the bond between them for the first time. It was a tenuous thing, built on the horrors they'd shared and the dreams they dared, stretched tight between two men who fought for ideals rather than personal gain. He took strength from it, and some of the chill in the wind went away. "Where will I get the information?"

"I'll bring it to you in the morning. You pick the place."

"My house." Franco answered without hesitation. "It's the most heavily guarded, and you've been seen there before."

Bolan nodded. "There's something else that needs to be taken care of. Along with the information, I'm having extradition papers from Dade County in Florida delivered for Ortega. Can you arrange it?"

"I think so, but Ortega will have to be in custody before we can enforce it."

"Leave that to me." Bolan pulled back into the shadows. "Take care of yourself, amigo."

"And you." Franco could no longer see the big man. *"¡Vaya con Dios!"* he called softly, knowing how out of place that must sound to a man who lived his life in no-man's-land, but unable to refrain from saying it. "And you don't fool me, my friend. You've found no home in the blood, either. Only an existence and a kind of honor few would understand, and for which even fewer would be willing to pay."

CHAPTER NINETEEN

"Boss?"

Costanza thumbed the intercom button by his bed. "Yes?"

"It's Ortega."

"Come." Costanza released the button and rolled from his bed. The call hadn't awakened him. He hadn't been able to sleep even after all the drinking and the tranquilizers. Too many things had gotten out of his control and his thoughts were filled with them. He shrugged into his robe and switched on a small table lamp, then reached for the bottle of tequila he'd left sitting on the bedroom's wet bar.

Ortega entered the room at the far end, walking past the mirrored walk-in closets and shoe trees filled with expensive imports. He carried a paper rolled up in his fist.

Not bothering to ask the man if he wanted something to drink, Costanza left the bar and joined him at the breakfast table in the center of the room. He sat in one of the plush chairs, while Ortega remained standing.

"I can tell by looking at your face that you don't have good news."

"No, Luis, I don't." Ortega leaned forward and smoothed out the paper.

Costanza recognized it as a map of the jungle surrounding Medellín. "The labs again?"

"Yes." Ortega pointed them out.

The narcobaron rose to his feet and threw the glass at the wall. It shattered into dozens of glittering pieces. "Five of them tonight?"

"Yes."

"That makes eight of them in the past two days. This is madness. Franco can't be doing this alone."

"No. Survivors have informed me that there are Americans helping Franco and the DAS."

"Their numbers?"

"Perhaps as many as forty men."

Costanza glared at his second-in-command. "Are they DEA?"

"If they are, they're men unknown to us."

"Are they soldiers?"

"It's possible. I've been told their moves are military in nature. The camps must have been mapped out previously, then they attacked."

"Who's in charge of this?"

"They speak of a big man, dressed all in black."

Memory of the graveyard voice touched the back of Costanza's neck. "And Franco?"

"He and Sigfrido were there, as well, but never were the three at the same camp."

"I want this man found, Esteban, and I want him found damn quick. If there's even a whisper of his name, I want it passed among my troops. I don't want them to believe they're being pursued by some phantom."

"They speak of this already."

"I know." Costanza paced the floor with his hands clasped behind his back. "This man is known to Franco. You can bet on it."

"I agree."

"I have a meeting in Bogotá tomorrow. Congress. I don't want to go there with an unclear conscience about these matters. If you can't find out who this man is, I want Franco dead before three o'clock tomorrow afternoon. He's scheduled to speak there."

"There's nothing to tie you to the jungle labs."

Costanza sighed as he turned to face his subordinate. "Esteban, the connection has already been made for Franco and our unknown attacker. Do you think either of them strikes blindly?"

Ortega shook his head.

"No. You yourself said they'd planned the attacks, even organized them before initiating them." Costanza stared at the stain on his wall. "They gain strength with every move they make. I can no longer simply sit by and depend on them to make a mistake, nor can I ignore the damage that's being done to my operation. La Araña is still missing in Miami. Our supply of cocaine has been restricted in some areas so badly that our customers will go somewhere else if we can't get product to them. We've taken several defeats. How long can we expect the men we have to remain loyal to us? I control the drug trade throughout Colombia, and many benefit from it. I bring new life to our country. I won't allow my dreams to drift away as if they're sand before the wind." He glared into his second's face. "It's my wish and my order that Franco die tomorrow by your hand. Is that enough to make it so?''

"Of course, Luis."

"Then see to it, Esteban, as you value your service to me."

Ortega nodded and left the room.

Taking another glass from the bar, Costanza fixed himself a fresh drink. He crossed the room to the window, unlatching the twin doors of bulletproof glass and stepping onto the veranda. The breeze called to him with sweet scents, promising him everything nature had to offer.

He sneered in response. He already had almost all that a man could take from others and from life itself. He'd be damned if he saw any of it taken away from him. He gave of himself and his wealth to the people. Franco and his unknown accomplice couldn't take away the good he was able to do. He was a god to some of the peasants. Their adoration for him had shone often in their eyes. No one, not even the invisible army backing the justice minister, could topple him from his place of power. No earthly force could stand between him and domination of those he chose to control.

In the distance he heard a soft rumble, and vibration shuddered through the veranda. It wasn't quite thunder—it possessed more power. He thought of the dormant volcano not far away.

"You and I," he whispered to the volcano. "We're sleeping giants, filled with terrible and swift power. You continue groaning in your sleep sometimes and cause bad dreams among the people who hear you, but I'll teach Medellín to fear the night again."

He toasted the volcano, drank and plotted, struggling to keep the fear from touching him.

DRESSED COMBAT CASUAL in jeans and a denim jacket, Mack Bolan watched the passengers disembark from the commercial flight.

Isaac Auerbach and Chaim Feldman were the third and fifth in line, wearing expensively cut business suits. People stayed away from the older man, avoiding the direct glare of the one burning eye. The black eye patch lent his face a severe look.

Bolan followed them with the compact binoculars, using the lamppost beside him as cover.

Once the men were inside, customs didn't hold them up for more than a few minutes, telling the warrior the fix had already been put in. He pocketed the binoculars as the two Israelis walked toward a rental car that was evidently waiting for them. He retreated toward his own car, an anonymous late-model American four-door station wagon. He started the engine and pulled out in pursuit of Auerbach and Feldman, following behind it at what he considered to be a safe distance. There was no doubt of their destination. Costanza had called the hounds home for the hunt.

Bolan rolled down the window and let the morning's heat wash over him. He unleathered the Desert Eagle and placed it on the seat beside him, the safety off.

Auerbach drove, speaking on a mobile phone as he adhered to the speed limit. Blinking his eyes to forestall the fatigue trying to pull them shut, Bolan kept to the right as they pulled onto a four-lane street.

Phoenix Force had been successful sidelining Caseros in Panama despite intervention by U.S. forces. That had been the primary objective of their leg of the mission. The secondary objective had arrived in Medellín. Technically neither Auerbach nor Feldman were wanted by the United States law-enforcement agencies. But the Stony Man mission required the elimination of the Israelis—temporarily or permanently— because of their link to Costanza. Bolan was here now to find out which way it would go.

Auerbach made no sudden moves. He signaled before changing lanes, hung up the phone and smiled as if he'd shared a joke with his companion.

Closing the distance now with the increased flow of traffic, Bolan drifted to within two car lengths of his quarry. A flash of light on metal was the only warning he got. He saw the van hurtle out of the constricted alley only heartbeats before it smashed into the side of the station wagon.

Glass shattered inward from the impact. The heavy car rolled from the force, coming up on two wheels. Brakes screeched as vehicles around them tried to stop and failed. The car following on his left crunched into his door and sprung the lock. A flatbed truck carrying crates of chickens slammed into the front of the station wagon, forcing the vehicle into a spin. The warrior found the .44 by instinct, curling up to cover his midsection and throwing his free arm across his face.

The cacophonic noise died away even as the station wagon settled on all four wheels again, replaced by car horns and angry voices.

The Executioner crawled free of the vehicle through the driver's window. Onlookers drew back when they saw the big pistol. The van's driver had already disappeared. He found Auerbach's sedan two blocks away parked next to the curb. Chaim Feldman gave him a snappy salute and a winning smile, then the car started forward again. Isaac Auerbach never looked back at all.

Unable to give pursuit, Bolan holstered his weapon and checked the occupants of the other cars. None of them appeared to be seriously injured. Keening sirens cut through the hissing sounds made by ruptured radiators.

Bolan turned away, leaving the car in the street because it couldn't be traced back to him. Auerbach had made a good call. If there had been any kind of gunplay the man would have become a fugitive in this country, vulnerable to the legal pressures Franco could bring to bear to have him forcibly deported. As it stood now, the man was just another unintentional observer of a mild traffic incident.

Bolan hoped Franco and Grimaldi were having better luck with their own attempts at whittling down Costanza's forces.

DISHEVELED AND DIRTY, wanting a shower more than anything else, Benito Franco walked into his office with Sigfrido at his side. "You must be made of iron, my friend," he told the DAS man as he sat in his chair.

Sigfrido knelt and brought out the liquor and glasses.

Franco waved it away. "I'm having breakfast with Dominga this morning. I don't want to worry her any more than I already do." He unbuckled his weapon and stored it in a desk drawer.

Sigfrido poured himself a drink. "You should reconsider wearing the weapon."

Franco laid it heavily on the desktop, rattling the phone with the force. "I despise this pistol, even more now than I did a few days ago." He looked up. "This represents chaos, the law of the beast. It makes me no better than Costanza."

"We fight for a world that holds more than that," Sigfrido said. "Don't lose sight of it."

Franco sighed. "I don't, but it gets so hard these days to see it clearly."

"Your mysterious friend sees it. That's why he wages war against the cartel with us instead of around us. The Americans have usually had their way in South American politics. This man doesn't appear to come from the same mold as Rodesney and his compatriots. He carries his own brand of thinking with him."

"Your opinion of him seems to have changed."

Sigfrido shook his head and sat on a corner of the desk. "No, I still know he uses you as bait, but he respects you for it."

"He saved my daughter."

"I know. I think he cares for you." Sigfrido tapped his head. "This man is smart, politically, but he doesn't seem to play political games. If he was a typical American espionage agent, he might have let Andeana die that morning. Politically it would have been the right thing to do. These jungle labs we've raided, they've built your popularity with the common people who live in fear of the drug lords. But had this man let Andeana die, even more sympathy would be at your feet. Maybe even those fence sitters in the congress would've been moved to join your efforts. But this man doesn't always go by his head—he listens to his heart first."

Franco put the pistol away again. He thumbed the intercom button. "Well, today we're going to put one of those fence sitters to the test."

"How so?"

"By asking for extradition against Esteban Ortega."

"And how do you propose to capture this man if you receive it?"

"He's supposed to be delivered to me."

Sigfrido's eyebrows rose in surprise.

"Yes, sir?" a woman's voice blared from the intercom.

"Place a call for me, Julita.'

"Yes?"

"To Bogotá, the president's office. Tell his secretary that it's very important."

"Yes, sir."

Franco sat in silence, brooding at the armored plating covering his windows, thinking that for a man who wanted only peace for his country he was surely walling himself away from it. Public exposure, instead of being a freedom, was now a dangerous thing.

The intercom crackled. "I have the president on line three."

"Thank you, Julita." Franco punched the flashing phone button and raised the receiver to his ear. "Hello."

The president was a robust man and had a voice to match. "Good morning, Benito. I'm told you have more good news for me."

"Yes, some, and a favor to ask, as well." Franco could almost hear caution invade the man's tone.

"Ask, and if it can be done, rest assured it will be."

"You've heard of the five labs that were raided last night?"

"Yes, only less than an hour ago. Your people are doing very good work. My acquaintances in the U.S. embassy are very pleased."

"That's good to hear," Franco said, "because the favor I'm about to ask concerns them."

"Does it have to do with the congressional meeting scheduled for this afternoon?"

"Only in some aspects." Franco shifted in his chair. "I need extradition papers to be allowed on Ortega."

Silence was the only immediate answer.

"Sir?"

"I'm thinking, Benito."

Franco gave the man time, remembering how he'd felt when Bolan had made the suggestion to him.

"You realize that allowing this will incur the wrath of Costanza?"

"Yes, but the man is on the verge of having many problems."

"You've tied the jungle labs to him, then?"

"No, not yet."

"You're taking a big risk, Benito. Costanza is a respected man in your city. He's sponsored churches, the Homes for the Poor of Medellín movement and various other causes that have endeared him to the populace."

"I think once the people realize where that money's been coming from, their love of him will wither and die."

"And if it doesn't?"

"There's no 'if it doesn't.' They will."

"Ah, Benito, Benito, I knew when I appointed you to your post that you'd be a man who put his body and spirit into these matters."

"Yes, you did, and at that time you promised to stand behind me."

"In anything that wasn't suicidal," the Colombian president amended.

"This isn't."

"You sound so sure."

"I am," Franco replied with more confidence than he felt.

An awkward pause followed, then the president said, "They say you're using American DEA agents in these strikes against the jungle labs."

"Are you asking me to confirm those suspicions?"

"No. I want nothing confirmed, otherwise I'll have to answer for it. The rumors will circulate again that our country has become a puppet government controlled by the United States."

"If that time ever comes, you may hold me accountable."

"Rest assured if that time ever comes, I'll do just that."

Franco balled his free hand into a fist but kept his voice calm. "You haven't let me know your decision about Ortega."

The man sighed into the receiver. "You have the warrants for his arrest?"

"They're being delivered from Miami this morning. U.S. marshals will be waiting for him in Miami after the DEA delivers him to them."

"This has all been arranged?"

"Yes."

"Why wasn't I notified before now?"

Recognizing the petty political jealousy the president was capable of at times, Franco said, "There were no plans until last night. This was unexpectedly dropped into my lap."

"Truly?"

"Truly."

Another sigh followed, this one sounding of commitment. "I don't like surprises, Benito. You know that. The job of running a country, especially one with as many problems as Colombia has, is an arduous and thankless task."

Franco reluctantly decided not to mention that conjuring up justice from chaos was no less so.

"If you have the means to take Ortega without blood," the president told him, "then you have my permission. I'll sign the necessary papers today just before we go to congress, so no word of it will leak out."

Franco held up a clenched fist of victory to Sigfrido. The DAS man smiled broadly. "Thank you, sir."

"Don't thank me yet, Benito. The carbon on these extradition orders could well be your death warrant, too. If you change your mind, let me know."

"I won't change my mind." Franco broke the connection and leaned back in the chair, lacing his fingers behind his neck as he stretched tiredly. "Well, my friend, we're going to have our day in court it seems."

"Yes, but be careful, because even though the 'courtroom' is your chosen battlefield, Costanza can't be relied on to play fairly."

"I know," Franco said, wondering if it was only him or if the room had grown suddenly cooler.

CHAPTER TWENTY

"Coffee?"

"Thanks," Mack Bolan replied, feeling awkward and out of place in Dominga Franco's kitchen.

The woman took two cups from a cupboard, placed them on a counter and filled them from a coffeepot on the stove. She handed one to him. "Sugar or cream?"

"Black." Bolan blew on the coffee and looked out the window overlooking the backyard of the Francos' new home. The curtains were towels, further testament that the house was only a temporary refuge for the family. The guards weren't visible, but they were there.

"Can I fix you something?" the woman asked. "Benito may be a while in returning home."

"No. I only came here to drop off some papers for him."

"Have you eaten?"

"No."

"Then you'll eat with us."

The warrior was made even more off balance by the invitation. Despite her genuine offers of hospitality, he knew part of the woman resented his presence. He represented a number of unpleasant possibilities. "Thank you."

She wiped her hands on her apron.

"How are things with you and your daughter?"

"We survive." She smiled sadly as she looked out the window. "The worst part is that Andeana can't go out to play. She loves being in the sun."

"Perhaps if she's closely supervised..."

Dominga shook her head. "No, not even then. We're living in a fortress now. The attack on our house has brought that realization to me if nothing else. I won't try to delude myself for even a few minutes."

"You're a strong woman, Señora Franco. Not many could make the adjustments you've made."

She looked at him, her dark eyes full of pain. "I'm strong only because I haven't been given a choice."

Bolan looked away from her, unwilling to confront the sadness he saw in her face.

"It's not all your fault, *señor*," she said in a softer voice. "Benito was caught up in this cause of his long before you found him. As his father was involved in it before him. They were both peaceful men in the beginning. But the job they do, the tasks they set before themselves, these things wear on the soul."

"I understand."

"I know you do. I can see it in your eyes when I look at you." She returned to the table, rolling out dough she'd been allowing to rise.

The warrior glanced down at the bundled papers sitting at the end of the cabinet. The information had come through, just as Barbara Price had said it would, and it was loaded, primed and ready. The only thing he needed was his sacrificial lamb. The thought turned his stomach sour.

Dominga washed her hands under running water, then dried them on her apron. "You must forgive my bluntness," she said. "My mother tells me I've lived too many years with my husband, learned to speak too much of what is on my mind with no one to tell me I can't. But I must say this."

Bolan waited in silence.

"Benito isn't as you are, *señor*. He isn't a soldier. He's a man trapped by his passions and the dreams his father passed on to him. I know from watching and from listening to my husband that you've enabled him to realize many of his recent accomplishments. He recognizes the dangers. It couldn't have been any clearer to him than yesterday when Andeana was almost taken away from us. But for all that, he finds himself still trapped, drawn like a moth to a flame. You and Sigfrido, you're two of a kind. You treasure the win over the fate of the individual. There are no acceptable losses in your wars, no peaceful withdrawals, only winning and losing. In Sigfrido, friend of his dead father, Benito finds the embodiment of the dream his father had for all of Colombia. In you, he finds the tools to get things done. I fear for him. I fear for his life. In your wars men fall and are replaced by other soldiers. But in my heart, should something ever happen to Benito, I want you to be warned that you can expect no forgiveness for your part. No one can replace Benito in my life." She turned away from him, her eyes filled with bitter tears.

"Some people in this life can't sit still when they see an injustice being done to others," Bolan said softly. "No matter what the challenge, no matter what the dangers, these people rise to the occasion, fighting to make us all better than we are. You can call them heroes or you can call them fools, but it really depends on which side of the fence you're sitting on when the dust clears. Not everyone has the strength to face their greatest fears and chance losing everything they hold dear to them. You should be proud of those who stand to be counted." He paused. "You should be proud of your husband. I am. As long as he needs me in this matter, I'll be there for him. More than that, I can't promise."

Her shoulders shook as she cried silently, leaning over the sink away from him.

Happy laughter sounded from the living room, then, "Mama, Daddy's home." A squeal of unbridled surprise followed.

Dominga looked up at him, tears streaking her face. "Please, if you could delay him until I compose myself... I don't want him to see me like this."

Bolan nodded, gathered the package of documents and left the room.

A SWIRL OF DUST covered the jeep. Luis Costanza turned away and held a handkerchief over his mouth and nose. When he looked forward again, the driver stopped the vehicle outside the church. Father Lazaro stood waiting for them.

Costanza got out of the jeep, shoved the handkerchief into his pocket and brushed the dust from his clothes. The morning sun burned hot and bright, scattering shadows under the trees. Children and their parents stopped what they were doing to watch his arrival. Only the animals stayed in motion. Without hesitation the narcobaron moved forward with purpose, allowing the anger that filled him to seethe through his body.

Two more jeeps bearing armed men parked beside the first, the wheels of the vehicle still rocking even as boot-clad feet hit the baked earth. Metallic noises filled the silence around the church as bolts were released on the weapons.

"To what do we owe this visit?" the priest asked. He kept his hands in his sleeves.

Costanza came to a stop in front of the older man, remembering Don Manolon for a brief instant. Both men, priest and smuggler, had been figures of power at different times in his life. Now both men were one with the dust at his feet, irritating and easily swept away. He backhanded the priest without preamble.

The old man hit the dirt, and the nuns rushed forward, crying shrilly.

"Tomás," Costanza called.

One of the men stepped forward, bringing an M-16 to his shoulder. Autofire filled the churchyard as bullets chipped branches from the treetops. Everyone froze, the more wary of the peasants dropping instantly to the ground.

"No," the priest commanded, waving the nuns back. The women seemed unwilling.

Costanza drew his pistol from his shoulder holster and pointed it at the fallen man. "Get back," he ordered. "Get back now or he dies."

The nuns retreated to the church as Father Lazaro tried to get to his feet. Stepping forward, Costanza put a foot on one of the man's hands, then added his weight. He smiled as the priest's face blanched with pain. "Now, you foolish old man," he said quietly, "we'll talk."

Father Lazaro looked at him without hate. "I'll pray for your soul, my son."

Costanza shook his head. "I don't need prayers, old man. I need answers." He snapped his fingers. Another man came forward, carrying the rolled map Ortega had presented to his superiors. "Do you know what this is?"

"It's a map."

"Yes, a map of this area. It contains this church and certain industries I find necessary in my business. You know of this?"

The priest didn't reply.

"Answer me, old man, or I'll have an arm of one of the nuns broken. And you had better not lie, or you'll surely send your soul to hell."

"I know of this."

"It took me almost all morning to figure this out. I searched for answers long and hard, trying to reason how Franco and his people knew of the labs. Then I realized this church was centered between them all. Eight of my labs. All lost, nothing salvageable. And for what?"

"So these people, God's people, wouldn't have to work in your fields and buildings anymore and fear for their immortal souls."

"Their immortal souls, Father? This is what you were trying to save?" Costanza knelt down, maintaining the weight on the old man's hand, and he pushed his face toward the other man's. "These people don't want their immortal souls saved, old man. They want something to eat. They want to survive. And you expect them to live in the jungle?"

Costanza looked toward the peasants and raised his voice. "Is that what you want, God's children? Do you want your immortal souls saved? Or do you want your bellies full at night?" Only the ringing echo of his voice answered him. "They don't answer me, old man. Perhaps they're afraid of offending you as I am doing."

"You don't offend me. You offend God."

Costanza smiled. "You're an ignorant peasant dressed up in the trappings of priesthood. If He walked the Earth today, don't you think I could find the money to buy even Him?"

"You speak sacrilege."

Costanza leaned on the foot trapping the priest's hand, smiling at the rictus of pain forming on the old man's face. "I speak the truth."

"Lies."

Costanza smiled. "I didn't come to hear you thump your Bible at me, old fool. I came here to find out who you told about the labs."

"Never."

"Then you shall watch the sisters be raped, each in turn, until I'm satisfied you're unrelenting in your choice. As you can see, I have many men. It would take a long time to slake their thirst for female flesh. Of course, I can understand if you aren't knowledgeable about these things."

"You're an abomination."

"And you're insufferable in your own right. Make your choice. Now."

Father Lazaro's head rested on the ground.

"Who did you tell?"

"I don't know his name."

"Liar."

"No. It's the truth."

"Describe him then."

"A tall American, black hair, blue eyes, scarred in many battles, dressed all in black."

A chill ran down Costanza's spine. He moved away from the priest and pointed to two men. "Get him up."

The men shouldered their weapons and moved forward, lifting Father Lazaro by the arms.

Costanza wiped his face with his handkerchief and jerked a thumb toward two trees growing close together. "There."

The men carried and dragged their burden to the trees.

Costanza followed closely, aware that every eye was upon him. Another man trailed him, carrying a burlap bag with something of considerable weight. "Hold him."

In response the two men held Father Lazaro with his hands straight out at his sides.

"People were killed during those raids on the labs," Costanza said as he took the burlap bag from the third man. "I don't know if you were aware of this, but I want you to know it now. You took lives through another by interfering in my business. You might as well have killed those men yourself. What made you do this thing?"

The priest's answer was flat and irrefutable. "God. God made me do it."

Costanza laughed. "You really think He did, don't you?"

"Yes."

"It doesn't matter. Even He will quail before me when He sees the power I wield." Costanza took a battery-powered nail gun from the burlap bag and held it up for inspection. It glinted in the sunlight.

Perspiration and dust streaked Father Lazaro's face, muddy droplets sliding down his chin.

Costanza put the nail gun over the palm of the old man's right hand and looked the priest in the eye. "I've killed men." He squeezed the trigger, nailing the bony hand to the tree trunk.

Father Lazaro groaned with the pain.

"You've killed men." Costanza nailed the other hand to the other tree.

The men moved away and the priest hung there, fighting the pain. Blood ran down the exposed parts of his arms and dripped inside the black cloth. The nuns cried out.

"There are no truly innocent men here, Father," Costanza stated, dropping the nail gun onto the ground. "We're both killers, you and I, and we both have others do our killing for us. Our hands are covered in blood." He turned to walk away.

The old man's thin voice stopped him. "You must still believe, my son."

Costanza faced him. "I don't know what you're talking about, old man."

"It's simple. You didn't kill me. If you truly wished to invoke God's wrath, you would kill me."

"Wrong. I want you to live as a message to this man in black and Franco. I want them to know they're next." Costanza smiled. "As for God, He has done nothing to offend me."

The long dormant volcano rumbled as Costanza seated himself in the jeep. He smiled. One triumph was his already and the day had hardly begun. He was still smiling as the nuns clustered around the priest vanished from his view.

ESTEBAN ORTEGA MADE his final circuit of the congressional building in Bogotá at 2:47 p.m. From his position on the second story, staring over the railing through the immense hole in what would have been the middle half of the floor, he could see everything going on below.

Luis Costanza had already put in his appearance, taking his customary seat. Justice Minister Franco hadn't arrived yet.

Ortega drummed his fingers on the polished wooden railing and ignored the flow of pedestrian traffic around him. He was no stranger to the meetings— Costanza had brought him several times. His manners, ground into him at an early age by an overbearing mother, had even proved suitable for dining with the congressman during thousand-dollar-a-plate dinners.

He pushed away from the railing and walked toward the maintenance door. The bribes were already in place. He'd spent several thousands of Costanza's dollars this morning on the staff alone.

Once inside the maintenance room, feeling trapped with the miasma of odors from cleaning chemicals and polishes, he counted three steps to his left, then let his fingers find the grooved slots of the air-conditioning duct. The screws had been removed earlier, and the panel slid away easily.

Taking off his jacket, he hung it on a shelf full of linens, then pulled on a dark brown sweater and stocking mask. He eased into the air-conditioning duct. The building was old and the architects had been generous with crawl space.

Ortega's breathing became labored, clouded with the scent of dust. Crawling through another access panel, he made his way across the ceiling of the second floor, overlooking the first floor. He immediately discarded the idea of using the penflash he'd brought with him. Even its dim glow could be easily noticed by anyone who happened to look up at the right time.

The duct was a squared pool of light less than ten yards away. A dark, rectangular bulk was next to it. The ceiling vibrated with the noise from below, and he worried that it mightn't continue to support his weight even as he eased himself into a sitting position next to the rectangle. He unfastened the clasps by feel and assembled the rifle inside the same way, then paused to look through the duct.

The duct was almost a yard wide on all sides, permitting a view of the speaker's box in front of the assembly and below the board. No one was there yet, but the numbers had grown.

Ortega pulled back his shirtsleeve and glanced at the luminous numbers of his watch. It was 2:53 p.m. The rifle was a .30-30 bolt-action piece of a kind with which he was familiar. The clip held five rounds, four more than he knew he'd need. He whistled tunelessly as he finished the assembly, then leaned forward into a prone position, putting the rifle to one side until he needed it.

Five minutes later Benito Franco walked into the room and sat to one side of the podium. Ortega slipped his fingers through the trigger guard of the rifle and drew it toward him. Something cold, hard and heavy touched his cheek in warning. He froze immediately.

"I wouldn't," a voice advised.

Ortega didn't. He slid his hand from the weapon. Even though he'd never heard the voice before, he knew he'd been touched by the whisper of death. No one else's voice could have been so cold and still.

CHAPTER TWENTY-ONE

Franco was amazed at how calm he became as he addressed the congress. Until this moment his knees had shaken and his voice had cracked. He couldn't help thinking it was only the calm before the storm.

"My friends," he said, "I've come here today to set right a great wrong." He paused to let the reaction he'd expected ripple through the crowd. "There is among us a man we've taken to our hearts who has done nothing but betray us and our country. He has caused untold numbers of deaths, murders, rapes, robberies, suicides and abuses."

The conversation from the congress members became an audible force, rolling in like the waves of an ocean.

"This man," Franco went on, "has been responsible for taking the lives of individuals and families. He has destroyed, corrupted or condemned all within his power. And his destruction continues every day, swelling into even more staggering numbers."

Aides walked from their posts now, swarming quickly down the aisles to hand out the photocopied sheets Franco had ordered. The sound of rustling paper filled the hall.

"You hold in your hands a statement of income for the individual I'm about to name. Look at the amount of funds rolling through his hands. Look at where he banks. Here. Switzerland. The Bahamas. And these are only the known places, only the known accounts. It's business, but the empire that exists now was created from the coca leaf and uncounted lives. To grow, this business must destroy more lives."

The justice minister locked eyes with Luis Costanza for the first time. The narcobaron's gaze was cold, distant.

"The man's name isn't on those papers," Franco said. "Yet. I'm going to give that to you. Unless he chooses to defend himself."

Heads started to turn. Already connections between some of the property and businesses named were being made to Costanza. Others who had been held in his grip of corruption knew from experience.

Costanza stood, regal-looking despite the unspoken accusations. "You libel and slander me, Minister Franco, and I want you to know I'll hold you accountable for your actions."

"As I hold you accountable for yours." Franco was surprised at the fire in his voice thundering from the speakers.

Costanza made his way through the crowd to the podium set up for rebuttals and questions from members of congress. He tapped the microphone to make sure it was on. "Those papers are filled with nothing but lies. I demand that you retract your words."

"I'll do better than that," Franco promised. "I'll offer proof. Show me one lie in those papers. I stand ready to defend them all."

The papers fluttered in all directions as Costanza threw them into the air. "Lies."

"Only truths."

"I've built homes for the poor."

"And taken their lives in return."

"I've given money to churches."

"Only to purchase souls."

Placing his hands on either side of the podium, Costanza said, "You try to make me out as an evil man."

Franco shook his head slowly. "I'm only showing what is truly there."

"I've helped this country become what it is today. I have worked hard to make it be something we all could be proud of. I've provided jobs, money, dreams for the people of Colombia."

"Wrong. You've kept the impoverished impoverished, you've only laundered money you couldn't spend and you've only given nightmares, not dreams."

Costanza stood silent.

"This country wears two faces," Franco said. "One is of hope, the other is of ruin. This country is exotic, beautiful, a place for peaceful people. At the same time an undercurrent runs through her veins. Death, destruction and despair are all foundations for the sewer you've helped burden us with." He paused. "I hold that against you. I hold against you the deaths you've been responsible for, the dreams you've replaced only with horror, and the futures you've squandered while feeding your own needs and ego." He lowered his voice. "And most of all I hold against you the fact that you tried to take the lives of my family."

Shaking his head, Costanza turned to the other congressmen. "Don't you see what he's trying to do here? He's trying to invoke your sympathies by making even wilder accusations." He looked back at Franco. "Perhaps that's what I should do at this point, talk about how you've wronged *me*."

Franco said nothing. He knew how damning the silence could be, and he let it work for him.

Costanza's features purpled.

The justice minister could almost smell the desperation in the man. Bolan had been right. The narcobaron valued his seat in congress highly.

"You paint me as some evil monster, Minister, filled with endless depravity. Would a being as powerful as you make me out to be tolerate your existence? Would I, then, put up with listening to your unfounded accusations when I could simply have you killed instead?"

A metallic screech ripped through the building, punctuating Costanza's words. The duct cover overhead separated from the tiled ceiling, fluttering down to crash against the floor. Seconds later a body tumbled through, arms flailing wildly.

The congressmen attempted to duck, seeking shelter. Only Franco and Costanza remained standing.

A rope snapped taut around the man's ankle, leaving him swinging in wide arcs six feet from the open duct. Many people recognized Esteban Ortega and his connection to Costanza, and the man's name circulated the stunned floor.

Franco returned Costanza's dark gaze full measure. "You tried."

SAM WATERSTON STOOD on the street with a dead mike in his hand as Luis Costanza walked through the cordon of men protecting him. A crowd had gathered before the congressional building, hissing and booing at Costanza's passage. Some spit at him.

Waterston grabbed his cameraman's arm. "You better be getting this, Tommy, or I'm going to kick your ass all the way back to Medellín."

"I'm gettin' it, I'm gettin' it. Now let go of my goddamn arm or you're going to fuck everything up."

The reporter knew he was no longer objective about his assignment. He no longer cared. His side still ached from where the bullet had burned through. Some of the people who had died at his table had been close friends, despite the careless way they treated one another.

Costanza, defended by his men, made his way toward the white custom-made limousine pushing through the traffic. Another person spit at him, and was punched by one of his guards, starting a miniwar that dragged a half-dozen people down.

"Can you get his face?" Waterston asked.

"I got it, I got it."

"Good. That son of a bitch declared war on us. I want him to know he can't fuck with the American press the way he thinks he can and get away with it. The bastard'll be shit from the *Washington Post* on down to the *National Enquirer.*"

"Don't you think maybe you're blowing this out of proportion, Sam?"

"Shut up, kid. Just do your thing with the camera and let me be the brains of this outfit." Waterston glared at the departing limousine. "You just got this assignment, Tommy, and the reason you got it is the same reason a lot of people I cared about aren't here anymore. That bastard had them killed."

"So if everybody knows this guy did it, why isn't he locked up?" The cameraman stood up, unhunching his shoulders as he looked around briefly, then started taping again.

"Like the man said inside the building when Franco nailed him—parliamentary immunity. As long as he's a member of congress down here, they can't do a thing to him."

"So he's still able to run loose and do whatever he wants to."

"Not for long," Waterston said, touching his wounded side. "They're going to run him out of town on a rail if they get the chance. Franco just gave him his walking papers."

The cameraman nodded. "Makes you wonder, though."

"About what?"

"About whether or not a guy with that kind of power is going to go peaceably."

Waterston shook his head. "No. Costanza's a gutter boy. He'll go down fighting. It'll take a big, rough son of a bitch to kick his teeth down his throat before he even thinks of giving in. And he's got a goddamn army to back him up." The reporter glanced down at his side and found the wound bleeding through again. It didn't matter. He was staying with this story until it was wrapped.

SEETHING INSIDE, Costanza lifted one of the phones in the limousine and dialed Alexander Constantine's office number. When the secretary came on the line, he was put through immediately.

Constantine sounded panicked. "I thought we'd agreed you were never to call me here. You can never tell when they might have this line tapped."

"Shut up," Costanza snapped. The crowd swarmed around the car, slapping at the windows now, getting braver. "The DEA has gotten extradition papers on Ortega. I assume he'll be flown out of here tonight and brought into Miami tomorrow morning."

"Jesus, how did they—"

"Shut up. I want him out of jail. I need him here. There are too many things that need to be done in Medellín. Do you understand me?"

"Yeah, but I think—"

"Don't think. Let me think. You get him out of jail and back here by tomorrow evening."

"God, Luis, I don't know if I can promise you that. It depends on what they have him up on."

"I don't want a promise, Constantine. I want it done. Either do it or I find someone who can. And he'll get all my business in the future. I also want La Araña found. You have some of my money up there. Spread it around." He broke the connection.

The limousine had almost come to a stop against the press of people. "Run over them if they don't get out of your way," Costanza barked into the intercom. The driver nodded and accelerated. The poundings against the windows and sides became more fierce, but the crowd parted.

His next call was to an associate in Panama. "Jorge? Luis. Do you have some product on hand?"

"Yes, I do, but now isn't the time to try to unload here, you know?"

"I know. But we're going to unload it, anyway. Use the women. American soldiers are always ready to associate with the local women when they're away from home. Find someone greedy, find as many greedy someones as you can, and sell them what you have. If necessary, tell them you'll let them have it on consignment, that they can send the money back to you."

"You might as well give it to them, Luis. Even if they can pay for it, they'll never get into the States with it."

"Some will be foolish enough and greedy enough to try, believe me. And it'll add a sour note to this triumph they're claiming. Understand?"

"As you wish."

Costanza hung up. American servicemen carrying cocaine back into the United States would be a newsworthy item considering that country's journalistic tendencies to hang their dirty laundry before the world. It might even buy him some time before Colombia became infested with even more reporters smelling blood.

With Ortega's problem administered to, with the Panama situation thrown back into the news, Costanza turned to the matter of Benito Franco. He leaned back in the seat and placed his next call to Isaac Auerbach.

CHAPTER TWENTY-TWO

Mack Bolan leaned into the phone booth and watched the night people pass by while he waited for the connection. Shadows had claimed the city, followed by a light rain that left the streets glistening in the street light and car beams. Sixties rock and roll from the tavern across the street drifted to him, moody and blue. Then Barbara Price picked up the receiver at the other end.

"It's me," the warrior said.

"We were wondering about you."

Her voice sounded tough, resilient, and it helped move the confidence level up another notch. "I've been busy."

"That's what we'd heard. The stories about Ortega and Costanza have broken on several of the news stations. There's a reporter named Waterston in Medellín who's raking Costanza over the coals and producing confirmed reports of drug deals himself. Others are jumping on the bandwagon with stories of their own. Looks like you've got your snowball running downhill."

"Yeah, but the farther it goes, the less control you have over it. There comes a time when you just hang on and pray."

"That's what we're doing here."

Bolan shifted in the cubicle. People mingled at the front of the tavern, talking and laughing. "How much flak are you getting from the other agencies over the release of information?"

"Enough. Hal's handling it, though. He's got the Man backing his play, and right now nobody wants to rock the boat until they see how things turn out in Panama."

"And Stony Man?"

"We'll keep the lid on. That's our lookout. You take care of your business."

"I heard about the freighter sinking in Cartagena."

"You can thank Phoenix for that when you see them."

"When will that be?"

"According to Katz, probably sometime early tomorrow morning. They're having to stay to the road to keep a low profile. Any long-distance traveling by air on their part will draw immediate attention. We haven't been able to assemble visas, IDs or drop zones for them yet. He asked about Auerbach."

"I've seen him."

"And?"

"Auerbach's still operational." The inner sense moved restlessly. "Guy's got a lot of moves. I underestimated him this morning. I won't make the same mistake twice."

Price's voice hardened. "You're still alive. Chances are Auerbach won't make the same mistake twice, either."

"That's a way of looking at it."

An uncomfortable silence filled the receiver.

"About the press conference tomorrow..." Price began.

"Franco won't back out of it. He's right. If he doesn't force the issue now, shake up the system Costanza is using to keep the city in check, make people wonder how much evidence he has, and Costanza will start covering up."

"He's taking a big chance."

"Yeah."

"Costanza may opt for elimination rather than a cover-up. Money has a way of outlasting political clout."

"Franco knows. That's one of the reasons he's moving on."

"Phoenix should be in Medellín by then. I wish there was more I could do."

Bolan changed subjects. He'd already done as much as he could to ensure the justice minister's safety tomorrow. There hadn't been much to work with. "Ortega should be arriving in Miami in the morning."

"At 9:13 a.m. I've already checked. U.S. marshals are scheduled to pick him up. Hal's riding shotgun on the operation himself. The Dade County D.A.'s going to try to get Ortega to roll over on Costanza. Maybe we can work on an extradition angle and apply some more political pressure from the U.S. A lot of the local law-enforcement people aren't happy about the idea of cutting Ortega free because of the policemen he killed there. Hal's posting a guard over Ortega to make sure he doesn't 'accidentally' hang himself while he's in jail."

"Any news on Able?"

"Leo and the boys are running into some strong interference trying to turn up Lyons or La Araña, both from Costanza's people and locals who might be involved. It doesn't look good."

"If he's anywhere in Miami, they'll find him."

"I know. I keep telling myself that."

"Stay hard, Barb."

"You, too." She broke the connection.

Bolan clenched his fist on the receiver, thinking about all the different fronts the Stony Man teams were forced to fight on to attempt the takedown of Costanza. And when it all was said and done, that's what it amounted to—an attempt. There were no guarantees, no promises, only a scattered handful of hopes.

He hung up the receiver and started across the four-lane street. Tall buildings surrounded him, lighted windows housing private worlds. Cars passed by him, their tires swishing on the pavement.

Without warning the shrill scream of a motorcycle's four-stroke engine roared to life. The warrior wheeled, reaching under his denim jacket as a solitary high beam singled him out. The bike bore down on him, the familiar bark of an Ingram subgun shattering the night.

RAIN FELL in a fine mist from the moonless sky. Father Lazaro paused, taking his hat from his head to turn his face up. The moisture left his hair wet, chilled him, but it refreshed him and gave him the strength to go on. God's tears, he'd called the rain upon occasion in his messages to his children. Now maybe it was so. There was a real evil upon the land, an evil that knew no bounds and had no heart. It had surprised him to learn how truly dark and powerful that evil was, and that he'd never seen it for what it was.

He clamped his hat back on, the movement made awkward by the thick bandages on his hands. They were no longer as white as when Sister Yanett had bound the holes in his palms. Red mud and wine-colored blood stained them now. In places the tape had started to peel back because of the humidity and his rough use of his hands in spite of the pain. He smoothed the loose pieces of tape back down as best he could. Then, gathering the reins of the donkey he alternately rode and led, he went on.

The way became harder. The hills became steeper. He held out in hopes that the way down to Medellín would start soon. He prayed constantly that he wouldn't be too late.

The sisters had argued with him as he'd packed the donkey to leave the church. They'd wanted him to let someone younger make the trip to warn Justice Minister Franco and the man in black. When they'd seen that he wouldn't change his mind or be swayed from his chosen course, they'd prayed for him, then helped him pack.

The earth trembled with a swelling vibration.

He fell onto the slick grass, catching himself on his injured hands. The pain crumpled him to the ground, anyway. He lay on his back for a moment as the agony rolled over him.

He knew it was the volcano. It simmered and toiled, readying itself for the day when the earth could no longer contain its fury.

Recognizing hunger pains amid the wild discomforts of his stomach from the cancer, he paused beside the pack animal and reached into the sack the sisters had given him and took out an apple. He bit into it, relishing the tart taste of it, then chewed slowly as he continued on.

He needed no light, no compass, no maps. He'd grown up here, studying the land as a younger man, sometimes spending hours from the church in times when he had questioned his faith. But he had wrestled those demons of uncertainty to the ground long ago. The world was filled with evils and men of God were needed to defeat them. If he had met a man like Luis Costanza earlier in his life, he'd have known this to be a fact even sooner.

A shadow stepped out from a tree, brandishing an assault rifle. A flashlight flicked on, blinding Father Lazaro. He turned his head away but didn't move his hands. It hadn't taken long to realize the night patrols around the jungle labs were unprofessional and fearfully jumped at any sound. Sometimes they killed only each other.

"Father," a quiet male voice said.

Father Lazaro looked back toward the flashlight. "Fico?"

"Yes."

The flashlight beam dropped to the ground, then extinguished. "What are you doing here, Fico?"

"I work here, Father."

"For Costanza?"

"It's work. My brothers and sisters go hungry if I don't help out."

"And you help out by carrying a gun? You're hardly more than a boy yourself."

"But I draw a man's wages." Fico seemed uncomfortable. "It hasn't been easy since Papa died."

"I know."

"I help any way that I can."

"I'll pray for you and your family for God's blessing, Fico."

The youth inclined his head, keeping the weapon across his chest in both hands. "Thank you, Father." He looked up, eyes bright in the darkness. "What brings you here at this time of night?"

"I'm going to Medellín on personal business."

"And it couldn't wait until morning?"

"No."

"This is a restricted area, Father."

"I see that now, my son. They're never clearly marked."

Fico's smile flashed in the darkness. "But I can get you through, no problem." He reached for the walkie-talkie belted at his waist.

"Thank you," he said, and led his donkey in the direction the youth pointed.

BARBARA PRICE PACKED quickly and efficiently. Only overnight items went into the carryon bag, as well as a fistful of makeup, a pocket recorder, pencils, pens and legal pads. The file on Alexander Constantine went into her briefcase. She looked around the small bedroom that she maintained at the main house at Stony Man Farm, wondering if there was anything she'd forgotten.

She took two suits from the closet, choosing from business attire rather than anything glamorous. Then she packed them neatly in a garment bag, zipped it up and laid it on top of the carryon.

"Knock, knock."

Price looked up and saw Kurtzman in the hallway outside the open door. "Come in."

The big man rolled his wheelchair inside the room. He looked worn and haggard, like a frayed and lumpy teddy bear.

She almost smiled at the thought. "Is it raining in Miami?"

"Beats me."

She took the trench coat from the closet, deciding it was better to be safe than sorry. "Who's minding the store?"

"Willis."

"Finally decided to let him do what he's getting paid for?"

"After I saw you leave with that familiar determined gleam in your eye."

She laughed. "And what do you know about determined eye gleams, familiar or not?"

Kurtzman spread his hands. "About a lot of people, not much. About you, I could write the book."

"You think so?"

"Yeah." He shifted in the wheelchair. "You wear your heart on your sleeve, lady."

"That's not a very safe place for it, now, is it?"

"Nope, but it cuts through a lot of bullshit, and if the wrong guy reaches for it, chances are he'll draw back a nub."

"So what are you doing here?"

"My bit for cutting through the bullshit."

"Meaning?"

"Meaning I know you made arrangements for a flight to Miami with one of the pilots just a few minutes after getting the phone call from Striker."

"Ortega's supposed to land in Miami tomorrow morning," she said. "I intend to be there."

"Why?"

"Mack went to a lot of trouble to put Ortega on ice. Franco risked his life. We know from the tap on his line that Alexander Constantine is supposed to represent Ortega for Costanza. I don't want to take the chance that Ortega will slip through our fingers because Constantine knows the right judges and prosecutors to grease."

"So you figure to take the guy on before he gets Ortega into the courts."

Price shook her head. "I'm not taking Constantine on. I'm taking him down."

Kurtzman nodded. "This guy isn't a clown, Barb. He makes his money dangerously. He won't think twice about getting tough with you."

"I know his type," she said as she gathered her things. "He's not as tough as you think. I used to be married to a guy a lot like him."

Kurtzman's eyebrows rose in surprise.

The trench coat folded neatly over her arm, she picked up her baggage. "Didn't know that?"

"No."

"I thought you might have peeked at my files."

Kurtzman shook his head. "I might make my living sifting through other people's dirt, but I don't prep myself for friends."

"Sorry."

Kurtzman shrugged. "You might consider taking a gun while you're down there, kid, in case some of Costanza's people object to your talking to Constantine."

"I don't carry weapons." Price regretted the harshness in her voice. It was a decision she'd made long ago, and it hadn't been easy. "Hal knows why. I'm a thinker, a political person who gets the job done with a word here, a nudge there. I don't do trench warfare. Doesn't mean I can't get my job done."

"I know." Kurtzman rolled out of the room.

Price followed him out and locked the door.

"You be careful down there, Barb."

She showed him her dimples despite the feelings of unease coursing through her. "Bet the Farm on it, guy."

"And if you need anything..."

"I'll call."

"Right."

Price left him behind, knowing she'd created a lot of questions in his mind. Before she reached the end of the hallway, her thoughts were squarely on Miami.

MACK BOLAN THREW himself to one side as the motorcycle whipped toward him. Slugs from the subgun chewed a ragged line of pockmarks in the pavement just behind him. He skidded on the street, dodging cars that suddenly braked to avoid him. He checked his forward motion with his free hand, swiveling his head to take in the other motorcycle team bearing down on him as he rolled under a stalled flatbed.

Forty-five-caliber bullets dug into the meat of the flatbed's tires. They collapsed immediately, sagging the weight lower. The warrior got to his feet on the other side, fisting the Desert Eagle in a two-handed grip.

The first motorcycle team completed a one-eighty in the stalled traffic, wavering for a moment before acceleration set them right again.

Crouched in a Weaver stance, the Executioner drew target acquisition on the cyclist as the bike roared between the line of cars toward him. He squeezed the trigger twice, keeping the sights centered on the biker's black face shield. He got an impression of Plexiglas exploding, then the motorcycle fell over, colliding with a car and spinning out of control.

The passenger staggered to his feet, the Ingram spewing death.

Bolan caressed the trigger again, sending another pair of 240-grain hollowpoints on their way. The twin impacts lifted the shooter from his feet and threw him onto the hood of a car.

Sparks flared from the iron frame of the flatbed as long splinters were gouged out by bullets from the second team. The Executioner dropped to a squatting position as he made his way to the front of the truck. He lost the cycle team for a moment, unable to find them in the maze of automobiles. Vehicles started up again in frantic motion, trying to get out of the death zone.

Hearing the motorcycle again, Bolan spotted it heading for the sidewalk, scattering people from in front of the tavern as it jumped the curb. He sprinted for the sidewalk himself, angling for a position that would put him forty feet from the cycle team.

Breaking free of his cover, Bolan took a side-on position to the cycle team, dropping the .44 into target acquisition. The motorcycle roared to life as he opened fire. The passenger's Ingram spit flame, but the Executioner stood his ground, firing until he emptied the Desert Eagle's clip, watching as the slugs struck home.

Out of control with a dead man at the wheel, the motorcycle slammed into the low wall of a department store, the bodies crashing through the bay window.

The empty magazine dropped onto the pavement between the warrior's feet. He rammed a fresh one home, snapping the slide back as he extended the weapon.

One of the bodies lay still. The other groped frantically for the dropped MAC-10, bringing it up as the guy fought his way to his feet.

Bolan put a single round through the helmet and dropped the corpse into the darkness. Not wasting time, knowing Costanza's men had to have followed him from the safehouse occupied by Franco and his family, the Executioner entered the nearest alley. The address was only a few blocks away. He ran, keeping the .44 in his hand.

CHAPTER TWENTY-THREE

The bar made Martin Flynn uneasy. It was rough-hewn, built by careless hands. The walls were a dull yellow that seemed bright compared to the rainy night outside. Crooked pictures hung from nails, depicting bullfights and fighting cocks. He would have bet that all of the dozen or so round wooden tables had known the bite of some kind of knife.

Even with the .38 tucked into the back of his waist-band, Flynn felt threatened. He was grateful Sharon had agreed to wait in the hotel room for them. The gym bag in his left hand carried the cash and drew the attention of many of the men lounging at the long wooden bar. Flynn turned to Virgil Bell only to find the guy surveying the interior of the bar with an air of amusement.

"What a dive," Bell said derisively as he stared at the walls. He looked at Flynn. "Can you believe this? I feel like we've been dropped into the middle of a seedy little Sam Peckinpah movie. I keep expecting William Holden or Ernest Borgnine to come busting through the door with a .45 in each hand."

Resisting the urge to slap some sense into his companion, Flynn replied, "Get a grip. This isn't exactly fun and games here."

Bell smiled maliciously. "Sure it is. You've just gotta be in the proper frame of mind."

"I'm not."

"That's your problem, buddy." Bell smiled again. "Me, I came down here to soak up a little sun, drink a little vino, eat a little cheese, get a little wild with the ladies and score a lot of dope."

"Christ." Flynn looked around and discovered that the bar's interest in them hadn't lessened. "Why don't you announce it to the whole fucking bar?"

"We did that the minute we walked in here." Bell took a table in the corner and laid his wet windbreaker on an empty chair.

Seeing the dark polished gleam of Bell's gun butt peeking up from his waistband, Flynn crawled in on the other side of the table and said, "Your gun's showing."

Bell shrugged. "You're getting hyper. Relax. Even if they do see it, it'll only tell them that we're serious gringos and that they'd better watch their asses around us."

Flynn kept his own coat on, shivering from the cold and the fear that had gripped him since they'd left the hotel room. Cashing the cashier's check had been no problem. He'd used his father's bank, had even gone through a bank officer his father had introduced him to during one of his infrequent visits to the country. The man had been only too happy to help. The .38 was a solid and uncomfortable weight at his back. He put the gym bag on the seat beside him. One of the waitresses approached them.

"Can I get you something to drink?" she asked in an alcohol-roughened voice.

Bell held up two fingers. *"Cerveza."*

When the waitress moved away, Flynn leaned across the table. "We're not here to drink, damn it."

"Listen, pal, if we don't drink, if we don't act like we're not relaxed, you might as well wear a sign that says I'm Itching to Do This Dope Deal So I Can Go Home."

Flynn cursed under his breath as he leaned back. The pistol gouged his back and forced him to change position. He kept his right hand on the gym bag.

The waitress brought the bottles of beer and set them on the table along with a bowl of tortilla chips and sauces. Bell paid her, adding a modest tip.

Flynn couldn't help wondering if it was because Bell didn't want to draw attention to the money they might or might not have, or if the guy was just that cheap. He opted for cheap. Bell loved attention.

Crunching a tortilla chip, Bell leaned forward and winked conspiratorially. "Know who I feel like right now?"

Before Flynn could hazard a guess a man pushed away from the bar and ambled over. The man was large, with a big belly straining at the buttons of his shirt. A long, flowing mustache drooped from his round, florid face. He looked at Flynn. "Señor Bell?"

Bell leaned forward. "Me."

The man switched his attention at once.

Flynn couldn't ignore the sour smell that emanated from the man. For a moment he thought the combination of odor and his own nervous tension was going to make him sick.

"We have business, no?" the man asked.

"Yes."

"Come with me."

Bell rose from the table, taking a final drink from his beer. "Be right back, buddy." He clapped Flynn on the shoulder.

Biting back on the impulse to tell Bell not to go, Flynn watched them cross the floor and walk into the bathroom. His eyes dropped automatically to his watch, logging the time. When two minutes had passed, he was unable to restrain the nervous energy that filled him. He got up, fisted the straps of the gym bag and started for the bathroom.

The waitress met him halfway across the floor. "Can I get you something else?"

He looked down at her, trying to be polite. "No, thank you."

"Something to eat perhaps?"

Using his hand to move her out of his way, he stepped past, hearing sounds of a scuffle before he reached the door. Flynn dipped his hand under his jacket and withdrew the .38 as he stepped through the doorway. His hands shook as he leveled the weapon.

The big man had one hand around Bell's throat. The other gripped a wicked-edged knife.

"Stop!" Flynn ordered. If he hadn't been so scared, he knew he'd have been embarrassed about the way his voice had cracked.

The man looked over his shoulder. Bell fought weakly, blood trickling from a slice along one cheek as his feet dangled above the floor.

Flynn thumbed back the hammer, aiming at the man's face. "Back off! Now, goddamn it, or you're history!" It was a struggle to keep his arms from shaking.

The man released Bell, who collapsed into a heap. "Okay, okay, don't shoot."

"Put the knife on the floor."

The blade clanked against the cracked tile.

"You okay, Virgil?"

Bell struggled to his feet, groping for something in the dark corner and coming up with his gun. "Yeah. The bastard took me by surprise. I didn't figure on him moving so damn quick." He massaged his neck and tried to clear his throat.

"Is this the guy we were supposed to do business with?"

Bell shook his head. "No. I thought Juan might have sent him since he knew my name."

"Where's your guy?"

"I don't know."

The bathroom door opened.

Flynn stepped back so that he could cover the door and the man.

A skinny Colombian stepped around the door and smiled. "Ah, Virgil, I see you've been keeping yourselves entertained while you waited for me."

"Juan, where the hell have you been?"

· The man shrugged. "Business, amigo, same as you, but I ran a little late. There have been some problems."

"I'll say there have." Bell sounded indignant, showing none of the fear he'd displayed only a moment ago.

"What am I supposed to do with this guy?" Flynn asked, incredulous that neither Bell nor the Colombian were taking any further notice of his prisoner.

"You have your choice, amigo," Juan told him. "You can kill him here for attempting to rob you, or you may let him go."

"He'll follow us."

"Not if we take his clothes," Bell said. "All right, asshole, out of those clothes." He waved his pistol meaningfully.

Completely confused as to how to feel now, Flynn watched in stunned disbelief as the man did as he was ordered.

"Now kick them over here," Bell said. When the man did, he gathered them under one arm and smiled. "Stupid bastard, this'll teach you to bring a knife to a gunfight."

Flynn thumbed the hammer down on the .38 as he tucked it back into his waistband. He backed out of the door, following Juan. All eyes were on them as they left the bar and clambered into Juan's ten-year-old Cadillac. The two Americans took the back seat with the gym bag between them. Juan slid behind the wheel and screeched the tires as they took off into the night.

"What's the problem you were talking about?" Bell asked.

"I haven't got your cocaine." Juan kept an eye on the traffic, checking the rearview mirror constantly.

Made nervous by the man's actions, Flynn checked to see if they were being followed. Nothing caught his immediate attention.

"So where is it?" Bell demanded. "We had a deal, Juan, and the last thing I need after going through what I just went through is a sob story and a hand job."

"No, no. No hand job, amigo. You'll get your product. It'll just take a little longer. There've been problems with the source."

"I don't want to hear about the price going up, either, or we'll take our money and run."

"Hey, does this look like the face of a man who'd let you down?" Juan presented his profile.

Flynn took the question under advisement. The money in the gym bag was becoming more burden than financial freedom. "How did that guy know us back there?"

Juan shrugged. "All I can say is that I knew of your friend before he knew of me. The street people knew he was looking to make a deal."

Bell didn't say anything.

Juan returned his attention to driving, pulling back into his own lane as the car swerved erratically. "I'll have the cocaine for you in the morning. I swear on my sainted mother's grave."

Sitting back in the seat, Bell asked, "Where?"

"In front of Medellín's Houses for the Poor. Do you know where that is?"

Bell looked at Flynn, who nodded. His father's firm had done part of the construction for Luis Costanza. "Yes."

"Tomorrow morning, then. At 10:00 a.m. They're having a meeting that will draw a large crowd. It'll be the perfect place to finish our transaction. Okay?"

"Okay." Bell smiled.

Unable to escape the wet chill that clung to him, Flynn pulled his jacket tighter around him, staring through the rain-dappled windows and wondering what tomorrow would bring. He asked himself if financial freedom was really worth all the risks they were taking, but his ghostly reflection had no answers for him.

"COSTANZA'S MEN HAVE the house staked," Bolan said as he closed the van door behind him.

Grimaldi and McPherson sat in the bucket seats up front. They looked at him. "What makes you think that, Sarge?" the pilot asked.

The Executioner shrugged out of the denim jacket, shoved a finger through the hole in the back that had been made by a .45-caliber bullet, then held it up for inspection. "A couple of teams followed me to the phone."

McPherson shifted in his seat. "Where are they now?"

"They're going to be a couple of teams short whenever they choose to make their move. Now we know for sure our security's been penetrated. All that remains to be seen is how badly we've been compromised."

The Mountie nodded. "With the number of agencies working this, it's not surprising. From what I've seen of Franco, he's a man who knows when he's got his claws in deep. They know it, too. They'll wait until the time is right.''

Bolan lifted a thermos from the floor and poured himself a cup of coffee. "Pass a warning among your men. The people lying in wait out there might try to whittle the numbers down some before morning. Have your people stayed paired up. They won't try an attack on the house at this point because it's too uncertain and too costly. I'll check in with Sigfrido next.''

Drumming his fingers on the steering wheel, Grimaldi asked, "So when do you think they'll try to take him?''

"Tomorrow morning. If Franco decides to do the speech, Costanza knows we'll have to move him out into the open.''

"Do you think Franco will press on after he finds out about this?" McPherson asked.

Bolan didn't even have to think about his answer. "Yeah, because at this point he doesn't feel like he has a choice. And you can bet Costanza knows that, too.'' He finished his coffee and dropped the cup into a trash bag, shrugging into another jacket for the brief meeting he planned with the DAS man. Then he stepped out into the night, leaving the silence of the van but carrying the mood with him. At this point none of them had any choices. He, Franco and Costanza were the focal points of a storm of violence that was about to erupt over the city.

And there were no sure bets on this one that there would be any survivors.

CHAPTER TWENTY-FOUR

Outfitted in jeans, tennis shoes, a flannel shirt, Kevlar vest and a yellow windbreaker with DAS markings, Mack Bolan blended in with the crowd that had come to listen to Justice Minister Benito Franco speak against the great evil strangling Medellín and the whole of Colombia. Almost three thousand people had turned out to hear him. They stood in the sections of the cross streets before a group of whitewashed Medellín Homes for the Poor. It was a sea of humanity spread across lawns and sidewalks, spilling out past the red-and-white barricades police had set up. Uniformed officers moved through the crowd constantly. As Bolan watched, some of the policemen broke off and moved the barricades farther back, trying to contain the growing crowd within the imposed barriers. Men, women and children—all had turned out to hear the man who'd captured their attention with his damning accusations of Luis Costanza, who'd been thought by many to be a great and good man. Conversations were a low rumble, like the grumblings of distant thunder fast approaching, pierced only occasionally by the impatient screams of a baby or the laughter of children.

An air of expectation had settled over the crowd, and Bolan felt it crackling around him like electricity. The morning was filled with possibilities, and everyone participating in today's event knew it.

Reaching up, he adjusted the radio headset he wore and scanned through the frequencies the security teams were using. The check-ins and confirmations trickled in like a never-ending litany. He pulled at the straps of the shoulder holster carrying the Desert Eagle under his left arm. The early-morning moisture hadn't burned off yet, and steam filled his clothing, making the leather chafe. He carried a CAR-15 slung over his left shoulder, but even that didn't make passage through the crowd any easier. There were dozens of armed men among them now. One more didn't matter. His pockets were heavy with spare magazines. More rode in ammo bags secured to the Kevlar vest and loosely covered by the windbreaker.

He looked toward the stage where Franco would speak, noting more than a dozen news vans resembling small metal islands amid the overflow of people. Cameramen were set up on top of the vehicles as they conferred with the reporters. No news helicopters had been allowed. The only two in the air belonged to the Colombian police.

The stage had been erected the previous afternoon and had been under constant guard since then. It was nothing more than wooden planks with an armor-reinforced speaker's podium wide enough for Franco to take cover in if there was time. Tangled cables of different microphones looked like a huge twist of spaghetti clinging to the front of the podium. Those were being checked by yellow-jacketed DAS electronic men now, making sure they worked properly and didn't hide anything lethal.

Behind it, almost directly in front of a large billboard proclaiming Medellín's Houses for the Poor, were the first of the buildings Costanza had donated to the city. They'd been constructed on the steep slopes, cutting into—but leaving more or less intact—the elegant and verdant jungle behind. The landscaping was impeccable, also donated by Costanza, serving to keep the jungle at bay while maintaining a beautiful view of it.

Bolan kept in motion, seeking in vain to work off the nervous energy that filled him. This wasn't his kind of operation. There were no controls for him, no absolutes. He was painfully aware of being just as much of a spectator as the people around him. He tightened his grip on the CAR-15's strap and worked the middle perimeters of the crowd, staying within a hundred yards of the stage, head and shoulders above most of the people around him. Grimaldi spotted him at the same time he saw the pilot.

Grimaldi carried an assault rifle and was decked out in one of the DAS jackets, too. A pair of stained plastic coffee cups were in his hands, and he offered one to Bolan. "I thought I was going to have to ask for a police escort to bring the coffee through." He peeled off the lid. "If you want cream and sugar, you'll have to get it yourself. I'm not going back again."

Bolan shook his head, unable to respond to the humor underlying the pilot's words. Responsibilities and the dangers of his war lay too heavily on him. Kevlar or no Kevlar, Franco was strapping on a bull's-eye when he took the podium today. And there was no denying the Executioner's involvement with the man's meteoric rise in the eyes of his countrymen, and in putting him in the danger zone where he now lived his life.

"There was no way around it, Sarge," Grimaldi said softly without looking at him. "With the stranglehold Costanza's got on this country, you could've spent months here chipping away at his operations. Hell, we all could have—you, me, Able and Phoenix—and never been as close to shutting Costanza down as Franco is."

"I know."

"And we could never have stirred up the desire for a better life in these people the way he has. Look at these people, Mack. Have you ever seen expressions like this before?"

"I know."

Abruptly the electronics men cleared the area. A man in a gray suit came forward and spoke into the microphones in English and Spanish. "Ladies and gentlemen, I give you Justice Minister Benito Franco."

Franco stepped onto the stage with a bright smile. The suit had been tailored so that even Bolan's trained eye had trouble discerning the Kevlar body armor. He waved as the audience came to sudden life. The applause was thunderous, drowning out all other sounds. Small children were raised to sit on their parents' shoulders so that they could see. When quiet descended on the crowd again, Franco began to speak.

ALEXANDER CONSTANTINE'S law office was everything Barbara Price had imagined it would be. The waiting room spoke of pretentious elegance, good taste and wealth. Filled with real plants, plush furniture, a wall-screen television, oil paintings and a broad choice of magazines, it seemed more like a showplace than a working environment. The carpet matched the decor and the color of the walls. The secretary was a redhead with a New Wave hairdo and even, white teeth. Her skimpy dress was made of neon-yellow spandex with matching yellow see-through hose clearly visible on the visitor's side of the glass-and-steel desk.

"Can I help you?" the secretary asked in a sultry voice.

Price couldn't help noticing that the voice was the same practiced come-on her husband's secretary had had years ago, the same secretary he'd had an affair with. She squelched the memories even though being here brought them roiling back. Kevin had been out of her life for a long time. She wanted to keep it that way. "No," she replied as she headed for the door.

"Hey, you can't go in there." The secretary stood, all the sultriness gone from her voice.

Price opened her Justice ID and flashed it at the younger woman. "Sit down and be a good girl." She gave her a false, pretty smile. "And just maybe you won't have any of the problems I'm handing out today spill over on you."

The secretary sat.

The second room was filled with legal books and three desks. Only one of them was occupied, and the woman glanced up. "You're not supposed to be back here," she said, getting up from her chair.

Price ignored her and made for the door on the left. It had Constantine's name on it in small bronze letters.

"Hey, lady, did you hear what I said?"

"Yes," Price replied as she twisted the knob and entered Constantine's private office.

The lawyer was on the phone, feet up on the desk as he slumped back in his chair. His shirtsleeves were rolled to midforearm, exposing his gold watch and a healthy tan. His free hand squeezed an orange-and-yellow tennis ball. Not a single blond hair was out of place.

"Mr. Constantine," the legal researcher said as she rushed into the room, "I tried to stop her, but she barged in here, anyway. I don't know why Steffi let her walk through."

The lawyer leaned forward, saying, "Frank, something's come up. Let me get back to you later." He replaced the receiver as he sat up straight in the swivel chair. He looked at the research assistant. "Get security up here."

"Yes, sir." The woman turned and hurried back to her room.

Price showed him her ID. "I wouldn't," she advised softly, "unless you're ready to take the heat."

THERE WAS NO MISTAKING the passion in Benito Franco's words. Bolan felt the same electric intensity in the crowd that had been generated by other men he could remember hearing—John F. Kennedy, Dr. Martin Luther King, perhaps a handful of others. All had made themselves heard at crucial periods of American history, and the effects—as this time—had been larger than the man behind those words. Behind the impassioned plea Franco was making lurked the urgent press of emotion, saying that if changes were to be made, the time was now.

Silence, except for the justice minister's ringing voice, held sway over the people. They listened. Even the children stopped what they were doing to pay attention.

"Friends," Franco's amplified voice thundered out, "I've come here today not as your minister, but as your neighbor. Together, we work hard to manage a living for our families. We work even harder to make dreams come true for our children and our loved ones."

Bolan scanned the crowd, knowing he could only react to a threat. As a bodyguard, he was trapped into responding to an action rather than initiating one. His flannel shirt was damp, clinging to him in spite of the coolness of the breeze circulating through the crowd.

"But there is a man in our community," Franco continued, "who has bled you and your families dry of hopes for years. This man has been a viper we have clasped to our breasts. We have believed his lies. We have held his untruths as gospel. In return he has given us crumbs from his plate." Franco pointed to the whitewashed houses behind him. "These are part of those crumbs."

A murmur ran through the crowd, low and vibrant as excitement flared through them. Heads nodded in agreement. Cameras mounted on the vans surrounded by the press of the crowd turned to play over the faces.

"Crumbs," Franco repeated. "The whitewash on those buildings might well have been applied over the black heart of the man I speak of." He paused. "These homes weren't even furnished in the hopes of forgiveness. Wanting forgiveness is something that has never crossed his mind. Forgiveness would mean that this person has stopped his trespasses against us. He hasn't.

They grow in number every day, and they grow ever more violent and costly. I often ask myself where it will end." Franco swept his gaze across the crowd. "And I find I cannot say. That's the thing that pains me most. There's nothing so horrifying as to look into your future and see only suffering."

A shuffling movement through the crowd drew Bolan's attention. He shifted, bringing the man into clearer view, recognizing him at once as Father Lazaro. "Jack," he said softly as he started through the crowd. There was no mistaking the disheveled appearance of the priest. The people parted reluctantly before the man, but there was no ignoring the cloth. The warrior found the way harder as he plotted a path that would bring him to the priest's side. Grimaldi followed close behind.

"In return for these buildings," Franco said, "in return for the generous amounts given to the coffers of the churches of our city, this man takes from us our dignity, our dreams, the futures of our children... and even our very lives."

"Father Lazaro," Bolan called as he neared the man.

The priest turned to face him, his eyes bloodshot and feverish. His clothes were torn and dirty. A gray pallor crouched under his skin. "You. The man in black."

"Yes."

Father Lazaro made his way back through the crowd.

Bolan noticed the bloody bandages on the priest's hands as they met. "What happened?"

"Costanza," the priest replied as he shook his head. "But that isn't important. What is important is that you and Franco know your lives are in danger. He hunts you now. He knows I gave you information about the jungle labs, and he's become like an animal, wanting only blood as his revenge. I must warn Franco.''

"He knows. We're watching over him.''

The priest pointed to the podium. "He's a target like this. Nothing more.''

Bolan shook his head. "No. He's more than that now. He represents the hope of these people.''

The priest removed his hat. His voice was solemn when he spoke. "And if he falls, he'll only be another martyr to mourn.''

Bolan couldn't disagree.

MARTIN FLYNN COULDN'T believe the number of people who'd come to listen to the speaker. He stood with Bell and Sharon on the outer fringes of the crowd, waiting for Juan to show up with their cocaine. The sight of the armed policemen shifting back and forth through the mass of humanity unnerved him. Visions of the bloody military movies he'd seen as a teenager kept running through his head in endless loops. He knew, at least cinematically, what a burst from an assault rifle could do to a person. He folded his arms across his chest as he glanced up at the circling helicopters, wondering if the men up there would radio the ground teams to pick them up if they saw the deal go down.

Sharon crowded in close to him, wrapping her arms around his waist. He carried the .38 in the pocket of his windbreaker today, in a readier position than last night. He blinked and yawned, more tired than he would have believed possible in a nerve-racking moment like this.

Bell moved closer, a cigarette dangling from one corner of his mouth. He checked his watch, then glanced at the podium. "I've been hearing all morning long how this sucker's probably going to be wasted before tonight." He shook his head in amused perplexity. "Goddamn country's main source of income and he's up there preaching against it."

Flynn didn't bother to reply. Bell had his own crazy, mixed-up perceptions of the world, and there was no use in arguing. Always before their group had enjoyed Bell's views on life because they were usually a 180 degrees opposite what was considered the norm. Now he felt jaded, irritated at the narrowness of Bell's mind. Flynn had given up a lot of fantasies before the sun had come up this morning, and he'd shared them with Sharon. He couldn't tell if it had made a difference in her mind. He'd been too wrapped up in his own self-discoveries, but she hadn't seemed to take this meet today with the same lightness.

"Hey," Bell said with a fresh smile, "here comes our boy now."

Flynn shoved his hand into his windbreaker pocket and stepped in front of Sharon. The gym bag full of money rested at his feet.

"Hey, *muchachos,*" Juan said, smiling. Bell exchanged a high-five with him, drawing the attention of only a few people around them. "My vehicle is over there."

Reluctantly Flynn followed the procession to a weathered Chevy van parked against the curb. He kept hold of Sharon's hand with the same hand that carried the gym bag. The other remained on the .38. He watched Juan and his companion closely. The speaker's words hammered like thunder.

"Cocaine is killing us and our children. We know it and we allow it to happen. We step over bodies now on our way to work and think this is normal. We listen to gunfire in our streets and thank God nothing is happening to us. We cower, we scrounge, we live without. Friends, we live every day in fear for our lives. Yet we do nothing about it."

The pain, sorrow and desperation in the speaker's voice was painfully evident to Flynn. He was torn between looking at Bell and Juan or looking at the stage. Glancing toward the speaker, he saw Sharon looking over her shoulder, too.

"Hey," Bell called out, "this stuff's the real thing. Pay the man, Marty, and let's be on our way."

Sharon squeezed Flynn's arm. He raised the gym bag and gave it to Bell, who swapped it for a backpack.

"A pleasure doing business with you," Juan said, touching his fingers to his hat in a salute. Bell jumped to the ground outside the van and nodded. He gave the backpack to Flynn. The van reversed and pulled back onto the street.

A silence, terrible and swift, drifted over the crowd as the speaker regarded them.

Drawn by the emotion emanating from the words, Flynn settled the backpack over his shoulder and walked back into the crowd with Sharon close behind.

"Hey, buddy," Bell said, "where do you think you're going? The hotel's back this way. We need to be at your old man's business in a couple of hours. With the traffic, we could have some problems, you know."

Flynn ignored him, hanging on the speaker's words, acutely aware of the cocaine he carried. He wondered why he wasn't afraid of the policemen. He'd dreaded this moment the whole morning, envisioned all kinds of scenes where they were all caught.

"Today, neighbors," the speaker at last continued, "today is the day we do something about it." He held up a clenched fist. "Today we gather and we strike Luis Costanza's name from our list of citizens. Today we start rejecting the white poison he pumps through our streets. Today is the beginning of our triumph!"

The crowd hooted and screamed its approval. Franco's name became a roar that gathered intensity, coming faster, stronger. The sound of clapping drowned out all other noise. Hats flew into the air.

Flynn watched, hypnotized by the strength of the emotional charge firing the people around him, amazed at the expressions on their faces.

Then an explosion went off on stage, throwing the man away from the podium as planks and splinters erupted into the air.

THE EXECUTIONER UNSLUNG the CAR-15, a yell of warning dying in his throat as he saw the wreckage of the stage. A half-dozen men in DAS windbreakers raced toward Franco, who lay unmoving. Screams of rage, fear and confusion rose from the crowd as people ran over one another in their haste to seek shelter. Bolan and Grimaldi stood their ground with effort, sandwiching the frail priest between them.

"Mother of God," Father Lazaro said as he crossed himself.

Small-arms fire followed on the heels of the echoing explosion. Vans and small buses had pulled up on the outside of the barricade. Guns blazed from the window, then men poured from the doors. The crowd went to ground on animal instinct. Uniformed Medellín policemen went down like hay before a scythe.

Bolan pushed Father Lazaro toward Grimaldi. "Get him out of here."

The pilot nodded, bending the older man low and leading him toward the stage and whatever safety remained.

Switching the selector to single-fire, the Executioner shouldered the CAR-15 and started choosing targets as the assassins tried to fortify their new position. Two shots punched into a man hiding behind a rusting Ford sedan, spilling the body out into the street. A third round caught another gunner in midstride, slamming into his temple and knocking him to the ground.

Bolan stoked the anger inside him, transmuting it into an elemental force that drove him on. He emptied his clip and reloaded as he fell back toward the stage area. Another rocket exploded in the crowd, throwing bodies in all directions. Spotting the grenade launcher, the warrior drew target acquisition on the man rearming it. He squeezed the trigger three times in quick succession. The 5.56 mm rounds staggered the man, probably flattening against a Kevlar vest. Bolan made the adjustment to the guy's face, let out a breath, then squeezed the trigger. The man jumped back, slapping a hand to his cheek, inadvertently lowering the grenade launcher to point at the ground. The launcher went off and the missile impacted at the guy's feet, the explosion blowing the man to pieces.

The angry buzz of the helicopters overhead dipped as they swooped down on the ground forces. Heavy .50-caliber machine guns opened up with their familiar roar. Ground erupted in grass-green and dirt-brown clumps as the helicopter gunners found their range. Then men dropped as the big rounds chopped through the cars and trucks they'd taken shelter behind.

Bolan dropped an empty magazine and shoved another home. He began firing at once, licking out with 5.56 mm lightning bolts in mechanical precision. The body count was staggering on both sides. The area was largely vacant except for the dead and wounded as the crowd dispersed. At least two rounds hit Bolan in the chest, stopped by his Kevlar vest, and knocked him off balance. He tripped over a corpse and went down, going with the momentum until he fell into a prone firing position. The targets were fewer now. The brave assassins had already paid the price—the others were seasoned enough to wait.

When the double whump went off overhead, the Executioner knew what they'd been waiting for. The police helichopper closer to the ground went down in flames, hit by a rocket from an approaching gunship. Another trailed in close formation.

CHAPTER TWENTY-FIVE

"I don't see that we have anything to talk about, Agent Price."

Ignoring the easy manner in which the lawyer dismissed her, Price said, "That's your choice, Counselor. Let's hope it's a good one."

Constantine steepled his fingers before him as he rested his elbows on the arms of his chair. His eyes never wavered from hers. She stood her ground, waiting.

Abruptly he leaned forward and hit an intercom button. "Forget security. I'll handle this."

"Yes, sir."

"And close the office door."

"Yes, sir."

After the door was shut, Constantine looked up at her and asked, "Now who the hell do you think you are?"

Price gave the man a cold smile. "Believe me, you're about to find out."

"You're a lunatic." The lawyer leaned forward in the chair. "I'll call security myself."

Striding over to the desk, Price knocked the phone away with her briefcase. "I don't think so. We're going to talk, Counselor. Me and you, man to man."

"I don't even know you."

"But I know you." Price placed the briefcase on the desk. "I know about the crooked deals you've been making over the past few months. I know about the slime you represent. I know you don't give a damn about the people you turn back out on the street. I know you've got virtually an unlimited amount of cash backing up every corrupt move you make."

Constantine stood, holding his palms out before him. "Hold it, lady. You're making a lot of unfounded accusations here. You need to stop and think about what you're doing."

Price was quiet for a moment, letting the silence become a palpable thing between them. The clasps snicked back on the briefcase. "I don't need to think, Counselor. I've looked at your file." She drew it out and tossed it onto the desk. It smacked as it hit, skidding into an inlaid ivory pen-and-pencil set.

Staring at the burgeoning manila envelope, Constantine made no move to pick it up.

Price closed the briefcase. "That's your copy, Counselor. Go ahead and check it over if you like."

He glared at her. "What's this about?"

Leaning across the closed briefcase, Price said, "This is about your future. This is about Luis Costanza and Esteban Ortega. This is about your proposed representation of said Señor Ortega. No other lawyer in this city would touch Ortega because he's so hot. No lawyer but you. You might have sold your soul to Costanza, but your ass is mine. That file gives me all the ownership I need."

"You can't come in here and threaten me like this."

"Sure I can. I just did. And it's no threat. It's a promise. Call me on it if you want."

Constantine reached for the file with trembling fingers. He leafed through it and his face blanched. He looked at her. "So what's the deal?"

"The deal is this—you don't represent Ortega. Let someone else do it. An out-of-towner won't have the grease you do. If you try to represent him, you go to jail. If we find out you've been trying to do anything behind our backs with another lawyer, you go to jail. If you get in contact with Costanza again, you go to jail. Catch the drift here, Counselor?"

Constantine nodded.

"Another thing."

He looked at her, his lips compressed into a thin, colorless line.

"You close up shop here. Find another state to make a dishonest living in."

"You can't do that."

"I can. I am. If you try to remain here, I'll freeze all those darling little Swiss bank accounts of yours as funds received from the commission of a crime. We both know what line of work Costanza's involved in. He's going down the toilet. You don't want to go with him." She paused at the door. "Have a nice day, Counselor."

BOLAN PUSHED HIMSELF to his feet, scrabbling for the headset he'd lost when he went down. Clamping it on, he adjusted the mouthpiece. Another explosion saw the second police helicopter become an orange-and-black fireball that evaporated into the sky. Bits and pieces of the wreckage rained down around him.

The helicopter gunships spun into the airspace over the stage like two angry wasps. Chain guns chewed through the landscape and tore tufts of grass free. Branches and small trees fell before the onslaught. At least three more rockets thudded into the stage, reducing it to kindling and starting fires. Another rocket speared into the billboard proclaiming Medellín's Houses for the Poor. Fire spread from one corner of the sign as the timbers gave way and it peeled back slowly, landing in a tangle of live wires that spit and sputtered.

The headset was dead. The warrior pulled it off and brought up the CAR-15, sighting in on the nearer Plexiglas bubble. He emptied the clip in single-shot mode, watching the bubble star from the impacts. As the other helicopter made a pass at him, he lowered the assault rifle and ran toward the stage.

Fighting in the streets had died down. Costanza had wanted his message spread, and his troops had done it. The only thing left was the signature provided by the attack choppers.

More rockets zoomed down, taking a heavy toll on the news vans lying in the middle of the kill zone like beached whales. One helicopter hung back, using concentrated fire to reduce everything man-made in the vicinity to flaming rubble. The other hovered closer to the trees, pursuing the unarmed civilians who'd gathered for Franco's speech.

Bolan pumped his legs, driving his body forward, deliberately keeping his mind off what had happened to the justice minister because there was no room in his thoughts for that. Costanza's assassins were turning the rout into a full-scale massacre.

Two DAS men staggered from the tree line, carrying a rocket launcher. They tried to set up in the open, but there was no time before the chain guns tracked across their position and knocked them to the ground.

Bolan changed directions immediately, throwing the assault rifle down as he pushed himself into an all-out sprint for the rocket launcher. The chain guns were locking onto him as he wrapped his fingers around the thick barrel. He heard the stomping impact of 30 mm rounds pounding through the ground behind him as he cut back like a wide receiver breaking into a reception pattern. He dived, clutching the rocket launcher to his chest as the chain guns swept by him, missing by mere inches.

Swiveling in the blood-covered grass, finding traction almost nonexistent, the Executioner lifted the rocket launcher and sighted on the gunship. The helicopter came around, heeling directly into his sights. Thunder belched from the chain guns as a row of 30 mm bullets slammed into the ground less than ten yards away, poking pockmarks into the grass. He waited until he had the cross hairs centered on the nose of the helicopter.

BREATHING RAPIDLY from the run to the building and from pulling Sharon behind him, Martin Flynn pushed through the glass doors and saw dozens of people taking shelter on the floor. He kept the backpack of cocaine gripped tightly in his other hand. Bell was right behind him. They were in some kind of public building, with wide hallways and high ceilings.

He saw a men's bathroom and went for it, wanting to get away from the prying eyes, almost sure everyone knew what he had in the bag. Once inside, he fell to his knees, gasping until he had enough breath to throw up, his stomach spasming as it emptied into a urinal.

"Marty."

It was Bell's voice, keyed up, anxious. Flynn shook his head, retching again.

"Marty, are you going to be okay? Because I don't think this is the time to let your guard down. There are some kill-crazy bastards out there, and the cops are going to be all over the place in a few minutes."

Flynn took the .38 out of his waistband and slid it along the floor away from him. He didn't want anything to do with the gun. Every time he closed his eyes all he could see was the dead bodies and the blood.

"Guess we must be living charmed lives to see us through that shit, right?" Bell leaned on a sink and laughed, a wild nervous sound that fit the maniacal expression on his lean face. His .38 dangled loosely in his fingers.

Sharon stroked Flynn's face with her palms. "Are you okay?" Her features showed her concern.

"Yeah." He nodded weakly, still in a kneeling position. Without saying anything, only knowing what he had to do to set things right in his mind, he reached for the backpack. Pulling it close, he took out the first pack, broke it open and poured the contents into the urinal. White powder piled over the drain until he pulled the lever. With a whoosh it started its way down.

"Hey, Marty, hey! What the fuck do you think you're doing?" Bell crossed the room and tried to take the backpack away from him.

Flynn hit him, knocking the guy onto his butt. He had the second pack open and dumped before Bell could scramble to his feet. He pulled the lever.

"You're crazy! Do you know what you're doing?"

Flynn emptied the third, not saying anything.

"Goddamn it, if you don't let go of that backpack, I'll shoot you!"

Flynn looked up. Bell had the .38 pointed at him. "You don't understand, do you?" He couldn't shut up, pushing himself to his feet as the rage, fear and pain pummeled him from inside. He pointed, not caring if his direction was right. Bell would know what he was talking about. "That man might have just given his life trying to make this country a better place to live. You and me, all of us, flying down here, making this buy this way, we're only helping keep the situation bad."

Bell shook his head, anger coloring his face. The barrel of the .38 never wavered. "I'm warning you, buddy boy, hand over the coke or I'll shoot you. Just because you get an attack of the guilts over some backwater politician getting axed down here doesn't mean I have to watch my future go down the toilet, too."

"I'm not giving you the backpack." Flynn was surprised at the lack of fear within him.

Bell thumbed back the hammer. "Then you're a dead man."

Flynn returned Bell's gaze full measure, then reached for another pack. He had no choice. Not if he ever wanted to put all those faces behind him.

"Don't!" Sharon's voice froze them both in place. She held Flynn's pistol in both hands, aiming it straight at Bell's chest. "Put the gun down, Virgil, or I swear I'll pull this trigger."

Flynn waited, not believing the turn of events, not wanting to breathe for fear of getting Sharon hurt.

Blood trickled from Bell's nose, crossing his thin lips. Seeing the thoughts race behind Bell's veiled eyes, Flynn said, "She means it, guy, and she knows how to use a gun."

Cursing, Bell placed his weapon on the floor and walked out of the room.

Flynn went back to the half-kilo packs of cocaine, tearing them open in succession and dumping them into the urinal. Sharon helped him. When the last had been emptied and flushed away, he reached for her and held her to him. Tears filled his eyes as she sobbed against him, knowing their worlds would never be the same again.

MACK BOLAN CARESSED the trigger of the rocket launcher. The missile whooshed away, streaming toward the attacking helicopter. When it impacted against the nose a heartbeat later, the noise of the chain guns died away, replaced by the hollow boom of the warhead. Skeletal remains of the helicopter hit the ground only yards behind him.

The second helicopter heeled over, sweeping back across the open area. The warrior got a momentary impression of a black eye patch on the face of the passenger—letting him know Isaac Auerbach had called the strategy on the attack—then it was gone before he could reload the launcher, vanishing into the distance.

He stood up in the field of death, gazing out over the collection of bodies and burning vehicles. The warrior dropped the launcher onto the ground, drew the Desert Eagle and walked toward the burning stage area. Keening sirens pierced the wails of the dying and the wounded. He tried to disassociate himself from the agonized faces before him and failed. This one had come too close to the heart.

"Mack."

Turning at the sound of Grimaldi's voice, Bolan saw the pilot standing in front of a small white church two hundred yards in back of the burning stage. He crossed the distance in a jog. People moved away from him, still stunned that the attack was over. "Franco?" the warrior asked as he came to a halt beside his friend.

"Doesn't look good, Sarge. There were too many internal injuries from the bomb blast. He's been asking for you."

Holstering his weapon, Bolan stepped into the church. His steps, even in tennis shoes, made echoes on the wooden floor.

Franco lay on the floor in the middle of the church. The young justice minister's face was lacerated with dozens of small cuts and a handful of larger ones. An abrasion over his right eye had swelled it shut. Blood stained his chin and neck, and his breathing was slow and shuddering, creating crimson bubbles. Father Lazaro knelt to one side, administering the last rites, bandaged hands clasped together as he prayed in a low voice. Dominga held her husband's head in her lap and trailed bloodstained fingers through his hair. She dabbed at his lips with a bloody handkerchief. Sigfrido stood behind her, holding little Andeana tightly as she screamed and struggled to get down, calling again and again for her father.

Dominga's face was rigid with shock, and tears slid down her cheeks. She looked away from Bolan, concentrating on her husband. Franco's bruised and battered features held only pain. He waved for Bolan to come closer. His breath rattled, seeming to hang for a moment as if it might not return, then went on, weaker than before.

Kneeling, the Executioner took the man's offered hand in his.

"We . . . fought the good . . . fight, eh, my friend," Franco whispered in a faltering voice.

Father Lazaro's prayer continued in a low undertone, slightly above the sounds of emergency vehicles approaching from outside.

"Yeah," Bolan said softly, "we did do that." He felt the man's strength ebbing from the hand that gripped his.

"And . . . it wasn't . . . all in vain."

"No."

Franco gasped, closed his one good eye for a few heartbeats, then fluttered it open again, having difficulty focusing it. "This isn't . . . your fault. You . . . would've stopped me . . . if you could."

"But I didn't."

"I . . . wouldn't have . . . let you. This . . . this was my war before I knew you."

Bolan gripped the man's hand tighter, trying to will life into him, knowing from experience that it wouldn't work, and knowing from experience that he still felt compelled to try.

"Even without me—" Franco drew a stubborn, shuddering breath "—the war must go on. Don't let this . . . become a hollow victory."

Bolan nodded.

"You must promise me this."

Bolan felt the hand tighten in his. "You've got my promise, Benito."

"*Sí, bueno.*" Franco rolled his head to one side, his final words for his wife's ears alone.

Feeling the hand relax in his moments later, Bolan knew that Benito Franco was gone, leaving him with a war to fight and a promise to keep. The Executioner took neither lightly.

* * * * *

Don't miss the exciting conclusion of The Medellín Trilogy. Look for The Executioner #151: Message to Medellín *in July.*

GOLD EAGLE

The Eagle now lands at different times at your retail outlet!

Be sure to look for your favorite action adventure from Gold Eagle on these dates each month.

Publication Month	In-Store Dates
May	April 24
June	May 22
July	June 19
August	July 24

We hope that this new schedule will be convenient for you.

Please note: There may be slight variations in on-sale dates in your area due to differences in shipping and handling.

GEDATES-R

TAKE 'EM NOW

FOLDING SUNGLASSES
FROM GOLD EAGLE

Mean up your act with these tough, street-smart shades. Practical, too, because they fold 3 times into a handy, zip-up polyurethane pouch that fits neatly into your pocket. Rugged metal frame. Scratch-resistant acrylic lenses. Best of all, they can be yours for only $6.99.

MAIL YOUR ORDER TODAY.

Send your name, address, and zip code, along with a check or money order for just $6.99 + .75¢ for delivery (for a total of $7.74) payable to Gold Eagle Reader Service.
(New York residents please add applicable sales tax.)

Gold Eagle Reader Service
3010 Walden Avenue
P.O. Box 1396
Buffalo, N.Y. 14240-1396

Remove from pouch

unfold once

unfold twice

and they're ready to wear

GES-1AR

Offer not available in Canada.

The curtain rises on a new cast
in the drug wars.

DON PENDLETON's
MACK BOLAN.

COUNTERBLOW

The upsurge in high-grade heroin on the West Coast is ringing
alarm bells all over Washington. It's clear there's a new player
at the table, someone setting up a Turkish heroin pipeline
through Pakistan. One man's war just found a new battlefield.

Mack Bolan has found a new high-stakes game to play in the
war against drugs in war-torn Pakistan, but he's not the only
one making the game rules....